THE UNKNOWN TERRITORY

(Gateskin Chronicles, Book 2)

Janice Spina

PUBLISHED BY JANICE SPINA

COPYRIGHT 2022
JANICE SPINA
Londonderry, New Hampshire

COVER BY JOHN SPINA

ISBN 978-1-7361673-6-6 (paperback)

LCCN 2022909249

ACKNOWLEDGEMENTS

A very special thank you to my wonderful beta readers, Patricia Bradley, Michelle Clement James, Michele Rolfe, John Spina and Frances Stewart for working tirelessly to read and review my work and for their helpful input. Their assistance is invaluable and appreciated.

Thank you to my husband, John, for the beautiful cover and for all the dinners he cooked that made it possible for me to write.

DEDICATION

This fantasy is dedicated to my husband, John, who has been patient enough to read this book about magic and fantasy in which he doesn't always believe. I think at the conclusion of this book he may now be a believer of fantasy and magic.

For all your support and encouragement, John, I thank you and love you dearly.

To all who believe in magic and fantasy

Contents

MAP OF TERRITORY OF NOELLA PROVINCE

CHARACTERS

Serena (14) - heroine of story, sister to Simon and Catalina

Simon (12) - brother of Serena and Catalina

Catalina (10) - sister of Serena and Simon

Solinara - Queen Fairy of Sovorotskina and mother of Serena and siblings

Gateskin - King Wizard of Sovorotskina and father of Serena and Siblings

Sovorotskina - Land of Goodness and Light, home of Serena and Family

Ressaphena - Goddess of Goodness and Light

Ramoforan- God of Goodness and Light

Noella - surviving child of Sovorotskina, during the capture of Taken Ones became Queen Fairy of Votovia

Sonovan - 1st King Wizard, husband of Noella, and ruler of Votovia

Noella II - descendant of Noella only child survivor of Legend of Taken Ones

Josoforan - King of Sovorotskina during capture of Taken Ones

Marolena - Queen Fairy of Sovorotskina during capture of Taken Ones

Hotenfaran - Wizard, uncle of Serena and siblings, brother of Queen Solinara

Procelina - Fairy, aunt of Serena and siblings

Arubane – adopted son of Procelina and Hotenfaran with many powers

Toleran - citizen guard of Sovorotskina

Miserva - citizen of Sovorotskina and wife of Toleran

Peteran - young son of Toleran & Miserva of Sovorotskina

Amora - Land of Faith and Love

Noderan - elder Amorans subject
(Became King of Amora)

Davora – wife of Noderan
(Became Queen of Amora)

Merlina - Land of Magic and
Mystery

Merlinans - citizens of Merlina

Merona - Land of Myths and
Legends

(Named after Fairy Princess
captured by EO)

Meronans - citizens of Merona

Votovia - Land of Peace and
Harmony

Votovians - peaceful but
powerful subjects of Votovia

Savina - Queen Fairy of Votovia, present day ruler

Cavelan - King Wizard of Votovia, present day ruler

Adolphin - son of king and queen of Votovia

Anatonia Noella - daughter of king and queen of Votovia

Soneran - member of King Cavelan's guard

Latoran - member of King Cavelan's guard

Sprites - little tree people who lived in the forests around Sovorotskina and the other villages

Spindle - tree Sprite, friend of Serena's

Abason - tree Sprite, father of Spindle, Head Counsel of Sprites

Anabal - tree Sprite, mother of Spindle

Micah - brother of Abason, captured by Evil Ones

Parotovina - Land of Darkness and Evil, home of Evil Ones

Beregina - Queen Witch of Parotovina

Kaposkaran - King Wizard of Parotovina

Parotovinans - citizens of Parotovina

Quilarena - Goddess of Darkness and Evil

Quilottan - God of Darkness and Evil

Mitteran - Head Guard of scouting party of Parotovinans

Leanna - wife of Mitteran

Allonso (Al) - son of Mitteran & Leanna

Tessa- daughter of Mitteran & Leanna

Kelleran – Gatekeeper of Parotovina

Francia – wife of Kelleran

Botular – Eyes & ears of King Kaposkaran (HOH – becomes citizen of Sovorotskina)

Zuri - King of Merlina

Zuleima - Queen of Merlina

Zayleen - daughter of King Zuri/Queen Zuleima

Zukan - son of King Zuri/Queen Zuleima

Zuriann - daughter of King Zuri/Queen Zuleima

Cantok – large wolf from Unknown Territory – migrated to Sovorotskina

Notak – mate of Cantok

Tankor – male cub of Cantok

Rattor – male cub of Cantok

Maku – female cub of Cantok

Rabbinels – creatures created by Queen Solinara and Hotenfaran to feed the wolves and fulfill the need of the wolves to hunt and forage for food

Quintaroon – a creature created by the Wizards of Parotovina

Catlings – cat-like creatures that roam the UT

Animals in King Gateskin Barn – chickens, cow – Milly

Acronyms:

EVIL ONES – EOs

TAKEN ONES – TOs

DESCENDANTS OF TOs – Ds

UNKNOWN TERRITORY – UT

Parotovinan Wizards – Head Wizard – Marno

Wizard #2 – Fortag

Wizard #3 – Wassor

Wizard #4 – Tornak

Wizard #5 – Kerno

Wizard #6 – Sufan

Parotovinans with powers

**Henno & Jenara – husband &
wife**

Danko – kind Parotovinan guard

VILLAGES:

Sovorotskina – Land of Goodness & Light – King Gateskin/Queen Solinara

Parotovina – Land of Evil & Darkness King Kaposkaran/Queen Beregina

Votovia – Land of Magic & Mystery - King Cavelan/Queen Savina

Amora – Land of Faith & Love – King Noderan/Queen Davora

Merona – Land of Peace & Harmony – Ruled by Healers

Merlina – Land of Myths & Legends – King Zuri/Queen Zuleima

PROLOGUE

Their eyes glowed in the darkness as they searched for food. These wolves had all gone beyond the Unknown Territory forcing them to hunt for food further out into the land. They came to the border of Sovorotskina and spied some men marching toward them.

The wolves' mouths watered at the thought of fresh kill. They salivated as they got closer to this new food.

The Parotovinan guards were on their way to Sovorotskina to bring back the shepherds and sheep and King Gateskin's daughter, Serena, per the request of King Kaposkaran. They had no idea what was living in the UT and that they would meet their fate in such a horrendous way.

The man in the front of the group spotted something ahead of them. He pointed and pushed his men back when he saw what it was! "Move back and flee for your lives, men!"

His scream and the screams of his men reverberated across the forest of the Unknown Territory.

Only the Sprites heard the cries. They were up in the trees bordering the Unknown Territory and hurriedly spread word to all the other Sprites about the carnage. They needed to warn one and all of these creatures and contact Abason, their leader.

"Are they a new breed of wolves?" Abason asked when word of the carnage reached him.

"We are not sure, Abason. The other Sprites who witnessed this said, "They are larger than dogs and much fiercer."

"Thank you for the warning. Tell the Sprites to keep watch over these creatures and report anything further to me. Tell them to stay away from them and don't let them see you."

"Yes, Abason. I will." The Sprite flew up into the neighboring trees and started spreading Abason's message throughout the rest of Sovorotskina.

***

Sovorotskina was a beautiful village, green and lush dotted with many farms with hardworking farmers who toiled their land and appreciated their blessings. The farmers had welcomed the new citizens to their land and helped get them settled. The new citizens of the Land of Light, Sovorotskina, appreciated the warm welcoming they had received from the villagers and the King and Queen of this wonderful land of plenty.

They were now all settled in their homes built by King Gateskin, his guards and the other villagers. They were happy to be away from the Land of Evil, Parotovina. Now they could bring up their families in safety and freedom. They toiled on their new farms and cared for their homes and family.

Peace was here for now, but for how long, they did not know. King Kaposkaran of the Land of Darkness,

Parotovina, was not happy he had not received any Taken Ones from the other villages to replace the ones who escaped with the help of King Gateskin. His men had been unsuccessful but he had a new plan. He had sent twelve guards to capture King Gateskin's daughter, Serena, and the shepherds and sheep that had escaped from Parotovina. His Wizards had been sending Serena messages of evil and images of the Gatekeeper's dead and tortured body. He knew if his Wizards could continue to do this, he would be successful in turning Serena to his evil ways. This feat would enable King Kaposkaran to gain control over King Gateskin who would be helpless over losing his daughter.

What King Kaposkaran didn't yet realize was King Gateskin was using his own powers to protect his daughter from these messages. King Gateskin was now the recipient of the messages instead.

Gateskin refused to let the evil king harm his daughter. He would continue to deflect these messages until he could come up with a spell to stop them completely.

He turned to his brother-in-law, Hotenfaran and his own wife, Queen Solinara. "I need your help, Hotenfaran and Solinara, to erase these evil messages I am receiving instead of Serena."

"Yes, Gateskin, I have been working on this very thing with my sister. Solinara always gives me credit for everything we do together. She is entirely too modest."

"That I know already. She feels as if she needs to give credit to everyone but herself. It is the only flaw my beautiful wife has," Gateskin guffawed as he winked at Hotenfaran.

"I agree with you there, my King!" Hotenfaran laughed along with Gateskin but never stopped working on his current project.

Queen Solinara listened to the exchange but didn't respond. She did, however, look over at her husband and brother, smirked and raised her eyebrows at them.

She was content now that she had become close once again with her brother, Hotenfaran, since the return of her family from the clutches of the Parotovinans. She couldn't thank her brother and his wife, Procelina, enough for their part in saving her family. She felt like a kid again as she and Hotenfaran set up a large shed a short distance from her home to house the materials to develop new spells to protect their village and all the other neighboring villages against a new threat which was coming their way.

They had herbs drying above their heads and on the walls of the massive shed. All kinds of tools, magic elixirs and spells were bottled on multiple shelves at their fingertips.

They spent hours daily working to create whatever they could using the Staglemite and other herbs and wild mushrooms along with a little of their powers mixed in to protect her daughter, Serena, from the evil King Kaposkaran who continued to send his vile messages their way. Solinara knew her husband Gateskin was taking on these messages and was becoming quite upset by them. She noticed he had become quieter the past few days. Solinara didn't like the look on his face which was pale and troubled.

Hotenfaran had nearly perfected a new spell to prevent Gateskin from becoming ill. He had developed some interesting incantations using the Staglemite found in the Cave of Crotesia Mountain when they were last there to rescue King Gateskin from the Parotovinan guards.

This Staglemite prevented and blocked messages from coming and going when a person was surrounded by it as in the cave. Hotenfaran discovered that if he held a small piece of it in his hand, he could enclose a message and send it one way for an individual to receive without others hearing it.

"Time is of the essence since evil doesn't wait," Hotenfaran said as he discussed what the next step would be with his sister. "Dear Solinara, we must try out this new spell to see if it is effective. Who do you think we should use it on? It has to be someone who you do not completely trust."

Solinara responded without thinking, "I know just the person we can use."

She decided to share what she knew about Botular with her brother. After all, he needed to know why she did not trust this man.

"Hotenfaran, I need to share some things about this man I have chosen to experiment on. His name is Botular. He is known to be the eyes and ears of King Kaposkaran. Botular was found inside the Cave of Crotesia by my children when they were on their journey with you and Procelina to bring back their father from the clutches of King Kaposkaran. This man had blended into the cave walls and Catalina, had stumbled upon him. Gateskin had brought Botular back with him to Sovorotskina so he could keep a close watch over him."

"Yes, I did see this man with Gateskin when we arrived back in Sovorotskina," Hotenfaran stated.

Solinara nodded and continued, "Botular professed to turn away from his evil ways and became a citizen of Sovorotskina. He told us reluctantly he had sent a message, before he arrived here, to his king about capturing my children. We have been keeping a close eye on him. He is responsible for the evil messages that have been directed toward Serena. Thank goodness Gateskin was able to divert them away from her and take them on himself."

"Hmm, I see. Like I mentioned, I did see this man but did not interact with him. I'm glad you shared this information with me. Now I understand why you moved Botular into the new cabin next to yours."

"Yes, I didn't trust him in the same house as my children."

"I don't blame you. Now that I know this, I will keep my eyes and ears on him too."

"Thank you, Hotenfaran. It's good to have you here, my brother. I have missed these times together working on spells and just talking. Let's not let the years pass us by and prevent us from being close."

"Yes, of course, Solinara. I have missed you too." Hotenfaran bent his head and looked busy to avoid letting his sister see the tears of happiness that glistened in his eyes.

Solinara excused herself and went in search of Botular. When she visited him in his little cabin, a short time later, he was surprised by her presence. She had focused and seen Botular through the door before she knocked.

She noticed part of him had blended into the table where he was sitting. She knew he had powers to do that and wondered how many other powers he might be hiding.

Botular hurriedly jumped up from his table where he was having a cup of coffee and nibbling on a biscuit and opened the door. "Oh, my Queen! I wasn't expecting you. What can I do for you?"

"How are you feeling, Botular? Have you received any messages from King Kaposkaran lately?"

"Oh no, Queen Solinara. I have not received anything since I have been in Sovorotskina, my new homeland." Botular hung his head and could not meet Solinara's eyes.

"Hmm, I see. Come with me, Botular? I would like to try something."

"What, try something? What is it, Queen Solinara? Did I do something wrong?"

The Queen did not answer him but commanded him, "Come with me, Botular."

Botular was anxious but followed close behind Queen Solinara. He tried to keep his thoughts to himself. He did not want the Queen to read his mind. He knew she had been trying to do that since he came to Sovorotoskina.

In fact, Solinara *was* inside his mind now and was reading what he was thinking. She did not like what she saw there.

Hotenfaran was waiting inside their shed with a small piece of Staglemite held tightly in his hand.

The Wizard pointed to the chair in the center of the shed. Botular nodded in assent and sat down.

"Now, Botular, please sit quietly and as still as you can. I am going to try a little spell on you."

"What? A Spell? What kind of spell? Are you going to turn me into an animal or something worse?"

"No, of course not, Botular. I just want to try something quite harmless. I assure you." Hotenfaran smiled to relieve his subject's anxiety.

Hotenfaran nodded at Solinara who came forward to assist him.

CHAPTER ONE

Later on, Queen Solinara went to find her husband to share what she and her brother had discovered about the surprising properties of Staglemite.

Before she told Gateskin the discovery, she said, "I feel something in the air." She turned toward her husband and asked, "Do you feel it, dear?"

"What, my love? What do you feel?"

"I have an awful feeling this isn't over with the Parotovinans. I think King Kaposkaran is not going to stop. He will send more of his men our way."

"Yes, my dear. I feel it too. His messages are becoming desperate in origin. He is sending them frantically now. My mind is trying to shut them out but he has some powerful wizards working on these messages. I am just relieved I am the one receiving them now and not our daughter."

"I was afraid of this, Gateskin. We have to stop him. I don't want you to get sick over this. I know how hard it is to keep evil at bay that is trying to eat at your brain and your very soul. I feel it emanating off of you. I see it in your aura now. It is becoming blacker. I don't like that at all. You must let me and Hotenfaran help you."

"Have you found a way to stop King Kaposkaran?"

"I think so. Hotenfaran is the one to discover what the Staglemite can do. He also has developed more spells with it. I have tried to assist him but he is much better at these things than I am."

"I wouldn't say that, Solinara. You are quite clever yourself. I have seen what you can do with your powers. Look what you did with the spell over the boundaries of our land. I could not get through it until you released the spell to allow me to come through." Gateskin laughed at the surprised face his wife made at him.

"Oh, Gateskin. You know very well you could have come through using your own powers over mine. You are being kind, my love."

Gateskin smiled and met his wife's eyes as he shrugged his shoulders.

"Do you want to hear about how we plan to stop the messages, Gateskin?"

"Of course, my dear. Please explain. I am all ears."

She smirked at him and began to explain. "You remember our new citizen, Botular?"

"Ahh yes, of course, my dear. I have been keeping an ear out for him as well as you have."

Before Solinara could explain to her husband about the new plan, a cry of help was heard outside. They ran to the window and looked out.

Serena and her siblings were standing in front of a large dog or wolf. It was growling and looking at them as drool dripped out of the side of its mouth.

Gateskin grabbed a large walking stick he kept by the door and raced out to help his children. But before he could, the animal stopped growling.

It bowed its head and shook it back and forth. It appeared confused but at least it wasn't as menacing now.

Gateskin got closer to his children and pushed them behind him. Serena spoke to him through mind control to explain what she was trying to do.

"Father, it's okay. I am talking to him. He is the same wild dog that was here before. You took him back to the Unknown Territory. Don't you remember?"

"Yes, I do, Serena. But what is he doing back again?"

"He is trying to warn us about something coming our way. He wants to help us. He said someone is trying to control his mind and make him harm me. He does not want to harm any of us. He is thankful to you for not killing him when he was last here. He knows he would have harmed us if you had not ostracized him when you did."

"Is it King Kaposkaran?"

"Let me ask him." Serena turned to the animal and asked him.

"He is not sure who or what is doing this. He has a family of his own that he wants to bring here to protect not only them but us too. He said he has many friends who will aid us if we need them. He also corrected me by saying he is not a dog but a large variety of wolf."

"I see. Okay. Ask him what he can do to help us?"

Serena looked at the large wolf. She nodded back to him in thanks.

"What did he say, Serena?" Gateskin asked skeptically.

"He can attack the men and cause them to scatter and go back where they came from. He said there are many men coming from the south. He also said the Sprites are making a lot of noise trying to frighten them. But it is not working. He introduced himself as Cantok. He said the Unknown Territory is a dangerous place to be even for him and his family now. He hopes you will accept his friendship and let him and his family stay in our woods. He can be your eyes, ears and nose."

"Please tell him I accept his friendship and his family to our village. We can build him a shelter to keep him out of the cold."

Serena relayed what her father had said to the wolf.

Cantok made a grumbling noise in his throat, nodded his head up and down, and bowed to King Gateskin.

The King bowed back to Cantok and showed the wolf where he would put a shelter for him and his family.

Gateskin turned toward Serena and requested, "Ask Cantok why the Unknown Territory is suddenly so dangerous."

Serena stared at Cantok who was looking over the area for his new home. She asked the animal this question. Her eyes opened wider and she gasped at his response.

"Oh no. This is terrible, Father. Cantok said there are many horrible creatures gaining power there. His kind were once the most powerful but someone has interceded and created these new creatures."

"Explain to him he will be safe here. If any more of his kind need refuge, they must swear allegiance to me and I will allow them to stay here too. I fear we will need all the friends we can get in the near future."

Serena looked at Cantok and sent her questions to his mind.

"Yes, he said he would ask them. He assured me they would be happy for your offer and to swear allegiance to such a kind and benevolent ruler as you."

Gateskin ventured closer to the animal which appeared to grow larger in size. He met the creature's eyes and extended his hand in friendship as he hovered it over the animal's huge head. The animal bowed down and let Gateskin pet him.

The children saw this and stepped forward to do the same.

If an animal such as this could smile, it would have looked like the expression Cantok had on his hairy face.

***

King Gateskin gathered all the villagers together and explained about the new occupants who were going to settle in Sovorotskina on each of their farms.

A few villagers stepped forward and voiced their concern, "We are not sure about these wolves on our property, especially since we have other animals housed here. Will the wolves attack us or our animals?"

But the King assured them, "No, they will not attack you or your animals. These wolves are kind and friendly. I will be sending my men to each of your farms to help you build a shelter and make sure the wolves are settled. If there are any problems, they will be dealt with by me."

The villagers agreed, but some grumbling could still be heard as they walked back to their homes. The King would make a note to keep a close watch on those who were still unsure of these new settlers.

CHAPTER TWO

Spindle waited for a chance to interrupt
the King. Being the Head Guard, he
knew he had a fierce responsibility to
keep his King abreast of what was going
on in the Unknown Territory.

He reported to the King's cottage prepared to tell him what he had seen. He had been on guard around the borders and told to stay there until further notice. But he felt it was even more important to report immediately to the King. He requested the rest of the men to stay put until he could tell them otherwise. He left Mitteran, his second in command, to stay with the men.

Spindle knocked on the King's door and waited.

"Ahh, there you are, my Head Guard. I know I told you to stay at the borders with the other men but I do need to speak with you. There have been some new developments."

Spindle waited until the King had finished explaining about the new inhabitants of Sovorotskina, the wolves.

"I will have to introduce myself to Cantok and his family and let him know

I do not taste too good, being made of wood."

King Gateskin laughed at Spindle's sense of humor. "I am sure he will not do that. If you want to stay in Cantok's good graces you need to talk to Serena. She is the only one who can correspond with the large wolf and his pack."

"Hmm, that's good to know, King Gateskin. I will definitely speak with her soon. But first, I must tell you about what I have seen in the Unknown Territory."

Gateskin listened and then responded, "I understand what you are saying about the wolves, Spindle. But I assure you they will not eat any of us. It was unfortunate they attacked the Parotovinan guards. I don't want to see anyone murdered in any way. The wolves may very well have saved us from an attack we did not see coming."

"Yes, that is quite possible, King Gateskin. But just the same, I will be wary of them until I see we are safe from harm."

***

The woods in the Unknown Territory were bustling with activity. There were more new creatures inhabiting it every day. Cantok moved carefully through his long-time home to gather his family and fellow wolves to spread the word about their new home in Sovorotskina.

There were fewer of the wolves than there once were because they had become food for the new creatures that roamed the land. Once Cantok explained what King Gateskin proposed, the animals all bowed in acceptance and followed Cantok to their new home.

There were many eyes watching the group of wolves as they traveled swiftly through the woods of the Unknown Territory known to many who lived there as the UT. This acronym was, however, unbeknownst to others.

Cantok sniffed the area ahead of them to make sure it was safe. They were almost at the edge of the woods bordering Sovorotskina. He could sense there were many creatures watching them. He did not turn their way but urged his fellow wolves to move quickly across the border into the village of Sovorotskina.

King Gateskin was at the border and opened it to welcome Cantok and his family and fellow wolves. He was shocked by how many of them there were. By what Cantok had told them he expected to only see a handful. There were too many for him to count. All the wolves bowed down to King Gateskin and followed behind Cantok and the King to their quarters.

King Gateskin had ordered his men to build shelters for all the wolves, one at each of the farms so that they were spread out for extra protection of his people. He told Cantok what he had proposed and the wolf directed his fellow wolves to find a shelter for each of their families. He also told them not to harm anyone unless they were the enemy, King Kaposkaran and his men or the creatures from the Unknown Territory.

Serena, Simon and Catalina saw the wolves walking into the village and rushed out to see them. Cantok came forward to introduce his family, his mate, Notak, and their three cubs, Tankor, Rattor, and Maku - Maku being the only female cub.

The three children were excited to meet the animals and moved forward, with Cantok's permission, to pet the cubs. The cubs were softer than the children expected as they petted their thick fur.

The cubs licked the children's hands and nestled into their arms for affection.

King Gateskin and Queen Solinara smiled at their children's reaction to the wolves. It looked like they would each have a pet to take care of with Cantok's permission, that is.

Serena spoke to Cantok's mind and was assured he was pleased to share his cubs with them.

"Father, Cantok said he must apologize for what he and his fellow wolves did recently in the UT."

"The what? What did he do?"

Serena's face blanched as she listened to what Cantok had to say.

Gateskin become concerned by his daughter's pale face and asked, "What did he say? Are you all right, Serena?"

"Yes, I feel a little sick but I will be okay. Cantok apologized for eating the guards who came to the UT. He only hopes they were not Sovorotskinans. If they were, he would understand if his kind were not welcome here."

"I see. Yes, I know about that already. They were Parotovinan guards. That was unfortunate. As long as he now understands that cannot happen here ever or I will have all of them eradicated."

Cantok bowed and grunted in agreement after Serena explained what her father had said.

Serena shook and shivered at the thought of what Cantok and the other wolves had done. Cantok sent words into her head to calm her and apologize again.

She looked at Cantok whose eyes were filled with regret and responded, "I understand you were hungry and had to eat. But it still is not something I would like to think about, Cantok."

The wolf knew he had to convince his new friend, Serena, he would never harm any of the Sovorotskinans. But he couldn't promise not to go after the Parotovinans again, if need be, to protect her and her family and his new home of Sovorotskina.

"Okay, I forgive you, Cantok," Serena said out loud, sighed and patted him on the head in friendship.

***

King Gateskin spoke softly to his Queen and discussed the new arrangement of the wolves. He expressed his concern, "We need to provide food sources for the number of wolves that are now living under our domain."

"No need to worry, my love. I will take care of their needs. I will conjure up some meat to feed them all daily. I will have your men carry some over to the other farms so that all the wolves will be well fed."

"But you must also give them some fresh food they can kill. They are used to foraging for their own food source, my dear," Gateskin added. "They are, after all, wild animals."

Solinara grinned and nodded, "Yes, I agree. I already have something in mind for them. I will work with my brother to come up with a new little creature the wolves can hunt for an extra food source"

"Hmm, I see. I am curious to see what you two come up with," Gateskin chuckled.

Solinara hugged her husband and said, "Don't forget we have something else to finish. Did you forget about Botular?"

"Oh, yes, I almost did. All this migrating of creatures to our land washed it out of my mind."

Gateskin turned toward his home but was stopped by his daughter, Serena, as she came up to him and asked, "Father, can we stay here with the cubs for a little while until they get settled in their new home? I have much to ask Cantok about the UT."

"UT? What is the UT? You mentioned this before." Gateskin looked confused.

"Oh, sorry. That is what Cantok calls the Unknown Territory."

"UT - that makes sense. Okay. Well, don't forget your chores and now you will have another one to do – take care of the cubs and make sure they do not come into the house. You must be careful about where they deposit their…You will have to pick it up and keep it away from the yard and house. You must also instruct

Cantok to keep his cubs away from the chicken coop, cows and vegetable garden."

"All right, Father. I will enlist Simon and Catalina to help. I'm sure the cubs can be taught where to go eventually." Serena giggled as she returned to the cubs who were looking around the area with noses pressed to the ground.

King Gateskin could hear Serena instructing her siblings what to do. He laughed at the shocked expressions on the faces of Simon and Catalina when they looked up at him. He nodded at them and walked away with a broad smile.

He would have to send word to the rest of the villagers about the wolves and how they would feed them and dispose of their waste matter.

He gathered his men and told them, "You will be visiting every farm in the village and delivering the meat the Queen will have ready for the wolves. If any villager needs more meat for their wolves, they are to contact me. I will keep my mind open for them to deliver their messages that way."

His men nodded in agreement and stood by until they were needed further when the meat was prepared and ready for disbursal.

King Gateskin opened his mind to the villagers and sent a message to them, "A new food source will be coming your way for the wolves to eat. If you have any questions, clear your minds and send the messages to me. I will answer any questions you may have." He asked, "If you are having any problems getting along with the wolves, please let me know." Gateskin waited a minute for any replies before continuing, "Okay, then if all is working out okay, I will sign off now." The King ended his mind message for the time being until someone contacted him.

***

Queen Solinara was working with her brother to conjure up this source of nutritious meat for the wolves. At the same time, they were developing a new creature for the wolves to hunt. They had to make sure that this creature was not dangerous to people.

The new creatures were to be called Rabbinels similar to a rabbit and a squirrel. They would be fast and be able to live underground. Since the wolves have such a powerful sense of smell, they would be able to detect these animals in the creatures' tunnels underground. Also, with the Rabbinels' speed the wolves could chase them at the same time giving the wolves some much-needed exercise and the thrill of the catch. It was important to keep the wolves happy and sated and at the same time fulfill their need to hunt and forage for food. The Queen and Wizard also added some extra vitamins and needed supplements to the creatures to keep the wolves healthy. They did not want the wolves to eat all the other little creatures who help to keep nature in balance.

Now all Solinara and Hotenfaran had to do was introduce this new creature to the woods and see if the wolves would be interested in them for food.

What they were unaware of was outside the border of Sovorotskina there were other hungry creatures lurking about.

CHAPTER THREE

Queen Solinara and Hotenfaran came out of the shed with two creatures in a cage. She also had a bag of the meat she had conjured for the wolves. She set the items on the ground in front of Cantok and his family to see what they would do.

Cantok sniffed the meat and the caged animals with interest. His family came alongside him and sniffed some more. The cubs began to salivate and drool could be seen dripping from their jaws.

King Gateskin stood by to observe this experiment. He grinned in relief when he saw the reaction of the wolves to both the conjured meat and the new creatures.

"Do you want to test the meat on Cantok and his family, Solinara?"

"Yes, I was hoping Serena would explain this to Cantok and let him decide if he wants to try some."

Gateskin called his eldest daughter over, "Serena, can you come here for a minute? I want to discuss something with you."

"Yes, Father. What do you have here?"

"These two items are food sources your mother and uncle have conjured to feed the wolves. Can you ask Cantok if he would be willing to test out the food sources?"

"Of course, Father. Let me ask him."

Serena looked at Cantok and sent her question to him.

"He would be more than willing to try them. He knows you are trying to make him and his family feel welcome by offering them these gifts of food. He also said his cubs are very hungry and need to eat."

Cantok put his nose into the bag and took a bite out of the juicy red meat that was there. He torn the meat apart, gulped and swallowed as his cubs watched. They salivated more profusely and put their noses into the sides of his mouth to get some too.

The wolf looked at Serena and nodded his head.

"He likes it, Father! He said it is the best meat he has ever tasted. He wants to know if he can taste the little creatures next."

Solinara stepped forward and opened the cage and let the creatures go. The Rabbinels raced for the woods with Cantok right behind them. They heard a scuffle and a cry of the animal being captured.

"What do you call these creatures, Mother?" Serena wanted to know as she watched Cantok.

Cantok walked back proudly with a creature in his jaws. He placed it in front of his cubs and mate and let them eat.

His mate ate her fill and let the cubs devour the rest of the creature. The wolves wiped their jaws on the ground as they swallowed the rest of the creature quickly.

"We named them Rabbinels. They are a combination of a rabbit and a squirrel," Solinara announced as she clapped her hands in joy that their experiment was successful. She thanked Hotenfaran and hugged him as they watched the wolves go search for the second creature who was hiding in the woods.

She pulled Hotenfaran back to the shed to create more of the creatures so they could begin to procreate on their own and provide plenty of food in the future for the wolves. They also worked tirelessly to produce enough meat to provide plenty for the other wolves on the neighboring farms.

Before long King Gateskin alerted his men, "The meat is ready for delivery to the farms. Please make sure the villagers know when they need more food for their wolves that all they have to do is call my name and give me their request."

The three children were fascinated by the wolves as they hunted for the second Rabbinel. They were hoping the Rabbinel escaped. At the same time, they wanted the cubs to get their fill.

Serena looked toward the shed and edged closer to see what her mother and uncle were doing. She wanted more than anything to learn how to do what they just did for the wolves. Serena didn't want her siblings to follow her. She kept looking over her shoulder to make sure they weren't looking at her. Fortunately, they were enthralled with the wolves as the animals continued to search for the second Rabbinel.

CHAPTER FOUR

Solinara left Hotenfaran to finish up in the shed preparing the food source for the wolves while she went back to the house to speak with her husband about the issues with Botular being untrustworthy.

"Ahh there you are, my love. I wondered how long you were going to spend in the shed working on the food source. I think we have enough to last for now especially since you created these new animals on which the wolves can feed. That was a brilliant idea by you and your brother."

"Well, I give the credit to Hotenfaran. He is the brilliant one here. I came up with the food source (meat) while he created the Rabbinels. It was quite clever of him to do that – combine two animals that the wolves love to eat. These creatures will provide the healthy food they will need. If we didn't create these creatures the wolves would decimate the population of other little critters around like squirrels, mice, rats and rabbits. They can still eat some of them too."

"I feel so out of my element with you two," he sighed. "Why are you looking so glum, dear?"

"Well, we never did get back to Botular and our testing of the Staglemite on him. I have been keeping an eye on him since he came. I still don't trust him not to contact King Kaposkaran."

"I know, Solinara. I feel the same. So, what did you and Hotenfaran do with the Staglemite?

Solinara grinned. "You won't believe what happened when we put the Staglemite into Botular's pocket without him noticing."

"Yes, please don't keep me in suspense, dear," Gateskin said as he leaned forward in anticipation.

Solinara laughed before responding, "It was quite comical, my love. We began to question Botular about his previous attempts to reach King Kaposkaran. He was hesitant to respond at first but then he got a strange look upon his face and turned to us."

Gateskin smirked but encouraged his wife to continue, "Please don't stop now."

"He couldn't stop talking. He went on and on about how evil his former king is and what he would do to him if he got his hands on him. He apologized for ever deceiving us and promised never to do that again. He even got down on his hands and knees and cried. He actually cried."

"I guess he was quite convincing then because of the Staglemite."

"Yes, I think that had a lot to do with it. It acted like a truth serum, a very effective one."

"That could be most valuable to us in the future," Gateskin mused.

Solinara nodded and continued, "Botular even jumped up and down and did a little dance when he was finished. He said he was relieved to get this off his mind and felt it was quite freeing to feel this way. He pledged himself to you and this land."

"A dance, you say? He doesn't look like the sort of fellow who would do a dance. That is strange and quite comical. Well, I still want to keep my eyes and ears open around him."

"Yes, I agree, Gateskin. I will continue to do so too."

"What about the Staglemite? Did you take it out of his pocket?"

"Oh, yes. We had to. He might do something with it to prevent us from hearing what he says if he does try to contact King Kaposkaran again."

"Did he know Staglemite was in his pocket?"

"I don't think so. At least I hope not. It could all have been an act if he did."

"Don't worry about that now, Solinara. I don't think he is that good an actor. After all, we did see through him right from the beginning."

"Yes, I guess you're right. But just to be safe, I will work with Hotenfaran on the Staglemite a little longer to see what else it can do."

"Good idea, sweetheart, but first, isn't it time for dinner?"

Solinara rolled her eyes at her husband and promptly went into the kitchen to create a special dinner for him. She planned to do a little work and magic to put it all together.

***

Gateskin went to look for the children to get them to clean up for dinner. When he went outside, he observed the children playing with the three wolf cubs. Serena was quite taken with the largest one, Tankor, and the two younger children with the smaller cubs. Simon was petting Rattor and Catalina was holding the youngest, Maku, the female.

The King beamed to himself as he called them in for dinner and patted each of his children on the head as they passed by him. The wolves went back to their shelter and probably to their own dinner.

Out in the woods the new animals, Rabbinels, were rapidly procreating as Solinara and Hotenfaran had programmed them to do. But when would they stop? The animals would stop eventually if there were too many of them. If they neared depletion, they would procreate rapidly again. Something in the woods at the border of the UT was watching all these new animals with large salivating jaws.

CHAPTER FIVE

Back in Parotovina King Kaposkaran was busy meeting with his powerful Wizards who were explaining what they were doing.

The Head Wizard, Number One said, "We have conjured up this creature using a man who was going to be killed soon anyway. We weren't sure if this experiment would kill him or not."

"Well, what did you discover?" King Kaposkaran asked in an irritated manner.

The Wizards, though powerful, feared their evil ruler and answered without hesitation. "We have created a new monster of sorts."

"Well, where is it?" King Kaposkaran asked impatiently as he looked around the dungeon room.

The Head Wizard walked over to a dark cell and turned a light on inside. As he did this a screeching sound was heard and he quickly backed away.

King Kaposkaran edged closer to get a better look. What he saw shocked him. Standing, at nine feet tall, three feet taller than he, was the strangest creature he had ever seen. It was multi-colored with spikes all over its slimy body and it had enormous jaws that dripped of saliva. Its eyes were glowing and looked at him with an odd expression of hopelessness and anger.

"What is its name, Wizard One?" The King spoke delicately so as not to soften the spell he was under just looking at the creature.

"We thought you might like to name it, our King."

The King sneered as he thought over what he would name this new creature.

"Hmm, let's see. What can I name you, my lovely creature?" King Kaposkaran leaned closer to the cell and whispered, "What would you like to be called?"

The creature with glowing eyes and dripping jaws of saliva looked down on the King and grunted. It tried to speak but was unable to do so. It shook its massive head and stamped its feet and shook the bars of the cell.

The Wizards and the King backed away for fear of their lives if the creature got out of its cell.

"Who was this man you used to create this thing?" The King directed his question to the six Wizards who were cowering in the opposite corner of the dungeon.

Wizard One stepped forward and answered, "It was the thief, Quintal, your highness." This Wizard backed away and joined the others in the corner far away from the creature.

"Quintal, you say. Let's make a name out of Quintal," the King mused it over and said, "It will be Quintaroon."

Looking inside the cell he directed his voice to the creature and announced, "From this day on you will be named

Quintaroon. Do you like your name, creature?"

The creature roared and spit saliva at the King as its eyes glowed brighter.

"Yes, I think it likes its new name," The King chuckled as he wiped the spit off his cloak and turned to his Wizards.

"I would like to see what Quintaroon can do. Are you ready to show me?"

The Wizards shivered in alarm. They had no idea what this new creature could do. They looked at each other and shrugged their shoulders.

"Don't just stand there, you idiots! Show me what Quintaroon can do! Now!"

The Head Wizard moved toward the King and said, "Dear King, we don't know what it can do. We just created it from Quintal. We gave it a fierce body, eyes and manner but beyond that we don't know. We didn't give it a personality or any other abilities."

"What do you mean you didn't give it any abilities? If you create a creature, you must give it some abilities. What else will it be used for if it can't do something?"

The Wizards gathered together and discussed what they would do next. They knew their King did not have much patience for lollygagging. They had to put their heads together and do it quickly.

King Kaposkaran cleared his throat and said, "Well, what do you have? I need to see something now or else I will open the cell and let Quintaroon show me what he can do himself."

The Head Wizard turned toward the King and announced, "We will give him some powers, your highness. Let us get close enough to him and put a few spells over him to do this."

The Wizards conferred and stepped close to the cell and waved their hands over the creature called Quintaroon. The creature sniffed the air and came closer to the Wizards.

Alarmed at Quintaroon's proximity to them, the Wizards hastily finished their spells and backed away from the cell.

King Kaposkaran reached over and pulled the key out of the Head Wizard's hand and opened the cell.

Before they knew it, the Quintaroon stepped out and swept Wizards Five and Six off their feet. It gripped the screaming Wizards in its clawed hands and squeezed them until they were dead. The rest of the Wizards ran out of the dungeon before they were next.

King Kaposkaran clapped his hands and laughed. Quintaroon looked at him, grunted and tried to clap his claws together too.

He waved his hands over the creature casting a calming spell. The King said in a soothing voice, "Good job, Quintaroon. You are now one of my subjects. You will do whatever I say. Do you understand? You will go back into your cell now and I will send you some food."

Quintaroon nodded and stepped back into his cell. He picked up the two Wizards he had killed and brought them into the cell for company. He didn't like being alone in the cell in the dark dungeon. He was afraid of the dark.

King Kaposkaran had his own powers, not as powerful as the Head Wizard or all the Wizards' powers collectively, but enough to keep this creature under his control.

Hurrying back upstairs to his castle he called the scullery chef to his quarters to discuss what to make for Quintaroon. He wanted his new creature to be strong and able to help him attain his goal of power over all the lands.

He looked around for his Wizards but they were nowhere to be seen. He chuckled to himself, "They were supposed to be fearless but even their own creation frightened them."

***

Unbeknownst to the King, the Wizards left the castle and went to their homes, packed up their families and raced into the woods to escape before King Kaposkaran would find them. They knew once Quintaroon was loose they were all dead for the King wouldn't be satisfied with just one creature. He would want more. They couldn't do this for fear of the lives of all the Parotovinans. They had to warn the other villages before it was too late.

CHAPTER SIX

Solinara was cleaning up the kitchen without her magic because she enjoyed working. She found it soothing as she gazed out the window at the woods.

She blinked a few times to assure herself that what she saw was real.

She dropped the dishes back into the sink and called her husband through his mind, "Gateskin, come quickly but keep the children inside."

Gateskin appeared at her side and looked over her shoulder at the scene playing out in the woods close to the wolves' shelter. He couldn't believe his eyes either. "What is it, Solinara?"

"I don't know. It suddenly appeared there."

Standing between the edge of the woods and his house was the strangest creature he had ever seen. It stood about nine feet tall and was multi-colored with spikes coming out of its body and a large jaw that dripped of saliva. He looked around for his wolves but did not see them. He only hoped they were safely inside their shelter.

The King stepped outside, closing the door and his wife inside for safety. He raised his hands up and pushed the air around him toward the creature. The creature looked up when it felt the air around it changing. It sniffed and spotted Gateskin several feet in front of it. The creature moved slowly forward and lifted its clawed hands up to protect itself as a defense.

Gateskin sent fire spells at the creature which stopped it in its tracks. The creature sniffed the air again which was full of the scent of its burning flesh. It turned around and ran off into the woods toward the UT.

Solinara appeared at the doorway and inquired, "Where is it, Gateskin?"

"It's gone for now but I'm sure it will be back with more of its kind. I need to put more spells over the UT border to keep them out. I don't know how it managed to get through. That is not good."

"Let me do that for you, Gateskin. I can use some new spells Hotenfaran and I have conjured. These spells will stop anything."

"Thank you, dear. While you are working on the UT borders, I will contact my men and send word to the other villages of this new danger. I fear that this is just the beginning. This is what Spindle recently warned me was coming."

King Gateskin called Spindle forward and gave him orders, "It is here, the creature you mentioned. I will need you close by to keep our borders safe and to warn the other villages of this creature."

"Of course, your Highness. I will do that right away. I will spread the word to the other villages through my fellow Sprites about this creature."

"Thank you, Spindle. Off you go." King Gateskin watched the Sprite fly up into the trees. A buzzing could be heard as word was spreading from tree to tree faster than he or his men could do that.

Solinara got Hotenfaran out of the shed to help her with the spells to protect the border. They put many spells, one over the other, to protect the borders. They felt assured even this giant monster would not get through.

Hotenfaran didn't ask any questions about the new danger until after they had finished with the spells. "What did this creature look like, Solinara?"

"It was too terrifying to think about! I couldn't believe my eyes! It was huge with spikes all over its body of many colors with a large jaw which could have swallowed a wolf whole. The scariest parts of it were its eyes – they appeared to look right through me with a surprising depth of intelligence. It was as if it was…"

"What, Solinara? What was it?"

"I felt as it if were somehow part human. It had a look in its eyes of intelligence only a human has."

"Hmm. I see. I feared that."

"What, Hotenfaran? What is it?" Solinara looked at her brother with consternation.

"It appears King Kaposkaran is up to more evil doings. When he didn't get his way capturing more Taken Ones or TOs and not being able to turn Serena his way, he has created this creature to try to destroy Sovorotskina."

"No, he can't destroy us! We are too strong for him."

"We must get a sample of its blood or saliva and analyze it to see if it is human or at least part human."

Solinara raced back to the shed with Hotenfaran close behind and picked up her bag of magic to collect the samples that were on the grass.

Hotenfaran got close to the area where Solinara said the creature was last standing and noticed some slime and blood streaks. He quickly swiped them up with a cloth as Solinara did the same with pieces of burned flesh nearby.

They disappeared back into their shed and began to test the samples.

***

The wolves who were deep into the woods of Skina Forest hunting, sensed something wasn't right. They sniffed the air and could smell the creature where it had been near their shelter. Cantok kept his cubs close by his side and guided them back to the shelter along with his mate.

Cantok kept his nose to the ground and followed the scent until it disappeared back into the UT. He ran back to his shelter and sent word to the other wolves to keep a lookout for any creatures in the border of the woods of the UT. He told them to keep their young ones safe inside their shelters until he could find out where the creature had gone.

Gateskin was deep in a meeting with Spindle and the rest of his men and the villagers. He told his guards, "Please stay close by the borders and if you see anything unusual, let me know right away." He told the villagers, "Be alert and stay clear of the borders and keep your family inside until the threat is over."

The guardsmen formed a border around the village between the border of Sovorotskina and the UT to try and keep everyone safe. They would be the eyes and ears of their King.

The King sent word himself along with Spindle's warning to the rulers of the other villages, "Be on the lookout for a tall, strange creature." He gave a more detailed description and continued, "I will send more of my men to you if needed."

He worked to strengthen the borders of Sovorotskina as he had instructed the other Villages to do to their own borders to ensure the safety of all subjects. He wondered how the creature had penetrated his barriers. There must have been a weak spot somewhere. He would look more closely at all the borders along the UT for any problems.

CHAPTER SEVEN

The Parotovinan Wizards arrived at the border of Merlina. They could see there was a strong spell at the border which they could not break. They tried different techniques to pierce it without success. They stayed there until they saw guardsmen heading their way.

"Please let us in. We are the Wizards from Parotovina here on our own accord. We do not plan to harm you or your people. We must speak at once to your King Zuri. It is of utmost importance."

The guardsmen nodded to one another and turned to their own Wizard to open the border for the visitors.

The Wizards thanked the Merlina Wizard for his assistance and stated, "We are here to speak to your King Zuri. He will want to know what we have to share. There is danger coming your way."

"What danger?" the Merlina Wizard questioned; his voice edged with suspicion.

"We need to share this only with King Zuri. Please, we must hurry. There is no time to waste. Lives are at stake."

The Melina Wizard led the Wizards to the castle of King Zuri and left them with more guardsmen to bring them into the King's Meeting Room.

After explaining about the creature, they had created, the Wizards waited to hear what King Zuri would say.

"What do you want me to do, Wizards?" King Zuri asked with a stern expression as he faced the four Wizards.

"I don't know, King Zuri. We are sorry for creating this creature. All we can do now is to warn all the villages of its existence and impending danger. It is most powerful and can destroy everyone in its way. King Kaposkaran will do all he can to destroy everyone in order for him to have control of all the villages."

King Zuri replied in a stern manner, "King Gateskin sent us a warning about this creature today. It is already roaming around our borders. You should not have created such a thing."

"Oh no, we are too late! King Kaposkaran didn't waste any time getting it out there. We know, your highness, we shouldn't have done this, but we were forced to do it."

"I see. We have known for a long time of the evil of King Kaposkaran. We know he cannot be trusted. Where are you going and what will you do now to rectify this situation?"

The Wizards exchanged worried glances with each other and the Head Wizard answered, "We fear for our lives and that of our families and must get as far away as possible from our King. We will go to King Gateskin who is the most powerful Wizard in the land. He will know what to do next."

"Okay, I agree. We have already built up our forces and strengthened our boundaries to keep this creature out. Now, you must hurry along. I will have my men provide you with supplies and wagons to transport your families. I am happy to hear you have changed your evil ways. Take care. May Ressaphena and Ramoforan, the gods of Goodness and Light, watch over you and take you safely into Sovorotskina."

"We noticed how strong your borders are. We couldn't break them with all our collective powers," the Wizards remarked.

"That is good to know. I wasn't sure if we had done enough to keep this creature at bay," King Zuri replied with relief.

"Well, it certainly looks like you did. Thank you, good King Zuri. We are grateful for your assistance." The Wizards bowed and left the castle and gathered their families into the wagons provided by the King. They used a little magic to move the wagons to the borders of the villages of Merona, Votovia and into Sovorotskina.

The Wizards had to stop at each border until the villages' guardsmen could have their Wizards open the borders. It took some quick explaining why they were in such a rush. But the villages noticed the wagons with King Zuri's emblem on them and gave them free passage without too long a delay.

As they traveled, the Wizards spoke through their minds to each other about what had transpired with King Zuri. They couldn't believe King Kaposkaran had already unleashed the Quintaroon on the villages. *How could he have done that so fast. We only left a few hours ago. Do you think the creature can fly?*

One Wizard looked up with wide eyes in alarm. *What did you do?* The Head Wizard asked in a stern and displeased voice.

The Wizards were only known as numbers. There were six of them in all before two had been killed by the Quintaroon. Now they were reduced to four. Wizard number two answered, *I didn't even think about it when I gave the creature the power to fly. I never thought it would live.*

The Head Wizard exclaimed, *Well, here we are now against a formidable creature with the ability to fly! How could you have done such a thing? Didn't we speak about this? We decided to only give the creature a creepy and intimidating appearance.*

The Head Wizard looked at the other two Wizards and asked, *what did you two give the creature for powers?*

One Wizard shrugged his shoulders and sighed. *I only gave it the ability to keep its fears as a man. They could come in handy.*

The Head Wizard nodded but looked at the other Wizard and waited for him to add anything further.

Nothing really. Just the power to disappear if he drank water.

What? Really? Head Wizard said as he shook his head and sighed heavily.

CHAPTER EIGHT

King Gateskin completed casting multiple spells of protection on top of what his wife and her brother had already done along the borders of Sovorotskina and the UT. He felt assured his subjects were safe from any further dangers that may come to their land.

He went back to the shed to speak with his wife and her brother to see how they were doing with the creatures' samples.

"Gateskin, come in. We are finding some interesting stuff here," Solinara said with elation.

"What is it, dear?" Gateskin asked as he stepped into the massive shed.

There were large tables spread with all kinds of paraphernalia. Along the walls hung many different tools that floated back and forth between Solinara's and Hotenfaran's hands to aid in their work.

Solinara was leaning over a sample of the burned flesh as she picked it up and put it into a container with fluid and moved it around.

Hotenfaran was working on the saliva samples as he did similar tests with a strange fluid that was changing colors as he mixed it.

"What are you doing, Hotenfaran? Why is it changing colors like that?"

"Well, it appears the cells in the saliva are colored like his body was. Didn't you say he was multi-colored, King Gateskin?"

"Yes, I did describe him like that. He had many colors all over him. Did you find any of the spikes that were covering most of his body?"

"No, but I will check the area carefully to see if I can find one. That's a good idea. There might be something important in the spikes to tell us more about it," Hotenfaran said as he concentrated on his sample.

"Gateskin, come close," Solinara urged him forward.

"What am I looking at, dear?"

"See this spot on the flesh. It is not an animal but belongs to a human. It is human flesh. It is underneath the scaly flesh and appears to have been protected by the outside layer which is tougher and thicker."

"Yes, I see this. How do you explain this phenomenon?"

"It looks like it is a human underneath the creature."

"What? Do you mean someone created a creature like this using a human for the form or base?"

"Yes, unfortunately, I do, Gateskin. It is a scary prospect, isn't it? Using humans to create monsters like this? Who would do such a thing?"

"Solinara, who do you think would do this heinous thing?" Hotenfaran announced as he looked at his sister and raised his eyebrows.

"Oh, I see, brother. I think I know. But what can we do to protect the lands from this creature? Who knows how many more there are?"

"Yes, I am working on this. It is inevitable there will be more to come. The evil King would not stop at just one."

***

Screams were reportedly heard by the Sprites inhabiting the trees in that area in the distance bordering the UT and Votovia which is west of Sovorotskina.

CHAPTER NINE

The screaming continued as King Gateskin enlisted several of his men to come with him to check it out.

Solinara and Hotenfaran closely followed Gateskin and asked, "What can we do to help?"

"Nothing. I am waiting to see if it is the creature again. Maybe it is making this sound to draw us into opening the borders."

King Gateskin came up behind his men as they formed a barrier between the village and the UT border waiting for further instructions from their King.

"Wait here, men. I will go closer to peer into the woods through my mind. There is no need for anyone to get harmed. If I need any of you, I will let you know. Stay here and close together."

The men nodded and stood side by side with Spindle flying above them in the lead in a formation tight enough that not even a feather could pass through.

The King looked into the woods and saw a terrifying scene play out in his mind. There were numerous bodies blooded and separated all over the woods. There were too many to count. Further back in the UT woods he saw the creature with its jaws dripping of saliva and blood. Its claws held onto one man and squeezed him until he stopped screaming.

The King shook his head to try to dispel this scene but it played back at him. It was not something he would ever forget. He told his men, "Go back to your homes and keep your families safe and let me know if you hear anything like this again."

The men dispersed quickly without further questions once they saw the shock on their King's face. They became fearful for their families and didn't waste any time hurrying home.

Spindle stayed close to the King in case he was needed. He knew his family was safely tucked away in their tree houses in Sovorotskina.

Solinara and Hotenfaran came alongside the King and supported him as they walked him back to the house.

When Gateskin arrived back home Solinara put her hands on his shoulders for comfort. "What did you see, my love?" Solinara asked softly. She was afraid to raise her voice once she saw her husband's face blanch.

Gateskin gazed around his home as he tried to dispel the horror playing back in his brain. He did not believe he needed a castle for a home as the other kings in the surrounding villages did. He was happy to have the large wooden house he had built himself. His home was his castle and that is where he needed to be right now to feel safe.

Once Solinara got her husband comfortably seated at the table, she asked him again what he saw. Solinara put a hot cup of her special brewed chamomile tea in his hands to calm him so he could begin.

Spindle stood at attention nearby and waited for any word from the King of what he needed him to do.

Hotenfaran sat next to King Gateskin and patted him on the arm. He asked softly, "Are you okay, Gateskin?"

Gateskin looked up when he heard Hotenfaran's voice. He shook his head and sighed heavily. He took a sip of the tea he just realized he was holding that was warming his hands.

Solinara exchanged concerned looks with her brother before she ventured to ask Gateskin another question.

"My love, are you receiving disturbing messages from King Kaposkaran again?"

Gateskin shook his head. "No, dear, I am not. In fact, they have ceased for a while now. I don't think we will have to worry about King Kaposkaran's men coming here. They are all dead."

"What? What did you say, Gateskin?" Solinara asked in a shocked voice.

Hotenfaran spoke up at this too. "What did you see, my King?"

The King shook his head back and forth and covered his face with his hands. Trembling could be seen coming from his hands.

Solinara wrapped her husband in her arms as she sat next to him at the table. "Oh, my love, please tell us what you saw. Get it out of your head and rid the scenes from playing back to you again and again." She knew what it was like to see something horrendous and not be able to get it out of your mind. She felt that way when she had dreams of her family being taken and slaughtered. Thank God her dreams were not a reality.

"This should not have happened to anyone. These men were coming here to harm us, I know, but I would not wish this horrific death on them by this creature." Gateskin took a deep breath before continuing, "Their bodies were crushed or torn apart by this monster. I saw it crush a man in its clawed hand. It was something I want to erase from my mind but I don't think I will ever be able to do that."

"Why were they coming from the UT border and not from one of the other villages?" Hotenfaran queried.

"It could be that since then all the villages have reinforced their borders to prevent the creature from entering. But the men and the creature could still go to the UT since this area was not protected."

"What about the Wizards of Parotovina? Don't they have control over the creature? They must have had something to do with its creation," Solinara asked as she was musing over the causes and effects of the creature. "They could have kept their men safe from harm if they were coming here to surprise us."

"Evidently these men were not told about the creature," Gateskin responded. "I think they were probably already on their way here before the creature was sent out."

"You may be right, my love. I bet King Kaposkaran did not even think about his men being in the way of the creature," Solinara said sadly.

Spindle nodded in agreement and saluted King Gateskin as he stood by sending his thoughts to the King to try to calm him down.

King Gateskin looked up at Spindle who was flying around him and saluted him back. "You are a mighty Head Guard, Spindle. It is comforting just to have you nearby. Thank you."

"I am here for you, King Gateskin, whenever you need me."

CHAPTER TEN

As they were discussing this creature, a rumble could be heard from the border of Votovia and Sovorotskina as if someone or something was trying to break through the border.

Spindle watched the wagons approaching the border and flew up to the trees to observe them. He sent word to King Gateskin that there were visitors coming.

King Gateskin went outside with Head Guard Spindle close by his side and reached out through his mind to his close friend, King Cavelan of Votovia, who had helped him in the last confrontation with Parotovina and King Kaposkaran. King Cavelan responded back quickly.

"Yes, King Gateskin. I'm sorry I didn't reach you before this. We were informed by King Zuri of Merlina we were to open our borders to the Parotovinan Wizards who are coming to see you with utmost important information about their new creature."

"Ah, I see. I just saw this creature in action and it was not a pleasant sight to see. It killed all the men from Parotovina who were coming to Sovorotskina to cause more trouble. It was not something I would ever want to see again."

"Well, that must have been horrifying, King Gateskin. I am so sorry you had to witness it. We haven't seen this creature yet, thank goodness. Our borders are strong as I am sure are yours. But the Unknown Territory is open and that is where it will reside with all the other creatures which inhabit that area."

"Yes, I'm sure it is. We do have some creatures from the UT, the wolves, who are living in Sovorotskina now. Evidently, there are other creatures in the UT who once used the wolves as a food source. Now with the new creatures living there, these other smaller creatures will become the new creatures' food source."

"The UT? What is that, King Gateskin?" King Cavelan asked in a confused manner.

"Oh, sorry, King Cavelan. The wolves told us that is how the Unknown Territory is known to them."

"Hmm. Okay. You can actually converse with these wolves?"

"Yes, well, at least my daughter can. For some reason I cannot speak with them. They block me out and only converse with Serena."

"Ha-ha, I bet Serena loves that. I would love to hear more about these wolves and see them for myself. Can we meet soon to discuss this more?"

"Yes, I think my daughter does like to have some power over me. Please come whenever you can but be careful of the creature. It is huge, standing about nine feet tall, with massive jaws, clawed hands and spikes that cover most of its scaly body. The strangest thing is, it is multi-colored."

"Well, I don't necessarily want to meet it but would like to see it from a safe distance."

"I saw it when it came to our woods behind my house. It was too close for comfort. I have since reinforced the borders."

"Happy to hear you are safer now. We all have to keep a lookout for it especially since you described it as so terrifying."

"The Wizards are here now. Thank you, my friend. I look forward to meeting you soon. We have much to discuss."

"That we do, my friend. That we do. Stay safe."

CHAPTER ELEVEN

King Gateskin instructed Spindle to guard the door of his home once everyone was inside. He would let him know if he was needed further.

The four Wizards from Parotovina stood next to their wagons with their wives and children safely tucked inside. They stepped forward with outreached hands to shake King Gateskin's hand in peace.

King Gateskin shook each Wizard's hand in turn and guided them into his home. His wife stood at the doorway to welcome them in, along with her brother.

The Head Wizard introduced his fellow Wizards to King Gateskin and his Queen and brother-in-law. Queen Solinara went out to welcome the Wizards' families inside for refreshments and to rest from their long trip.

Queen Solinara laid out a table full of all kinds of food and drink and gave the children a table of their own on which to eat along with her own children. Serena, Simon and Catalina made the Wizards' children at home and soon they were all talking about their favorite things to do and what powers they had, that is, after Serena got the message from her mother that it was okay to share their powers with these visitors.

King Gateskin put a BE spell (Block Enchantment) that created a wall between the children and the adults' tables in order that they could discuss in private the reason why the Parotovinan Wizards had come to Sovorotskina.

King Gateskin opened up the conversation by asking, "Did you have a safe trip here, Head Wizard?"

The Head Wizard looked solemn and concerned but nodded. "Yes, we did, King Gateskin. Thank you for asking." He bowed his head and then continued, "We Parotovinans have not always been kind to the other villages. Please be assured that was not our choice. We have had to live under the evil King Kaposkaran for too long in fear for our lives if we did not do his bidding. This thing he requested we do was the last straw. We could not do another evil thing."

"Okay. I understand. Now tell me what brought you here after all this time?"

"We…created a formidable creature in size and strength but King Kaposkaran was not satisfied with that. He wanted the creature to do more. We think it must be able to fly now because it arrived here before we did even though we left before King Kaposkaran knew we were gone."

"Who gave the creature the power to fly?"

The Head Wizard exchanged wary glances with his fellow Wizards and shook his head at them before continuing, "It wasn't any of us. We were requested to give it more powers by the King but we just went through the motions and did not give it any more. It must have been King Kaposkaran who gave it more powers."

"It appears to be almost human. Did you use a human to create it?"

The Wizards exchanged surprised glances at each other before the Head Wizard answered, "Yes, we did. How did you know? The man we used was going to die the next day. We thought that we would give him a chance to live in another form."

"My wife and brother-in-law are powerful and surmised it from samples they collected. We can discuss that later if need be. Tell me, do you think that the man knows he is no longer a man?"

"Yes, I think he does. I saw a fearful and beseeching look in his eyes after we made him."

"I saw something in his eyes too but it was not helpless. It was more fierce and powerful. I think it now knows that it is a powerful being and is no longer fearful."

"Yes, I think that was going to happen inevitably, King Gateskin. Unfortunate for all of us he knows he is powerful and can control us instead of the other way around."

"I agree, Head Wizard. Please tell me why you do not have a name? I would like to call you by your name and not Head Wizard. It is not very personable."

"I know, King Gateskin. Our King wanted it that way. He did not want to think of us as humans but rather as powerful objects he could control. Let me begin by introducing myself and my fellow wizards to you by name." Pointing to himself he said, "I am Marno. Wizard two is Fortag, Wizard three is Wassor, and Wizard four is Tornak."

"It is a pleasure to meet you, Wizards, Marno, Fortag, Wassor and Tornak. We have much more to discuss but I know you are tired from your long journey as are your families. Eat and drink up and I will set up some sleeping quarters for you in our extension used for guests. After you have rested, we will talk some more about this creature. I'm sure my wife, Queen Solinara, and her brother, Hotenfaran who is a powerful wizard in his own right, have much to ask you."

Queen Solinara and Wizard Hotenfaran nodded and escorted their guests to the extension with their families that was now ready for them.

***

King Gateskin had almost forgotten about Spindle who was still outside his door. He brought out a plate sized for the Sprite and apologized for keeping him there. "I must apologize for letting you stay here so long, Spindle. You must be starving. Here is something to keep your strength up. I can't have my Head Guard weak from hunger and unable to do his job. Once you finish eating, please return home and get a good night's sleep. I will need you fresh and ready tomorrow for whatever comes our way."

Spindle's mouth watered as he looked at the plate of food in the King's hand. He responded, "No problem, King Gateskin. I am here for you as long as you need me to stay outside your door for protection. Thank you for this appetizing-looking meal. I have to admit, I am starving. I will leave the plate here and return home afterward. See you early tomorrow morning, my King." Spindle saluted Gateskin and dug into the food.

Once Spindle finished his dinner he called to Serena in his mind. She responded back, curious to know what he wanted.

She came to the door and watched Spindle fly up into his family's tree. He pointed to the plate that sat there on the step and smiled. He blew Serena a kiss and disappeared into the highest branches.

Serena blushed and threw Spindle a kiss in a mind message up into the tree which made him also blush a greener shade than the leaves around him.

CHAPTER TWELVE

Solinara, Gateskin and Hotenfaran sat at the large table in their kitchen/dining area sipping the Queen's potent chicory coffee. She had also baked, with some magic, her tasty biscuits to go with the coffee. They were all full from the large dinner she had served to their guests but not too full to enjoy the coffee and biscuits.

Solinara looked at her husband's face that now appeared less stressed but still showed some concern. She was relieved the messages had stopped from King Kaposkaran but now there was another problem – the creature. She could see her husband trying to work things out in his head. She tried not to interrupt his thoughts but she had much to ask him.

Gateskin could see that his wife was doing her best not to read his thoughts. He could see she was anxious to know more about this new creature but so was he.

Turning towards her he asked, "My Queen, what is it you need to ask me?"

"Oh, Gateskin, there is much we need to know about this thing. What powers does it have and are there any weaknesses we can use against it?"

"Well, that is something we will find out soon enough, my love. We must let the Wizards and their families rest first before inundating them with questions. We must also get them lodging so that they can stay here. This will be their new home. They cannot go back to Parotovina ever again. King Kaposkaran will have them tortured first to find out what we know about the creature and then kill them and their families."

Hotenfaran stood up and excused himself, "I must get back to my wife. She is probably pacing the floor and dying to ask me a million questions about the creature. I can help you tomorrow with setting up the Wizards' houses, King Gateskin."

"Thank you, Hotenfaran. We'll talk more about that tomorrow. Have a good night's rest."

Solinara kissed her brother and hugged him. "Thank you, Hotenfaran, for all your help. I couldn't have done any of this without you. I think you should go home and rest and fill Procelina in on everything. Bring her with you tomorrow for breakfast. There will be much more to learn about this strange creature in our land at that time."

"Same goes to you, Sister. We work well together, just like the old days," Hotenfaran chuckled and waved goodbye to Gateskin as he left their home.

Gateskin sighed heavily and said, "I think you two make a perfect pair of inventors. There is no limit to what you can do together."

"Oh, my dear. You flatter me too much. But I love it. Thank you. Now it's time for us to get some rest too." Solinara pulled her husband to his feet and wrapped her arms around him as she led him to bed.

***

The next morning everyone was up early especially the Wizards' children. They were keeping busy in the yard as breakfast was being prepared. They had been introduced to the wolves by Serena, Simon and Catalina. Serena had gone outside ahead of the guest children to prepare the wolves for the onslaught of affection from the Wizards' children they were sure to receive.

Cantok nodded and accepted with grace and patience all the attention he and his family had to endure. It was all new to him but he loved Serena from the moment they became friends. He would do anything to please her and keep her and her family safe. They had saved him and his family and fellow wolves from being slaughtered by the many creatures that inhabited the UT. He only hoped he could keep everyone safe in

Sovorotskina from these creatures and especially the newest one that had somehow recently broken through the barrier of the border.

CHAPTER THIRTEEN

Spindle reported to the King bright and early the next morning. "What can I do for you, King Gateskin?"

"Did you have a good night's sleep, my little man?"

"Oh, yes. The food you gave me made sure I did. I slept for eight hours without a dream until this morning."

"Good to hear, Spindle. Now, what I need for you to do is introduce yourself to Cantok and his family. See Serena about this first. I will call you when I need you. Okay?"

"Of course, King Gateskin. I will do that. I have been curious about these wolves and look forward to meeting them as long as they don't eat me."

"No worries about that, Spindle." Gateskin went inside with a smile on his face and a little chortle.

Spindle went over to Serena and inquired about the wolves, "Good morning, Serena. I would like to make my acquaintance with your wolves."

"Hi, Spindle. I haven't seen you around. Is my father keeping you busy?"

"Well, I am his Head Guard. That is my job to keep busy protecting and whatever else he needs me to do."

"Yes, of course. I almost forgot. But I do miss you, my friend."

Spindle's face brightened at Serena's words and he felt tongue tied. "Yes, I miss you too, Serena. I have some time now to spend with you and meet your wolves if you will introduce me and please tell them not to eat me. I don't taste very good."

Serena giggled and said, "I assure you, Spindle, they will not want to eat you. They have tasty meat and a new creature to eat that is much more appetizing."

Spindle followed Serena over to the wolves' shelter and waited for the wolf to look down at him once Serena sent her thoughts to its mind.

Cantok nodded at Serena and cast its golden eyes on Spindle's little body. He responded to Serena and she stated back to Spindle what he had said.

"Cantok said, he is glad to meet you. He is quite impressed that such a little man as you were given the auspicious position of Head Guard. He thinks you are quite an interesting little fellow to get to know."

"Really, he said that? Tell him I am impressed with him too. He is an incredible creature and quite handsome for a wolf."

"I don't think I want to tell him that part."

"What part?" Spindle was confused.

"Well, you said in other words that wolves are not attractive. I don't think that would make him happy at all," Serena warned.

"Oh, I see. Well, then tell him he is the most attractive wolf I have ever seen."

"Have you seen other wolves?"

"Umm, no, not really. But tell him this anyway. I'm sure he is the most attractive one of all. Please tell him so he won't want to eat me."

Serena laughed out loud at Spindle's words. Cantok looked at Serena with a confused expression waiting for an explanation of what was said.

She explained and watched Cantok's face widen into a wolf smile, if you could call it that.

Spindle watched in amazement and laughed too as Cantok's expression changed into one that was not threatening to him.

"See, I told you. He is not interested in eating you, Spindle!" Serena laughed again as she hugged the Sprite much to his surprise and delight.

As they were laughing over Spindle's fears the three cubs came out of the shelter along with their mother. Spindle jumped back and looked at them in amazement.

"Wow, Cantok has a family?"

"Yes, isn't it wonderful?" Serena beamed as if she was responsible for the family.

"Can I pet the cubs?" Spindle looked at Cantok as he flew above them and raised his hand above the cubs' heads and waited for Cantok's response.

The large wolf nodded his head at Spindle and the Sprite relaxed and laid his hand over each of the cubs' heads.

"They are so soft, Serena."

"Yes, I thought the same thing, Spindle. I was as surprised as you. They are really sweet too." She proceeded to introduce each cub to her best friend.

Spindle relaxed and sat on the grass as the cubs tried to sit on him. He had to stand up quickly or be smothered by them. He hopped up on their backs and gave them each a scratch behinds their ears which they liked even more.

"I think you have made some new friends, Spindle," Serena giggled in delight.

"Yes, I think I have." Spindle couldn't contain his relief and surprise.

Arubane, adopted son of Wizard Hotenfaran and Fairy Procelina, appeared next to Cantok and looked into the wolf's eyes, nodded and smiled.

Spindle whispered to Serena, "Look, I think Arubane is speaking to Cantok. I thought only you could do that."

"Hmm, so did I, Spindle. Let's go see what they are discussing so intently."

Cantok looked at Serena and nodded. She asked him what they were talking about.

"What did Cantok say?" Spindle couldn't contain his curiosity.

"Well, it seems Arubane can converse with the wolves too. He learned how by watching and reading my mind and that of Cantok. Arubane asked him about the UT and its creatures."

"Are there more creatures like the new one we saw, the Quintaroon?"

"Not yet, but Cantok thinks they could be more soon. The creatures he knows are the ones that are like large cats. He said they are called Catlings. They used to prey on the wolves' cubs for food. That is why Cantok and his fellow wolves abandoned their home in the UT."

"Oh wow! That is awful. These cubs are so cute. I wouldn't want anything to happen to them. They are sweet critters."

Serena laughed at the way Spindle spoke so tenderly about the wolves. She thought to herself, *Spindle has such a kind heart. No wonder I love him.*

Spindle observed Serena as she grinned and appeared deep in thought. "Is everything okay, Serena?"

"Oh, yes. I…uh, yes. Everything is just fine, Spindle. I was just thinking about the wolves after what you said about the cubs being so cute. They really are sweet things. We must protect them from the Quintaroon. I am sure it would love to use them as its food source."

Spindle thought about that and then responded, "No I don't think it would need them now. It has the Catlings to eat and their young."

"Well, as long as it has a food source it won't bother us or the wolves, for now anyway."

"Yes, for now. Who knows what will happen if there are more Quintaroons? Then they will run out of food and come this way."

Serena shivered at the thought and shook her head. "No, we will have to take care of it before anything like that happens."

"I agree with you, Serena. We must do something to stop it. King Gateskin must have a plan and I will help him carry it out."

***

While the children and Spindle entertained themselves with the wolves and cubs, the Wizards sat down after full stomachs to discuss the creature with King Gateskin, Queen Solinara, Wizard Hotenfaran and Fairy Procelina.

King Gateskin began by asking how it all came about.

The Head Wizard, Marno, began, "We need to explain from the beginning and apologize for anything we were forced to do that caused your family harm or discomfort."

King Gateskin nodded to Marno and waved his hand for him to continue.

"We were called to the King's palace to discuss some new ventures. King Kaposkaran had requested that he wanted to control all the villages eventually. As you know he instructed us to collectively send evil messages to your daughter, Serena. We did all we could not to do that but he could read our minds and knew if we were doing that or not. Thank goodness, King Gateskin, you diverted the messages and took them on yourself. We knew you did that but the King did not."

"Yes, I could not let my daughter receive such vile pictures in her head. It would have destroyed her. They nearly made me too sick to go on as it was. But I learned how to take care of them. But that is not important now. Please go on."

Marno continued, "We also tried to contact Botular at the same time per the King's request to have him try to undermine your authority and control over your people."

"I did not know that. Botular has been under my close watch and did not show any signs of anything like this."

"That's good to hear, King Gateskin. I was worried about Botular. He can be quite wily and untrustworthy at times."

King Gateskin replied, "I will continue to keep my eyes and ears on him. Thank you, Marno, for the warning."

Marno continued, "When things were not going as the King wanted, he instructed us to create a monster that would be used to frighten all the villages into submission."

"Ahh, yes. This is what I have been waiting to hear. What did he request you to do?"

"Well, we six put our heads together and came up with this new creature."

"Six? There are only four of you?"

"Yes, unfortunately there are only four now. We will explain about this shortly."

"Okay. Please go on."

"We had a man in the King's dungeon who was scheduled to be tortured and hung at daybreak. We thought we could give him another chance at life if we took his body as a vessel for the creature."

Wizard Marno looked across the table at his fellow wizards and said, "One of you take over explaining what you added to this experiment."

Wizard 2, now known as Wizard Fortag, took over the dialogue. "This man was surprisingly strong and still healthy but we supplemented his diet over the next day or two as we worked out what we would do to ensure he was at his healthiest to withstand our magic."

Wizard 3, now known as Wizard Wassor, picked up where his fellow wizard left off, "We asked the man many questions about his habits, weaknesses, allergies and fears. He told us many interesting things which we used in our incantations."

Wizard 4, now known as Wizard Tornak, took over the explanation, "We did not tell King Kaposkaran what we had done about the questions we had asked the man named Quintal. We tried to explain to Quintal what we were going to do – save his life in a way and make him into something else. He was happy to know he would not die but at the same time apprehensive about what he would become. He didn't have any family to worry about but still wanted to know more about what we were going to do to him."

Wizard Marno picked up the dialogue from here and said, "Yes, the man did have some problems mentally and psychologically too. He was not especially intelligent and did not have any common sense. He also did not have a conscience. He was known to murder and steal in order to live day by day. This is the reason why he was locked up and scheduled to die."

Wizard Fortag added, "Quintal was anxious to begin but we told him it would not be until he was rested. We left him that night and told the King what we planned to do with him so his demise would not go forth."

"King Kaposkaran did not like the idea of using this man. He wanted us to create something completely new and different," Wizard Wassor explained.

"We convinced the King to go along with our plan and that he would be pleased with the results. We thought by using this man we could control more of what we put into him and use some of his weaknesses against him, if need be," Wizard Tornak added.

Wizard Marno detailed their plans to create a creature they could somehow control this way without the King knowing. "If the King did not have all the information about this creature, then we could be in control and limit him from harming anyone."

Everyone listened intently and did not interrupt as they waited for the complete story to unfold about this creature.

"It was clever of you to think of that, Wizard Marno," King Gateskin complimented the wizard.

"Thank you, King Gateskin. We all thought that was the best thing to do. We needed to have some control over what we created. We also did not trust King Kaposkaran to leave our creature alone. We knew he would interfere and try to change it to put it under his control. It looks like he did that already."

"Yes, I agree. It looked like it was under someone's control when I looked into its eyes. It turned away from me and ran off as if someone was telling it to leave."

Wizard Marno listened to what King Gateskin said and queried, "What did its eyes look like? Were they clear and focused or glazed over?"

King Gateskin gave this some thought and replied, "What I noticed right away was that its eyes looked human. They were clear and focused but then became glazed over before it suddenly turned and ran off."

The wizards exchanged anxious looks.

CHAPTER FOURTEEN

Wizard Marno nodded to his fellow Wizards and stated in a shaky voice, "King Kaposkaran was definitely controlling the creature. He even named it using the man's name, Quintal changing it a little to Quintaroon."

"Quintaroon? That is a strange name. Do you think King Kaposkaran added any other powers besides the ability to fly to this Quintaroon?"

"Yes, I am sure he did," Wizard Marno responded in a whisper. "Most definitely he did. I am sure he put the creature under his power completely. Quintaroon will do his bidding no matter what. We cannot stop the creature."

"We will discuss that at greater lengths, Wizard Marno. I assure you. Now are you going to tell me what happened to the two other wizards?"

"Oh yes, I almost forgot about poor Wizards five and six. Their names were Kerno and Sufan. They didn't deserve to die like that." Wizard Marno shook his head and tears threatened to fall.

"Take your time. I'm sorry for your loss," King Gateskin bowed his head in sympathy.

"It's awful what happened. I have a hard time talking about it but I did promise to explain what happened. It was right after we turned the man into the creature. Quintal was confused and didn't know what was happening to him. He struck out at our fellow wizards because they were the closest to him. He was angry. The rest of us backed away in time when we saw his hand sweep out and grip them in his claws."

When Wizard Marno couldn't go on, Wizard Fortag continued, "Quintaroon gripped them so tightly he squeezed them to death. He then threw them down on the ground."

Wizard Wassor added, "There was nothing we could do to save them. They were already dead, King Gateskin."

"Also," Wizard Tornak stepped forward to add, "Quintaroon then picked them up and brought them back into the cell with him."

"That is strange," King Gateskin announced, in confusion.

"What is strange, King?" Marno looked at Gateskin with a furrowed brow.

"Oh, I think it is strange that the creature just happened to capture Wizards five and six, in that order."

"Umm, yes. That is kind of weird when you think about it. But we always stood in this way in front of the King when we met with him. I would always be the closest to him. He expected us to do that so he would know who was the Head Wizard and so on. Each one of us has certain powers, some stronger than others."

"That is interesting, Wizard Marno," King Gateskin stated with a serious expression.

Wizard Marno continued with embarrassment, "We ran out of the dungeon after that. We were frightened we would be killed next. I think King Kaposkaran was too fascinated by what Quintaroon had just done to notice we were missing right away. We ran to our homes and gathered our families and belongings and fled the area. We stopped in Merlina and asked for assistance from King Zuri. He was most helpful to us. He had already been warned about the creature by you. He offered his help by loaning us wagons to house our families and belongings and opened up his borders and allowed us to pass through. He even told the neighboring villages we were coming their way and to let us pass."

"I see," King Gateskin said. "King Zuri is a kind and benevolent ruler. He has had a most difficult time keeping his village and subjects safe from evil King Kaposkaran and his Parotovinans soldiers."

"Yes, I can see that. But for some reason King Kaposkaran never bothered him as much as he did you and your subjects, King Gateskin. I think that is because you are the most powerful ruler in the land."

"Thank you for your kind words, Wizard Marno. All the rulers in this land of Noella Province have their own powers. Collectively we are stronger than we are apart. King Kaposkaran knows this and tries to break us apart little by little. So far, we have not let him be successful. We continue to be stronger than he is but now with this… I am feeling some doubt in our abilities to keep our land safe."

Wizard Marno leaned closer to King Gateskin and laid his hand on the King's arm. "I assure you, King Gateskin, we will work with you to keep everyone safe in this beautiful land. We are in your debt for giving us and our families asylum from this ruler."

"You are welcome, Wizard Marno and company. We are pleased you came to us with such honesty. We will need everything you can do to help keep our villages safe from this creature."

Wizard Marno beamed and shook King Gateskin's hand in friendship. The other three Wizards did the same. They left the King's home and went back to their new homes that had been recently built by the King and his men. With the help of a little bit of magic.

They whispered amongst themselves as they walked away. They were frightened more than they let on to the King because they knew it was not going to be easy to destroy this creature especially now it could possibly fly.

King Gateskin observed them as they went to their homes. He felt strongly that they were keeping something from him about the Quintaroon.

CHAPTER FIFTEEN

King Kaposkaran sent a command to the Quintaroon to return to Parotovina immediately. The creature did not respond because it was deep inside the UT and exploring the area. The other creatures that inhabited the place were hiding. They were not nearly as large or formidable as this new creature was to their territory. They sniffed and walked around the place where the new creature had just been trying to get a sense of what it was and what it could do.

These creatures were getting larger than the wolves that had fled the territory and had procreated quickly to take over the UT from the wolves. They now fortunately had help from King Kaposkaran when he sent food for this new creature to eat. This meat had been filled with nutritious and magical properties that helped to increase their size and strength. They snatched it up before the Quintaroon could eat it. They knew they would need to be larger and stronger to fight this formidable creature. They did not want to lose control of their newly acquired land.

Quintaroon sensed there were others living in this land. It prowled around and noticed a few small hairy creatures with large heads that burrowed into the ground when it came near them. It tried unsuccessfully to pull them out of the hole where they had just disappeared. It was hungry and had not found anything to eat. The man who controlled it promised to leave it some food but still had not done that. It sniffed the air and growled letting off some of the anger it felt was building up inside.

The other creatures watched it and were pleased their young had escaped this monster's clutches. They noticed its sharp claws and teeth and wide jaws. It could swallow one of their little ones in one gulp. They had to do something to stop it.

Quintaroon continued to search for food and finally found some large frog-like creatures and it swallowed several whole. This food source looked plentiful around a pond where it had found them. At least it would not starve for now.

***

King Kaposkaran was getting frustrated when he did not get a response from his creature. He kept trying to reach it to command it to come back to Parotovina. He was also upset about his Wizards' disappearance. They were cowards after two of them were killed by the Quintaroon. He chuckled to himself as he replayed the scene in his head. He was proud of the new creature and wanted the Wizards to create more of these creatures. He would have to find them.

He instructed his men, "Search the village and the surrounding area and do not come back until these cowardly Wizards are found."

The King had many powers but could not do as much as his Wizards could do. He didn't know how to create this creature but could add to its powers and control it. He wanted an army of them to send out to each village to decimate them all. He wanted control of Noella Province. It would no longer be called by that name. His name would be all over the land.

They would fear him once he had control of all of the villages. His creature would be all he needed to keep the villagers in line. He would control all of the UT eventually too. He knew that was where his Quintaroon was living for now. It was the safest place for it to live and be at his beck and call when needed. He had sent his men to the area to drop off the food source for it. He didn't know if it could live off the UT on its own. He would have to keep it fed until it could break through the borders and it could then eat whatever it wanted in the villages. There were already too many villagers living there. They needed to be culled out. He chuckled to himself at the thought of his creature eating some of the people there.

He wanted to control the Quintaroon and couldn't do that so far away. He decided to call out to the mind of the creature to try once again to get it to come back to Parotovina. He waited and waited without any success. He wasn't as experienced or knowledgeable as his Wizards were at doing this. What was he going to do if it did not come back? Where were his men who were supposed to bring the shepherds and sheep back to him that had escaped out of his village? And, where were the other guards he sent to find the Wizards? Why hadn't any of them returned? He needed the Wizards and he needed them now. He would have to use his own powers as best he could to contact them wherever they were and command them to come back.

If they did not answer he would have to send more men to find them all.

CHAPTER SIXTEEN

The Parotovinan Wizards gathered outside their newly built cottages and shared the messages they had been receiving from King Kaposkaran. They were jumbled up but the recipients knew exactly what he wanted from them. They could tell by these mixed messages that the King's power to send mind messages was not good.

The Head Wizard, Marno, calmed his fellow Wizards down by saying, "Do not listen to these messages. It is King Kaposkaran trying to draw us back there. We are safe here from him. He can't harm us now. We are under the protection of the good King Gateskin. He promised to always protect us as citizens of this great land of Sovorotskina.

Number two Wizard Fortag spoke up, "But we are not officially citizens yet. Do we have to pledge an oath to King Gateskin in order to do that like we did in Parotovina?"

"I will have to ask King Gateskin about that," Marno responded.

"Okay, but do we have to cut ourselves too and pledge with our blood like King

Kaposkaran had us do?" Number three Wizard Wassor exclaimed in a voice edged with anxiety.

"No, I don't think he would have us do that," Marno said. "This king is not like our former king. He is kind and benevolent. It is sad we have only known one king that is evil who has filled our lives with fear and foreboding. It is time for all this to end."

The three other Wizards visibly relaxed and sighed collectively in relief.

The fourth Wizard Tornak expressed his concern still when he said, "I think King Kaposkaran is having a problem with the Quintaroon. Maybe he can't contact it."

"It is a *he*, don't forget that, Tornak. I know we can't think of Quintal as a person anymore but he is still in there. We may be able to reach the human side of him whereas King Kaposkaran cannot."

"Yes, I think you may be right, Marno. That is why he is becoming anxious and insisting we come back immediately. He does not know what to do on his own. He still needs us," Fortag exclaimed.

"Hmm, that could be a good thing. We may be able to get control of Quintaroon now before the King figures out how to do that on his own."

"Yes, Marno. I agree," Wassor said happily.

"Let's put our heads together and figure out a way to contact the Quintaroon before he harms anyone else," Marno stressed with urgency.

Marno invited his fellow Wizards inside his cottage to work together on a spell that would do what they needed to do – control the Quintaroon and turn him back to Quintal once and for all.

Wizard Tornak began by explaining, "We have to reach the human through his weaknesses. Remember all the things he told us. Pick one and we will work through them until we can reach him."

"Yes, Tornak, that just may work," Marno stated with a smile.

There was a knock on the door causing the Wizards to stop working on their spells and turn toward the sound.

Marno got to the door quickly and opened it to find King Gateskin. "Wizards, I need a word with you. It looks like I interrupted something important. What are you up to?"

Marno stepped back to welcome King Gateskin into his home. "Welcome, my King. I'm sorry we did not meet you again to thank you for our lovely cottages. Our families are quite comfortable and grateful to you and your men for building them so quickly."

"It was my pleasure, Wizard Marno. My pleasure indeed." Gateskin looked around the table at the three other Wizards who wore intense expressions.

"Is there a problem? You all look like you were into something quite intense the way your faces are wearing anything but happy expressions."

Marno coughed to cover up his concerns and put on a relaxed expression. "Oh no, King Gateskin, we are all fine. We were just talking about how fortunate we are to have come here. We also wanted to ask you about how we would become citizens of Sovorotskina."

"Ahh, yes. That is why I came here to see you. I want to present each of you with a certificate showing your citizenship. But, at first you must take an oath."

"See, I told you," Wizard Fortag said.

"Yah and now comes the blood part," Wizard Wassor stated with raised brows.

King Gateskin snickered and tried to keep a chuckle out of his voice when he said, "No, there will not be any bloodshed in this kingdom. In fact, if you are ready, I have the certificates with me and can perform the ceremony right now with the help of my Head Guard, Spindle."

"Head Guard? I didn't see anyone with you, King Gateskin," Marno said as he looked around.

Spindle was standing behind King Gateskin at ease and waiting to be summoned forward. When he heard his name, he flew up onto Gateskin's shoulder and bowed to the Wizards.

"Oh my, I didn't see you, Spindle. We have heard a lot about you since we arrived. Everyone is talking about how brave you Sprites are. I have never heard of such bravery from creatures as small as you."

Spindle bowed again and said, "Well, I thank you, Head Wizard, Marno. I appreciate your kind words. Yes, most Sprites are quite small. I am the largest of them but still small in your eyes."

King Gateskin waited for Spindle to finish and then began, "Now Wizards of Parotovina, are you ready to become citizens of Sovorotskina this very day?"

The Wizards stood at attention and waited for what they had to do next.

Marno stepped forward and said, "We would be honored to become citizens, good King Gateskin. We have waited many years to be free and now we finally will be."

Spindle held the certificates and waited for the oath from each Wizard to be said before presenting each one.

"Repeat after me, Wizard Marno, I promise to honor and protect this land of Sovorotskina until my dying day. I will do all I can to assist King Gateskin in all things he requests to keep my fellow citizens safe."

Each Wizard repeated this oath and received a certificate from a beaming Spindle.

Marno wiped away tears of joy and noticed his fellow Wizards did the same. He turned to them and said, "Let us thank King Gateskin of this wonderful land of Sovorotskina for this honor. We are truly grateful!"

Wizards Marno, Fortag, Wassor and Tornak bowed to King Gateskin and said, "Thank you, good King. We are indebted to you until our dying days."

King Gateskin shook each Wizard's hand and said, "Well, I am pleased to welcome you as new citizens to Sovorotskina, Land of Light. Now please share with me what you are so worried about."

Marno welcomed King Gateskin to his table and began to explain about the messages they had been receiving from King Kaposkaran.

CHAPTER SEVENTEEN

Gateskin and Spindle left the Wizard Marno's cottage and returned to meet with Solinara, Hotenfaran, Procelina and Mitteran who were waiting for the King in his home.

Queen Solinara, always the perfect hostess, had laid out a mixture of different pastries and coffee for all. Gateskin had sent a message to her mind to get prepared for a long meeting.

Solinara greeted her husband but stopped short of hugging him when she saw his face. He looked as if he carried the weight of the land on his broad shoulders once again.

"What is wrong, Gateskin?" Solinara whispered.

"We need to discuss what the Wizards just told me about their former King, Kaposkaran."

Solinara handed Gateskin a hot cup of chicory coffee to restore the color to his cheeks which were quite peaked.

"Thank you, dear. I need this or maybe something a little stronger in a while."

He looked at his family sitting at the table, for they were all his family outside of his children. He knew he could depend upon each one of them to help in times of great need. This was one of them.

They looked up at him and waited for him to explain.

"I performed a Citizenship Ceremony on the four Wizards. They are now officially citizens of Sovorotskina. While I was there, I knew there was something going on by the look on their faces. I completed the ceremony with the help of Spindle before asking them what was wrong."

Spindle nodded and grinned at everyone and waited for King Gateskin to continue.

"It appears King Kaposkaran is trying to reach the Wizards for assistance with the Quintaroon. He evidently cannot reach it or he, whatever it is now. I sat with them to see what they had to offer for spells to contact the creature before the King was successful. They suggested we use his weaknesses to reach his human side and bring it out from the creature."

Wizard Hotenfaran asked, "How did they plan to do that? What are the Quintaroon's weaknesses by the way? They never did share this information with us when they were here."

"Yes, I was aware of that. I wanted to wait until they were more comfortable here and certain of their safety before asking them about that."

"What did they say, Gateskin?" Solinara was getting anxious to know.

"Well, the man, Quintal, had a few weaknesses the Wizards kept inside of the creature to enable them to control him in case the King went beyond their powers, which he did. King Kaposkaran did not give Quintaroon the power to fly.

The Wizards confessed that one of them did that."

"Oh no, not a good idea," Mitteran stated with a shake of his head.

"Yes, they know that now but it is too late. It knows it can fly and get around quicker. So far it hasn't tried to fly over the boundaries yet but I will be putting spells higher up in the sky to expand the boundaries so it will not be able to do that. I already did it in the back of our house here. That is where it was first seen."

"Good idea, Gateskin," Fairy Procelina exclaimed with relief. "I have not seen it yet but don't look forward to doing that either."

"Yes, I hope you don't, Procelina. It is not something you will ever forget once you do," Solinara expressed with a shiver.

"If you need my assistance, King Gateskin, I am available to do whatever you need," Procelina stated in a strong voice.

"Are you sure you want to do that, my dear?" Hotenfaran said as he looked at his wife with concern. "You are now a mother. I don't want anything to happen to you. Besides, Arubane needs you and so do I."

"I will be fine, Hotenfaran. No need to worry. You know me. I am always careful and now extra so being a mother," she smiled and sighed happily at the fact.

Hotenfaran patted her hand and smirked back at her. "I know you will be fine because I will be there with you to help with the spells."

"Of course, you will. I wouldn't have it any other way," she guffawed.

"Sorry, Gateskin. We do get carried away. Please tell us more about this creature and its weaknesses," Hotenfaran apologized.

"Yes, let me continue by sharing its strengths first then its weaknesses. We already know the first one. Here is what the Wizards shared:

1. Can fly
2. Formidable size and strength
3. Dangerous claws and jaws
4. Can become invisible when it drinks water

Here are its weaknesses:

1. Fear of the dark
2. Blinded by bright light
3. Fears rodents like squirrels, mice, rats
4. Has allergies to nuts

"What do the Wizards plan to do now?" Mitteran asked.

"Well, they are working on some strong spells by using its weaknesses and sending these spells to it in the UT. They say they have opened up a channel to reach it and will let me know when its thoughts come back to them."

"Okay, we may know something soon, I hope," Hotenfaran said as he mulled over the situation.

"I hope so, Hotenfaran. I certainly hope so. I know I can depend upon you, Procelina and Solinara to help with the spells if the Wizards need anything."

Hotenfaran and Procelina nodded their assent, "Of course, we are always available if needed."

"Yes, I am here too if they need me," Solinara said then giggled when she thought about the third weakness and exchanged smirks with her brother. "Do you know what number three means, Hotenfaran?"

"Hmm, yes, I think I do, Sister! It was fortunate we created those Rabbinels.

They may become the thing we need for the creature's undoing."

"We will see, Brother. We will see!" Solinara smiled and winked at everyone at the table.

Laughter could be heard throughout the room by the children who were coming back from playing with the wolves.

"What's going on, Father?" Serena looked intense as she observed everyone at the table.

Simon and Catalina stood by their sister's side and waited for someone to say something.

Gateskin smiled at his curious and intelligent children who did not miss a thing and said, "Oh we were just having a good chuckle over some things to relieve the tension we have been feeling since we returned."

"I see," Serena snickered and nodded as she walked back to her room with her siblings close behind.

"I guess this meeting has come to an end, if you know what I mean," Gateskin announced as he nodded to each member at the table. Enough had been said without the use of a Soundproof Spell.

Everyone nodded in silence and excused themselves. It was clear that it was no longer safe to discuss any more with the children nearby.

CHAPTER EIGHTEEN

Botular was trying to keep his head straight. King Kaposkaran was sending messages to him faster than he could decipher them. He did not dare answer him. He knew King Gateskin was watching him and listening in. He knew Queen Solinara and Wizard Hotenfaran tried to trick him with the Staglemite. He put on a good show for them though. He only hoped they hadn't figured that out yet. He managed to bring some of the Staglemite out of the cave with him without anyone knowing. He planned to use it to keep his thoughts away from the King, Queen and Wizards. He felt like all eyes were on him everywhere he went. He kept to himself and stayed in or close to his cabin. He also used his powers of blending into his surroundings, when need be, like now.

He watched Wizard Hotenfaran, Fairy Procelina and Guard Mitteran leave the King's home. They wore serious expressions and their minds were flooded with all kinds of things. He couldn't quite make out what they were.

He grabbed his head and passed out when the King's messages became too strong. He didn't remember anything after that.

Hotenfaran felt a presence and alerted his wife, "Procelina, look around. Do you see anything? I feel we are being watched."

His wife used her powerful eyes to gaze in front, behind and around them and spotted Botular leaning up against the King's house. When she saw Botular fall over, she gasped, "He was there all along. I never saw him. He was spying on us, Hotenfaran."

"Yes, I see him now. It looks like he passed out. I wonder what caused him to do that? Why was he here?" Hotenfaran sighed.

"No worries, I kept my thoughts protected by the Staglemite you gave me, dear. All is safe from him. Gateskin did mention him to me and that we should all be wary of this man. He is not to be trusted."

"I agree, especially after seeing him there. I hope he did not enter the house when we were talking. Do you think he did?"

"No, Hotenfaran. I think he came upon us by accident. He probably blended into his surroundings so we wouldn't see him and think he was spying on us."

"We must tell Gateskin right away. But first let me revive him and ask him what he was doing here?" Hotenfaran pulled out his Pepper Salts.

"Good idea, my love. I want to see what he has to say for himself."

Botular sat up abruptly after Hotenfaran waved some Pepper Salts under his nose. He looked around startled. "What happened?"

"That's what we want to know too, Botular," Hotenfaran inquired as he lifted the man up by his cloak.

"I...I don't know what happened. One minute I was walking along and the next I was here with you."

"Well, I think you may have some more explaining to do to King Gateskin. Let's go see him now."

"No, no, I am okay. I don't need to see him. I have nothing to share. I don't know what happened."

"Listen, Botular. I saw you here. You had blended into your surroundings and then appeared on the ground. What were you doing and why did you faint?" Procelina queried.

Gateskin came to the door to see Hotenfaran and Procelina standing there holding up Botular by his cloak a foot or so off the ground.

"Well, look who we have here? What's going on, Botular? What have you been up to?"

"I....I… um, nothing really. I was just out for a walk and for some unknown reason must have fainted. I can't understand what happened. The good Fairy and Wizard here found me and brought me to with his magic Salts."

"Did he now? Hmm, come in, Botular. It has been a little while since we have had a nice chat."

"Do you need us, Gateskin?" Hotenfaran and Procelina asked, waiting to be invited in again.

"No need for you to come in again. Please go home to your son, Arubane. He must be worried about you both."

"Okay, King Gateskin. If you need us, we will come back. Just send us a message. You know we will answer quickly."

"Yes, I know you will. Thank you for finding Botular and helping him regain his balance."

"Our pleasure to assist him." Procelina winked at the King and took her husband's hand as they walked home to their son.

"I was not unbalanced, King. I was just out for a walk and fainted. I am here with all my faculties, I assure you."

"Yes, I'm sure you are. Now please hand over the Staglemite if you will. I can see it in your pocket. We need to have a chat, a serious one at that."

"That is clever, King Gateskin. You spoke in rhyme."

"Okay, Botular. Let's get serious. What caused you to faint? Are you receiving messages from King Kaposkaran again?"

"No...um...I ...yes. I am. They were becoming too strong with an urgency I could not contain. He is angry with me and the Wizards for escaping. He wants us back."

"I'm sure he does, Botular. But you will never go back there, correct?"

"Oh, yes, your Highness. I mean no, I will never go back there for he will string me up in the square like he did to the Head Gatekeeper, Kelleran."

"I would think that alone would convince you to turn away from him and his evil messages. What did you think I would do when I learned about this fact?"

"I didn't think you would know about it. I tried to keep the messages inside me and not let them out."

"Well, that didn't work even with the Staglemite in your pocket. Do you know why?"

"No, I don't know. What did you do, my King?"

"I cannot share that with you. It appears you deceived my wife and her brother recently."

"What? What do you mean I deceived them?"

"Well, first of all, you did not share that you already had some Staglemite in your right pocket when they placed Staglemite in your left pocket. Having two pieces there prevented an exchange of true feelings from you. In other words, you lied about everything."

"I didn't mean to do that. I didn't know they had put some into my pocket. That is a surprise to me."

"Now, is this all the Staglemite you have in your possession?"

"Well, I…"

"You do realize I can find out where it is, don't you? I can see it in your mind right now."

"I may have some more tucked away somewhere."

"I will have my men search your cabin and things until they find it. You will stay here under my watchful eye until they finish the search."

"Okay. I'm sorry, King Gateskin. I didn't mean to upset you. I really am trying hard to rid myself of these messages but I can't get them out of my head. I think I may go crazy from them soon if I don't do something."

"Sit down and have some coffee while we wait. I am disappointed in you, Botular. I thought you had changed. I don't know what to do with you."

"Can I suggest something, King Gateskin?"

The King looked at Botular in disbelief. "What did you say?"

"I'm sorry I am not trying to be disrespectful, King Gateskin. I wanted to suggest that you find a way to stop these messages that the King of Parotovina keeps sending me before I go crazy. I can't stand them anymore."

Gateskin studied Botular's disturbed expression with concern and listened to King Kaposkaran's messages holding the Staglemite close to the man's head.

He was surprised at how strong they were and insistent on getting Botular's attention.

"Let me see what I can do. The Wizards may have some suggestions also. Sit tight for now while I have my men begin the search of your cabin."

Botular clasped his hands over his ears and cringed as the messages assaulted his brain once again.

King Gateskin called the Wizards and Spindle and his men to his home. He gave Spindle directions, "Take a few men with you and search Botular's cabin thoroughly for Staglemite. Bring all that you find to me. Also, if you find anything else out of the ordinary, bring that too."

Spindle nodded and flew off to complete his duties with his men following behind him.

The Wizards arrived right after Spindle left and waited as the King spoke to them through their minds so as not to alert Botular.

"Botular is receiving serious messages from King Kaposkaran that are making him sick. He fainted outside my door. What can you do to help him?"

"We will do what we can, King Gateskin, to erase these messages and put a block to keep anymore from getting through. King Kaposkaran is getting more anxious about reaching us. When he couldn't reach us, he used Botular as a way to get to us."

"Yes, I agree, Marno. Do what you can and let me know if it works. I will keep Botular here until my men complete the search of his cabin for Staglemite. Stay in touch with me and let me know as soon as you can that it is done."

"Yes, King Gateskin. We are at your service," Head Wizard Marno expressed with serious concern. He only hoped he would not fail to do this task as King Gateskin requested. He looked at his fellow Wizards and headed back to his cottage to work on the spells.

Once the search was completed Botular was to be allowed to return to his cottage until otherwise summoned.

CHAPTER NINETEEN

Spindle returned after a short time and brought along a few more pieces of Staglemite and a scroll that was blank that he and his men had confiscated from Botular's cottage. He handed these items to King Gateskin and bowed.

"Is there anything else I can do for you, my King?"

"Ahh, this is perfect, Spindle. You are an excellent Head Guard. Thank you for finding the Staglemite. Hmm, this scroll is interesting. There is no writing on it. I think it could be like the one Queen Solinara gave me not long ago."

"Yes, it may be the very same thing. That means the writing will appear to the person for whom it was intended."

"Yes, I agree, Spindle. Please go fetch Botular once again. I shouldn't have allowed him to go back home too soon. I need to know what this says."

"Yes, King, right away!" Spindle flew right through the door and disappeared before the King could look up at him again.

He smiled to himself and said, "I can't believe this little man. He has more power in his small body than I have in my whole being. I am just glad he is on my side."

A short time later Spindle knocked at the King's door and waited with Botular next to him.

"Thank you, Spindle," King Gateskin exclaimed sternly as he looked at Botular who had hung his head in shame and refused to meet Gateskin's eyes.

"Come in, Botular. Spindle, please stay outside my door for now and I will let you know if I need you."

"Yes, King Gateskin. I will be right here at your beck and call."

"Botular, sit down."

Gateskin sat next to him and pulled out the blank scroll. He slowly unrolled it and laid it on the table in front of Botular.

Botular's eyes opened wide with alarm and stuttered, "What…? How…how did you get that?"

"Evidently, you left it out in the open in your cottage. Since it is blank you thought it was safe there."

"I...never saw it before, King Gateskin. I don't know what it is."

"You don't? Well, I do. I think it is a scroll that came from your former king. Now, what I want you to do is take it in your hands and read it to me."

Botular looked at the scroll and shook his head. "I can't, King Gateskin. I can't look at it. It is too frightening to see."

"Well, let me be the judge of that, Botular. Pick it up and read it to me now!"

Botular's hands shook as he tried to grip the scroll but couldn't open his fingers to grasp it without losing it.

Gateskin picked up the scroll and placed it into Botular's hands and waited.

Botular squeezed his eyes shut and refused to look at the scroll.

"Open your eyes now and read it to me!" King Gateskin commanded.

"I...didn't know I had this until I opened my backpack. It was inside. I don't know who put it in there or when," he sighed heavily and tried to go on.

"Botular, what does it say?" Gateskin probed with even more force in his eyes and voice.

"It...it is from King Kaposkaran. He said, "'You are to infiltrate Sovorotskina as soon as possible. My Wizards will keep a watch over you. Get into King Gateskin's good graces and convince him you are his friend and my enemy. Once you do that, you are to put a spell on him and bring him back to me. If you do not return, I will send other men to find you and...well, you know what will be done to you.' It was signed, King Kaposkaran, Ruler of Parotovina."

King Gateskin sat there shocked at this revelation. He never expected this. How would King Kaposkaran have known that we would take Botular into our village so readily? Is there another spy about that I have to uncover?

"I see," Gateskin said, "now tell me who are you working with, Botular?"

"I'm not working with anyone, King Gateskin. I don't know what you mean. I came here because you wanted me to come to be your eyes and ears like I did for my former king."

"Are you saying you did not know King Kaposkaran wanted you to come here? Then explain why you were still in the cave waiting for me to find you?"

"I really don't know. Maybe the King put a spell over me and controlled my movements until you found me. He must have had help from the Wizards 1-6 to do this and with the scroll. Maybe you should ask them about it."

"Maybe I will. Now, for the moment. You will stay here until I summon the Wizards. Let's see what they have to say about this."

***

Head Wizard Marno sat at his table with his fellow Wizards deep in concentration when he received an urgent message from King Gateskin. He looked up at his fellow Wizards and exclaimed," We have been summoned to King Gateskin's home once again. He said it is urgent we come immediately.

Fortag shrugged his shoulders and said, "What could be more important than what he just gave us to do to help Botular?"

"That I don't know, but are you going to ignore this summons? I wouldn't dare. King Gateskin is benevolent but he does have a temper and I don't want to be the one to disobey his orders after just becoming citizens."

Wassor and Tornak agreed, "We will follow you over there, Marno. We don't want to take a chance that we will be deported back to Parotovina to our deaths."

CHAPTER TWENTY

King Gateskin requested the four Wizards sit at his table alongside Botular who held his head in his hands and didn't look at anyone.

Marno observed Botular and tried to read his mind. He looked up at King Gateskin as the King called his name.

"What? Oh, sorry, King Gateskin. I was deep in thought and didn't hear you. What can we do for you?"

"It appears Botular has been keeping secrets from us. I had Spindle, along with a few guards, search Botular's cottage for some Staglemite which he kept hidden from us. During the search, Spindle found this scroll."

The Wizards picked up the scroll which was once again blank. Marno touched it with his fingertips and spread a spell over it, to no avail.

"There is nothing here, King Gateskin."

"I know, Marno. Botular must hold it in his hands for the message to appear."

Looking at Botular who hadn't met the Wizards' eyes yet, he instructed, "Pick up the scroll and read it to the Wizards, Botular."

Botular shook his head to clear it of the continuing onslaught of messages and finally looked up. He gripped the scroll once more and read it aloud then hung his head again.

Marno looked surprised at what the words implied. We did not know anything about this, King Gateskin, I assure you. This is a trick by King Kaposkaran to discredit us. We had nothing to do with this."

Gateskin looked at the other Wizards and waited for them to say something too.

Fortag sat up straighter and met King Gateskin's eyes. "We did not know about this, I agree with Marno, King Gateskin."

Wassor and Tornak also nodded in agreement and sat back to think about what this scroll meant.

"Who do you think helped the King do this if you were not responsible?"

"Marno suggested, "Well, let me see. He did have some other men who had some powers but not as much as ours. He could have sent this along with their help and tucked it inside Botular's backpack with a spell."

"What can you do to find out more about this, Marno? I know I already gave you one job but these two are connected. You may have one spell that will take care of stopping both the messages Botular is receiving and finding the creator of this spell on the scroll."

"Yes, King Gateskin. We may be able to do that. I agree with you. I think they are connected."

"Well, off you go. Botular and I are not finished chatting."

The Wizards flew out of the room as quickly as they could once Gateskin opened his door. They never looked back.

"Now, where were we, Botular?" Gateskin leaned in close to him to get Botular to meet his stone-cold gaze.

"Look at me, Botular? How many chances am I supposed to give you before deporting you back to Parotovina?"

"Oh, please don't do that, King Gateskin. I will never live a day there again. In fact, King Kaposkaran will have me tortured and killed and hung from the square like Kelleran, the Gatekeeper. I can't go back, please!" Botular begged with tears in his eyes.

"I am well aware of that fact, Botular. But what I can't understand is why you keep trying my patience and pressing me to do just that."

"I know. I'm sorry. I apologize again, King Gateskin. I truly do. Please forgive me. I promise not to do anything to disfavor myself in your eyes. In fact, I can help you find the person responsible for creating the scroll if it wasn't the Wizards."

"How would you do that, Botular? Do you know something you are not sharing with me?"

"Well, not really. But I know of one powerful person in Parotovina who would do anything to put himself in a favorable light with the King."

"Who would that be, Botular?" Gateskin peered closely to look at Botular's eyes to try to detect another lie.

"I will have to think about this some more and maybe I can use my own spell to find him."

"Him? Do you know it's a him for sure? There may be some powerful woman doing it too. I know that for a fact having three powerful women in my household," Gateskin tittered.

"As soon as I know, I will share that information with you. I want you to trust me. I know this is the only way to do that."

"Well, let me tell you something, Botular. If you can find out who the creator and planter of this scroll is, then maybe I will trust you." Gateskin stared seriously at Botular, still not sure he was ready to put his trust in this man.

"I will do my best, King Gateskin. In the meantime, what about these messages I am being inundated with by King Kaposkaran? How can I live with this pain? I can't think straight."

"The Wizards are working on that now as we speak. They should have a solution to your problem and clear them out soon. Once you are free you will be able to think more precisely about working on what we just discussed. Now you are excused. I will wait to hear from you soon, Botular. If I do not, I will come looking for you again."

"I expect nothing less, King Gateskin. I will do all I can to succeed in gaining your trust and being a good citizen of Sovorotskina."

Gateskin closed the door after Botular left and sat down at the table where he found his wife with a cup of chamomile tea.

"Ahh, just what I need, my love. How did you know? Did my meetings disturb you and the children?" Gateskin look a few sips of tea which revived him somewhat.

"No, or course not. I was busy preparing and canning the vegetables you left for me this morning. The children are out playing with the cubs who are growing quite large day by day. I don't think Serena will be able to pick them up much longer."

"Good. That's good to hear."

"Are you listening to me, Gateskin? What is going on? Do you need my help dealing with Botular again?"

"No, I think I have things under control with him. I gave him a job to do and also one for the Wizards. I hope to have everything done soon."

"Well, you know I am here if you need me, my dear. You look tired. Why don't you go lay down and rest a bit before dinner? I will prepare one of your favorites."

"Favorites? Stew? Chili? Vegetable casserole?" Gateskin asked with curiosity.

"It will be a surprise. Now, go into the other room and rest. I will keep the children away so you can take a little nap."

"Thank you, Solinara. You take good care of me. I know that is not an easy thing to do either," Gateskin snickered.

"That is an understatement, dear," Solinara chortled back at him.

"What did you say, Solinara?"

"Nothing important, Gateskin. Go to sleep now. That's an order."

"Okay, okay. I look forward to dinner."

Solinara went back to the kitchen and began preparations for a hearty stew for her husband. She knew he was under much pressure with the situation with Botular. She had heard every word but never let on to Gateskin. She would do her own spells to keep a watch over this troublesome new citizen and help to ease her husband's mind.

The next time she peeked into the room to check on Gateskin, he was sound asleep. She would let him sleep for another hour and then wake him for dinner. She wanted a little time to work on some spells. She planned to contact her brother and sister-in-law for their help. One fairy is powerful but if you combine two fairies and a wizard you get unspeakable powers.

CHAPTER TWENTY-ONE

King Kaposkaran sat at his table sipping coffee as he waited for his men to bring in the two villagers who were known to have some powers.

Two guards cleared their throats as they stood at attention at the doorway of the King's dining room.

King Kaposkaran looked up and invited them in, "Come in. Don't just stand there! Where are the villagers?"

The two guards stepped aside to reveal a man and a woman who had been standing behind them.

Pointing at the two, the King waved his hand and said, "Well, come forward."

The couple shivered as they moved closer to the King who frightened them with his tone and steely-eyed look.

"Introduce yourself and tell me what powers you have."

The man spoke first, "I am Henno and this is my wife, Jenara. We have lived in Parotovina all our lives. I didn't know I had any powers until I was in my teens. That is when I discovered I could make things disappear and reappear somewhere else. I can also send messages through my mind."

"I see," the King said as he smiled, pleased to hear this. "What about you, Jenara? What can you do?"

The woman was timid as she bowed her head and didn't meet the King's eyes. Her voice was like a whisper as she responded, "I can read minds and send messages that way too. Also, I can blend in with my surroundings."

"Hmm, good to hear, Jenara. Now I want you both to sit with me at my table. We have a lot to discuss."

The two guards stood by waiting for further instructions from their King who turned toward them and commanded, "You two can leave now. I don't need you anymore."

The guards bowed and left, relieved to be free from the King's watchful eye for the time being.

King Kaposkaran began by explaining to Henno and Jenara what he wanted them to do. "I have a creature who is living in the UT, Unknown Territory, if you do not know what that means. It is refusing to come back here. I need you to summon it and get it to come home. If you can do that, I will reward you both handsomely."

Henno responded after meeting his wife's eye, "We will do your bidding, King. Is that all you require from us?"

King Kaposkaran rested his chin in his hand as he contemplated what else he would require them to do. "Well, there will be more to do but first I need the Quintaroon here."

Henno nodded but appeared confused. "Quintaroon? What is that, my King?"

"Oh, of course no one knows about this creature but me and my Wizards who are absent."

"Oh, I see," Henno said.

"It is a creature that was created by my six Wizards. They have since disappeared. Well, two of the Wizards are dead by the hands of the creature while the other four are missing."

"Dead? What happened to them?" Jenara asked in a quivering voice before she could stop herself. She bowed her head and waited for a reprimand from the King.

"Yes, Jenara. They are dead. The Quintaroon squeezed them to death. This could happen to anything or anyone that gets too close to it."

Jenara shook her head and looked at her husband. They spoke to each other through their minds. "What are we doing here? He will surely kill us or it will do that. How can we work for this man?"

Henno responded, "We must do as our King asks of us. We cannot refuse or we will be put to death like the Gatekeeper. Remember what happened to him for going against the King's wishes."

Jenara nodded and said, "Yes, Henno. I will never forget that. Once we help the King, he will never let us go. We will be forever under his watchful eye. He will have us do horrific things. I cannot do that. I would rather die."

"I know my dear. But what other choice do we have? If we don't do as he requests, we will die. Why did you not tell the King about your ability to fly?"

"I was fearful about that. I didn't want him to know about this ability."

"Yes, I understand. You were smart to avoid mentioning it, Jenara."

"Oh, Henno, I know we shouldn't have used our powers. Someone saw us and reported that back to the King. Now we cannot deny him anything. I wish you could make us both disappear out of Parotovina and into another village. I don't feel safe here now."

"That I know, Jenara. I will keep this in mind when we need to do that. But, for now we must do as the King asks. Let's work together to get this one thing done for him. Then we will leave this village forever."

Jenara tried not to smile and covered her mouth with a yawn instead. She felt the King's eyes on them.

"What are you two discussing so intensely?" King Kaposkaran queried.

"Oh, we were just discussing the creature. It must be quite fierce to be able to crush the two Wizards in its hands," Henno stated.

"Yes, it is powerful beyond belief. There is no end to what it can do with your help."

Henno looked at the King and asked, "What can we do? We do not know anything about creating creatures."

"Oh, I think you can learn though. We will work together on this. Now, concentrate and send messages to the UT. Call out to Quintaroon and see if he answers you."

"He? Is it a man?" Henno asked, thoroughly confused.

"Well, let's just say it was, at one time. Now it is more than that. Much more than that for sure," King Kaposkaran tittered.

Jenara glanced at her husband in shock. He sent a calming message to her, under a protective curtain so the King couldn't read his thoughts, "Relax, my love. Don't let him see you are afraid. He will prey on your fear and so will the creature. Now let's concentrate as the King instructed and get this creature here. Then we will disappear forever like the Wizards did."

Jenara nodded and calmed down as she sent her first message to the Quintaroon.

***

Queen Beregina came into the room as the couple stood ready to leave. She asked her husband, "What is going on here?"

"Oh, my dear. I have found us a couple of new wizards. They are to do my bidding with the creature."

The Queen looked closely at the couple who avoided looking into her eyes. "Look at me," she commanded the couple.

Henno said, "Sorry, my Queen. I did not want to offend you by meeting your eye. My wife felt the same."

"You are to obey the King and me at all times. Now stay alert. King Kaposkaran will need you again."

King Kaposkaran instructed Henno and Jenara, "You can return home for now. If I need you again, I will summon you through your minds. Stay available and listen for my commands. You must not share any of this with anyone else. Do you understand me?"

"Yes, we do, King Kaposkaran," Henno and Jenara said in unison, bowed to the Queen and King and exited the room backwards.

Once outside the castle Henno said, "We have to be careful, Jenara. The Queen is even more devious than the King. She will be watching us closely."

"Yes, I think she is, Henno. I fear her more than him. That is why I sent a special message to the creature."

"What special message did you send to Quintaroon, Jenara?"

"I sent one that would enable us to escape without the creature coming after us."

"Oh no, Jenara. What did you do? You may have sealed our fate."

CHAPTER TWENTY-TWO

In the UT creatures were keeping their distance from the Quintaroon. They were somewhat smaller but growing by the day after eating the food they found in the woods. They did not realize the food was for the Quintaroon to keep him strong and fit.

Quintaroon looked around. He could smell the creatures around him. He moved slowly through the woods to search them out. He was hungry, for the insects and small critters he ate did not satisfy him.

The cat-like creatures moved farther into the UT to escape the new creature who was bearing down on them. They gathered their young and burrowed into the spaces underground they had created for their young and waited.

Quintaroon sniffed the earth around where there was a mound of freshly dug dirt. He used his claws to dig deeper but stopped when he heard a message in his head.

"What was that? Who is calling me? Is it the Wizards or the King who created me? What do they want?"

Jenara's message kept repeating in the creature's head. "Return to the Land of Parotovina now at the request of the King."

"Why should I return? I am happy here in my own land without anyone telling me what to do. Why would I want to go back just to be under the King's control again?"

Jenara had put another message inside the first message that told the creature, "Stay where you are. It is not safe to come back to Parotovina. The King is going to kill you."

Quintaroon shook his head to get the words out of his head. He was confused. *What did that mean? Does the King want me back or not? Will he kill me if I go back? Who is saying this?*

***

While Quintaroon stood apart from where he was digging to concentrate on the messages, the cat-like creatures known as Catlings were escaping down deeper into their tunnels and out into the forest where they had a larger camp set up with the rest of the Catlings. They had to come up with a plan to outwit this new creature who was a threat to them and their young.

Once the Catlings arrived back at their base camp, they gathered together to discuss what they would do to protect their young and their territory. They had lived here for many years and now that the wolves had left there was more room for them but unfortunately, less food. The wolves' cubs had been their food source.

A loud sound was heard as the creature came bounding toward their camp. What were they going to do now? How would they protect themselves?

Quintaroon looked between the trees and could see a large gathering of cat-like creatures in the mouth of a cave. "Hmm," he thought to himself, "I have found a food source to keep me full for a long time."

Just as Quintaroon moved forward, another message came louder and more forceful into his head.

***

The King sent his men with a command to Henno and Jenara to send another message to Quintaroon.

"Return to Parotovina now at the King's command. If you do not return your food source will be stopped."

Henno and Jenara looked at each other in confusion. "Food source? What food source? "

Henno ventured to ask the guards, "What food supply is King Kaposkaran talking about?"

"One guard responded, "The King sent several of his guards into the UT many days ago to drop off the food supply for the Quintaroon. They have not returned. He does not know what happened to them. Maybe Quintaroon ate them too along with the food they brought with them."

Jenara visibly shivered at this and shook her head at Henno. "We cannot do this! We are going to die along with the guards who did not return. The King may send us into the UT next to deliver the food to Quintaroon if it does not respond soon."

"Don't worry, Jenara. I will get us out of here before he requests us to do that. Now just relax. The King will pick up on your anxiety and respond negatively. Don't encourage him to do what you just said."

Jenara tried to keep the tears at bay and calmed herself down the best she could as they both listened to the King's request.

"You must do as the King requests. If you refuse, we will have to bring you back to the castle. We don't want to do that. We know how strong a punishment he will mete out to you both, if you refuse to do his bidding," a guard responded kindly, surprising them both.

"What can we do then?" Henno asked the kind guard.

"I suggest you do as King Kaposkaran commands. That is the safest way to stay alive. I know, for that is what we all do in order to keep our families safe and ourselves until…"

Jenara looked at the guard and queried, "Until what?"

The guard whispered so the other guards couldn't hear him, "Until we can escape safely out of Parotovina with our families."

Henno smiled and nodded. "I may be able to assist you with that. This is what we must do."

The kind guard told the other guards, "Wait outside while I further instruct these two powerful citizens."

Henno spoke softly to the guard and explained, "I have powers that can get you out of this evil land if you help us in turn."

The guard nodded and said, "I will do all I can to help you if I know you are telling the truth. It is important you do not try to fool me. It would cost my life and that of my family."

"I would never do such a thing," Henno exclaimed in surprise. "Why would I do that?"

"I'm sorry. I cannot trust anyone in this land. I have learned to be skeptical about everyone and anything that is being said."

"I don't blame you. Um, what is your name?"

"I am Danko, one of the King's Head Guards. He trusts me with his life. Or, at least he did up until now. I will be a wanted man if I do this."

"Yes, but you will be a safe and free man along with your family. Isn't that what you want, Danko?"

"Yes, I do," Danko responded with a determined expression.

"Then, do as I say and we will all be free."

Danko nodded and left with his men to return to the castle. This time he felt uplifted by Henno's words. He could feel his heart beating rapidly in anticipation.

***

Quintaroon was confused by the new message he received. *What did that mean? Food source? What food source?*

CHAPTER TWENTY-THREE

Back in Sovorotskina the Wizards were working on spells as requested by King Gateskin. They had come up with one to erase the messages that Botular was receiving from King Kaposkaran or at least to lessen them until they disappeared altogether as the spell took effect.

Marno looked at his fellow Wizards and asked, "Which one of you put a spell on this scroll?"

"What?" Tornak asked in shock. "You actually think one of us did that?"

"Well, by the looks of the scroll and spell it had to be someone as powerful as one of us."

"Well, I know I did not do it," Wassor stated strongly and gave Marno a frown that was full of menace.

"Neither did I, Marno," Fortag responded sternly.

"Nor I," Tornak retorted with furrowed brows.

"Okay, I believe all of you, but if not one of us then who?"

"Wait a minute, Marno. What about Wizards Five and Six, Kerno and Sufan? They could have done that a long time ago."

"Yes, it could have been one of them, Wassor. They are not here to defend themselves though. But it does look like their work," Marno surmised as he wrinkled his face up more than it was already.

Tornak and Fortag nodded in agreement.

"Well, that is settled. We can report to King Gateskin who we suspect created the scroll. I doubt if there is anyone else as strong to do that left in Parotovina," Marno stated as he felt relieved it wasn't one of them.

***

Botular wracked his brain trying to come up with a name to give the King. He had to convince King Gateskin he was to be trusted. But he couldn't think of a single name. He only told the King he knew of a man who was powerful. It was a ploy to give himself more time to think this over.

All of a sudden, a spark was felt inside Botular's brain and he gasped in surprise. "I've got it! It had to be one of the Wizards – numbers five or six who did it. They were in the castle the day before I left with the guards. I saw them speaking with the King," Botular sighed in relief. He had a name or names to give King Gateskin that would get him off the hook. He knew if he didn't come up with something to explain the scroll, he would be deported to Parotovina and to his death. Now if he could only stop the messages he kept receiving from King Kaposkaran. They were becoming more numerous and filled with anger and exasperation.

***

Queen Solinara met with her brother and his wife to develop a spell that would help her husband deal with everything that had come his way. He was exhausted from all the stress he was feeling since the creature appeared and now Botular was causing him more.

Gateskin woke up from a quick nap and saw the three with heads together in deep concentration.

"What's going on here? Did I miss the meeting of the minds?"

"Oh, Gateskin. How are you feeling, dear?" Solinara said, sweetly hiding any thoughts in her mind from being read by her astute husband.

"Yes, I am much better, thank you. Now what is going on here? Is there something you would like to share with me?" He watched his wife's eyes and tried to read her thoughts as he waited for her to respond.

Solinara came forward and wrapped her husband in her arms and whispered in his ear for only him to hear, "You will not feel any more stress, my love. You will feel only strength to take on all the problems that may come your way."

Gateskin stepped back and looked at Solinara. He suddenly felt stronger and stated, "We have much to do. Are you here to help me with the Quintaroon?"

Hotenfaran sent a message using the Staglemite to his wife and his sister, "Nice work, Solinara. Now we can get down to work without any further worries. The spell worked to erase the strain and the messages that Gateskin had kept in his mind from King Kaposkaran."

Gateskin observed the three speaking to one another through their minds. But he was unable to read the messages being shared.

"Now stop that right now, you three. What are you discussing without me? We are to work together on these things. Please do not hide anything from me."

"Sorry, my dear. We wanted to ensure you were feeling better. We are working out some spells to keep Botular in line and maybe the Quintaroon too."

"I see. Is there any need to keep me in the dark?" Gateskin asked, watching their expressions carefully.

Hotenfaran spoke up first, "No, my King. All is right. We will help you in any way you need us. What's first on the agenda?"

Procelina winked at her husband and squeezed Queen Solinara's hand under the table.

CHAPTER TWENTY-FOUR

Botular hurried over to see King Gateskin with the news he had to share about the scroll. Before he could get to the King's door, the four Wizards flew up the stairs, pushed him aside and knocked on the door.

"Hey, what are you doing? I was here first."

"Out of our way, Botular! We have urgent business with the King!" Wizard Marno exclaimed with a steely gaze.

"Well, so do I. I know who created the scroll and I plan to inform the King. He is my king too!"

King Gateskin came to the door when he heard raised voices. "What's going on here?"

The four Wizards bowed and Marno explained, "We have news for you, King Gateskin, that is of utmost importance."

"Yes, well come in. What about you, Botular? What are you doing here?"

"Well, I...um I also have urgent business to discuss with you, King Gateskin!"

Gateskin looked at the five and shook his head. "One at a time, please. Botular, you will stay outside until I finish with the Wizards."

"Yes, your highness. I will do as you ask." Botular bowed but had a disgruntled expression on his face which he did his best to hide from the King.

Once inside the Wizards got right down to business. Marno explained, "We have come up with a spell to keep the messages from coming to Botular from King Kaposkaran."

"Ahh, that is good news, Marno. But I feel you have more to say. What else do you want to share?" King Gateskin watched the four Wizards' faces for a sign of what it could be.

Fortag cleared his throat and began, "Well, we have discussed the blank scroll and have come up with two names who could be responsible for its creation."

"Who are they?" Gateskin couldn't hide the urgency in his voice to learn the responsible parties.

"We think it was Wizards five, Kerno, and six, Sufan, who were responsible."

"You *think* they are responsible? How do you find out if they actually were?"

"Well, there really is no way to know for sure, King. I apologize for that. Since they are not here to tell us one way or the other," Wassor stated sadly.

"We might be able to find out if we could see their bodies and try to extract their last memories from their dead brains," Tornak explained.

"How would you do that?" The King waited for further explanation.

"We would have to go back to Parotovina and find their bodies," Tornak added.

"No! No way are we going back there! Are you crazy, Tornak?" Marno shouted.

"I don't think it would be a good idea either, Tornak," Fortag and Wassor exclaimed together.

"I agree with you," Gateskin stated. "It would be too dangerous. After all, King Kaposkaran is trying to reach you. If you go there, you will walk right into his hands."

"Yes, what were you thinking, Tornak. Do you want us all to die?"

"No…I …I'm sorry. I don't know what I was thinking! But it appears to be the only way to solve this problem."

"It's all right. At least we have an idea who did it. Now, let's work on getting Botular's mind clear. Let's get him in here," King Gateskin instructed with a firm tone.

"Okay, King Gateskin," Marno agreed and the other Wizards nodded.

King Gateskin opened his door and called out to Botular who was sitting on the bottom step with his head in his hands, looking clearly upset for being shut out.

"Come in, Botular. We need to speak with you."

"Yes, King, I have something to share with you too."

"First, the Wizards are going to spread a spell over you to clear your mind. Are you still receiving messages from King Kaposkaran?"

"Yes, he is getting frantic because he cannot reach me. I can't take much more of his rantings!" Botular sighed heavily.

Marno guided Botular to the table and told him to sit down. "We need to have you quiet and settled here for a few minutes as we put the spell over you."

Fortag requested, "Fold your hands on the table and sit back."

Botular nodded and folded his hands on the table as he waited for further instructions.

"Good. Now close your eyes, Botular, and try to relax and clear your mind. Don't give into the messages," Wassor instructed.

"It's not easy to do, Wizards. He is sending them too fast and louder than before."

"Relax, and take a deep breath, Botular. We will do the rest," Tornak said.

King Gateskin watched and waited until the Wizards were done with their spell.

The Wizards spread their arms out toward Botular and waved them over his head in a circle. They began pulling streams of brilliant white light out of his head and twirling them around their arms and tying them into knots.

Out of thin air a large pot appeared on the table. In this pot is where the Wizards deposited the knotted streams of light. Once they were all inside, they closed the pot with a heavy lid and stepped back.

"Open your eyes, Botular," Marno instructed. "How do you feel?"

Botular shook his head and blinked his eyes in amazement. "There is nothing coming into my head now. It is all quiet. Thank you so much, Wizards."

"That figures," Tornak chuckled and stifled himself when Marno gave him a shocked look of warning.

King Gateskin stepped closer to Botular and told him, "Stand up. Do you feel all right?"

"Yes, I do feel much better. My head is clear of the King's message at last! I can't thank you all enough for what you did for me. I promise to repay you in my own way sometime."

Botular shook each Wizard by the hand and then the King's.

"Was there something you wanted to share with me, Botular, before you leave?" the King queried.

"Oh, yes. I'm sorry. I almost forgot. I know who did the scroll."

The Wizards looked at Botular in surprise as the King waited to hear what the man had to say.

CHAPTER TWENTY-FIVE

Back in Parotovina King Kaposkaran had his men bury the two Wizards, Kerno and Sufan, in the local grave site. Their bodies were beginning to stink up the dungeon even more than it already reeked.

The King had been unable to reach the Wizards or Botular. It felt like a lost cause. He knew they were never going to come back for fear of being hung in the square. Of course, he mused, I would use them in any way I needed first before doing just that.

Henno and Jenara, the powerful couple, were nowhere in sight. He feared they too had escaped. He sent for more of his guards to report to his Meeting Room for further instructions.

A few of the guards were feeling the fear more than ever now since Danko, their leader, was not with them.

"What are we to do? Danko isn't here. Where did he go?" one guard expressed his concern.

"I don't know. I haven't seen him since that couple left here. Maybe he went with them to their home to make sure they stayed there."

"Maybe, but I saw him in deep discussion with the couple before they left. I think something is going on."

The men marched forward as instructed to meet with King Kaposkaran, fear and anxiety filled their hearts and minds.

King Kaposkaran told them, "At ease, men. I have some new instructions for you. I need you to find the Quintaroon in the UT. It is not answering me or Henno's and Jenara's requests to return here. Who is in command here?"

The most senior guard who stood in front of the rest stepped forward when commanded, "Yes, your highness. I am in command of the men and will do your bidding."

The King did not ask his name nor did he care. He only wanted the man to obey, whoever he was. He gave the guard his most fearsome stare and continued, "Okay. You will lead the men into the UT, find Quintaroon and bring him back here."

"Umm…King, how do you want us to do that? He is dangerous and can eat all of us. We have nothing to protect us from his claws like the Wizards he killed."

"Well, that is true but you will take some food with you and entice him to eat it. It will be soaked with a sleeping potion. Once he falls asleep you will tie him to a wooden stake and drag him back."

"How many men do you want me to take, King Kaposkaran?" the senior guard's voice shook with anxiety.

"You idiot! You will take as many men as you can to ensure that you do not fail my request! Do you understand?"

"Yes…yes. We will not fail, your highness."

"I pray you do not. If you do fail, you will become food for the Quintaroon."

The men whispered amongst themselves in terror and shook their heads at the thought.

"What are you waiting for? Get the ropes and stake and move out now!"

"Yes, King Kaposkaran. We will leave at once. Come on, men. Let's get going."

The contingency moved along reluctantly and still whispered about what would surely be their march to death. They had told their families, if they did not return, to run for their lives into the woods and escape to other villages.

CHAPTER TWENTY-SIX

Spindle went to King Gateskin's home when he received a request from the King.

"Please come in, Spindle. The Wizards and Botular are just leaving. I need to speak with you."

"Yes, King. I am listening."

Gateskin waited for the Wizards and Botular to leave and then turned to Spindle.

"The Wizards have cleared Botular's mind of King Kaposkaran's messages but I fear the King will not let this pass. He will try something else."

"I see. That is good to hear about Botular. What can I do to help you, my king?"

"I need you to speak with your fellow Sprites and tell them I need their ears to pick up anything that is coming our way. I know the evil King is not finished. He will keep trying to get to us and especially my daughter, Serena. We are not safe."

Spindle flew up to sit on the King's shoulder when he heard this about Serena being in danger once again. "I will keep Serena safe at all costs, King.

Do you want me to stay by her side whenever she is outside this house?"

"Yes, I think that would be a good thing to do but first speak with the Sprites and have them listen for anything unusual happening in Parotovina. I feel the King is planning something. He has been unable to reach Quintaroon to bring him back to his command. That will not stop him from succeeding to get Quintaroon somehow."

"Yes, my King, right away. I will have Mitteran keep a close watch on the borders with the other guards."

"Yes, good thinking, Spindle. That is why you are my Head Guard."

Spindle flew into his home tree and spoke to his father. He knew Abason would take care of sending the King's message to the other Sprites.

Now that this part of the King's request was completed, Spindle flew back to find Serena to guard her with his life.

***

Serena was in the chicken coop collecting eggs and jumped when Spindle suddenly appeared beside her.

"Spindle! You nearly scared me half to death and I almost lost these eggs. My mother would have been quite upset with both of us!"

"Sorry, Serena. I didn't mean to frighten you. I was just coming to see you. Do you need any help?"

"No. I doubt if you could lift the pail of milk I just pumped from Milly. It's quite heavy. I planned on coming back for it with Simon's help. But you can come with me to deliver the eggs. My mother is planning something special for my father. He has been under a lot of strain lately with the Quintaroon and other stuff too numerous to mention." Serena sent word through her mind to her brother to pick up the pail of milk as she walked back to the house with the eggs and Spindle.

"Yes, I understand," Spindle said. "He is still concerned for your safety too. He asked me to keep an eye on you to ensure you are not in any danger from King Kaposkaran's messages again."

"Oh that! I haven't received anything since my father pulled them out and took them into his own head. But I think the Wizards, along with my mother, have taken care of that now."

"That's good to hear. But I have my orders and I am not leaving your side until King Gateskin says otherwise." Spindle stuck out his chin in defiance.

"I see. Okay. Well, you can help me with some other chores then. I have to look over the yard and pick up any stray poop the cubs may have left behind. Let me give my mother the eggs and then we can begin the cleanup."

Spindle waited for Serena to come back and responded, "Wonderful! I've always wanted a job as a pooper scooper!" Spindle guffawed and held his nose as he smelled one nearby.

"Ha! You have a super nose. I hadn't even smelled that one. You will make a super pooper scooper, Spindle!"

"Ha!" He scrunched up his nose, bent over and scooped up a good-sized one with a small shovel, Serena conjured out of thin air for him to use, and threw the poop into the woods.

"They are getting better about going into the woods. But every so often they can't wait to go and drop a few before they get beyond our yard."

"Don't you think that this is the job of the parents, Serena?"

"Well, dogs do the same thing. They must be taught to go farther away from the house."

"Yeah, I guess you're right, Serena. It's just not a pleasant thing to do."

"I know. But Father gave me and my siblings the job and we must follow through. It could always be worse."

"Worse? What could be worse than this?" Spindle shook his head and scooped up another one. "I only hope that the wolves learn quickly to move out into the woods to drop them when they are grown up. I don't like to think about scooping larger ones than this."

Serena giggled, "I agree, Spindle. But it is much more fun doing it with you. You make me laugh and not think too hard about how bad they smell."

"Yeah, I guess so. I hate to say it but I'm enjoying working with you too, Serena," Spindle blushed as he smiled at her. His smile took on a grimace as his eyes opened wider in alarm.

Serena noticed Spindle's facial expression of horror. "What's wrong, Spindle?"

"Don't look now but there is a large cat in the woods coming toward us. He is huge, as large as one of the wolves."

Serena stared at the spot where Spindle was pointing. When she saw it, she moved backwards toward her house, never taking her eyes off of it.

Spindle pushed her into the house and told her, "Tell your father, quickly."

The Sprite kept his eyes on the cat as it prowled and headed right for him.

Spindle spotted Cantok who was coming up alongside the cat to intercept him.

Cantok pounced onto the unsuspecting cat just as it turned to leap at Spindle. The animals wrestled with claws and teeth barred. A loud growling could be heard that brought King Gateskin outside along with his wife. Serena looked out the window along with her brother and sister as they watched the wolf and cat fight.

Serena sent a message to the wolf, "Please be careful, Cantok. You can take him."

Cantok nodded at Serena as he grabbed the cat by the throat and shook him back and forth until it stopped moving.

King Gateskin moved closer to the cat to make sure it was dead. He patted Cantok on the head and laid his hands over the cat to feel for a pulse. There was none.

"Where did he come from?" King Gateskin looked at Spindle and Cantok as he asked this.

"He came from the woods behind Cantok's shelter. Thank goodness Cantok was nearby to help. I don't know if I could have kept him at bay for long."

"You were brave, Spindle. Thank you for protecting Serena. I'm sure you would have come up with something if Cantok hadn't come by."

Spindle bowed to King Gateskin and smiled in relief. He nodded to Cantok in thanks.

Cantok sent his thoughts into Serena's head as she came out to inspect the cat.

"You are welcome, Spindle. Cantok was happy to help," Serena relayed and turning toward her father she queried, "What kind of cat is this, Father?"

"I've never seen one before. It must be from the UT. I've heard there are many creatures inhabiting the area since Cantok and his fellow wolves migrated here."

"Let me ask Cantok, Father. He must know what it is."

Cantok nodded and answered Serena. *It is what used to eat our young when we lived in the UT. But it has grown much larger than I remember. Something is making it increase in size. They are called Catlings.*

Serena responded and repeated what Cantok had told her about these creatures called Catlings.

"Very strange indeed. There must be someone feeding them to increase their size and strength. I have a feeling I know who that is," Gateskin stated, with a stern expression.

Spindle whispered to the King, "I think I know who you mean, my King. He is up to no good again. I will ask my fellow Sprites if they have seen or heard anything about these creatures."

"Yes, please do that right away, Spindle. I think we may have more of them soon. They are getting through our barriers somehow."

CHAPTER TWENTY-SEVEN

Abason was waiting for his son to report what his Sprites had told him.

"Spindle, you must report back to King Gateskin about what I am going to tell you."

Spindle listened intently.

"There are more Parotovinan guards coming this way. They are carrying a large wooden stake and ropes. It appears they are hunting for something – must be the Quintaroon. None of the Sprites have seen it lately. It must be hiding somewhere underground."

"Thank you, Father. I will tell King Gateskin right away, but first I must ask you something else per his request."

"Yes, son. I'm listening."

The Sprite conveyed what the King had said about the Catlings and his altercation with it and waited for his father to respond.

"Were you in danger?"

"No, Father. Lucky for me Cantok came to the rescue. I would have had to fly away and try to distract it until help came to put it down."

"Yes, I know about these creatures. That is something else the Sprites have noticed. The cats are getting bigger than ever. Someone is helping them get that way. I will ask them to watch the Catlings to see what they are eating and let you know as soon as I find out."

"Thank you, Father. This has become dire. If one gets through our barriers, there will be others. We must all be vigilant."

"Be careful, my son. You have an auspicious job that puts you in great danger. I don't share half of what you do with your mother. She would not be able to handle it all."

"It's all right, Father. I am safe and doing the best job I can as Head Guard. I know it can be dangerous but I want to do it. I promise to stay safe. Don't tell mother about this Catling. I don't want her to worry about me."

"Of course. I know. I won't say a word. Just be careful, Spindle. Okay?"

"Yes, Father. Let me know when you hear about what the men are doing and what the Catlings are eating as soon as possible. King Gateskin is waiting."

Spindle flew back to the King's home to keep an eye out on the border behind the King's house while he waited to hear from his father.

Gateskin was watching the land behind his house as was Cantok who was patrolling the area with some of his fellow wolves. Cantok had sent word to his fellow wolves around the village to keep an extra careful watch over the borders to ensure the safety of the villagers.

Serena was staying inside but kept her mind open to Cantok in case she had to relay a message to her father.

Things were quiet as they all waited. The only sounds that were heard were an occasional mooing from Milly the cow or clucking of the chickens in the coop in the barn who were unaware of any danger coming their way.

CHAPTER TWENTY-EIGHT

The Sprites watched over the wife and three children of Kelleran, the Head Gatekeeper of Parotovina, as they moved stealthily through the UT toward Skina

Forest outside the Village of Sovorotskina. They had escaped Parotovina and the clutches of King Kaposkaran after the death of Kelleran.

"Watch out behind you!" one Sprite yelled to the family. This Sprite swooped down along with the help of many other Sprites, who heard his warning, and gripped the collars of the family pulling them up into the trees for safety.

The Catlings pounced but were too late as they tried to grab the edges of the family's cloaks. They growled deep in their throats and raised their large paws up the trees as they tried to climb.

The Sprites watched their attempts which were so far unsuccessful but one smaller Catling was trying harder and managed to reach the lower branches close to where the Sprites and rescued family were perched. Loud noises could be heard as the trees vibrated sending the lone Catling down to the ground where it tried once again to climb.

The Sprites conversed, "We cannot keep it from reaching us. We must move the family from tree to tree until we reach the border of Sovorotskina. We can get word to Abason and he will find help to bring the family out of here safely."

"Yes, I will send word immediately to Abason," another Sprite announced as he kept his eyes on the Catlings as they moved from tree to tree watching the family being passed forward.

Abason received the warning quickly as it had been passed throughout the trees. He called Spindle home to report what he had heard.

***

Spindle was helping Serena do her chores picking vegetables from the garden when he heard his father's call. He looked at Serena and explained, "I must leave you for a short time. You better go into the house until I return. I will tell your father, though, before I leave."

"I am perfectly fine here, Spindle. You need not worry about me. I am safe here with the wolves patrolling the borders."

"That may be so, Princess, but I cannot take a chance. Please go into the house. I will be right behind you."

Spindle flew up behind her and followed her until she was inside. He met with King Gateskin and quickly explained, "My father has an urgent message for you that he said you would need to receive right away."

"That is fine, Spindle. I will keep Serena safely inside until you return. I am not as worried now with the wolves on patrol. They have proven how efficient they are in killing the Catlings if need be. I am anxious to hear what your father has to say. Go now."

Spindle bowed and flew up into his family's tree where his father was waiting for him.

"Thank goodness, Spindle. I was worried you did not hear me. I know my hearing is not as good as it used to be but I know yours is. I was afraid I didn't hear you respond."

"No problem, Father. I heard you and came as quickly as I could. I had to make sure Serena was safely inside with her father before leaving her."

"Yes, yes, of course. I understand you have an auspicious responsibility to do the King's bidding at all times. But what I have to share is of the utmost importance to King Gateskin too."

Abason explained from his perch in the family tree in Sovorotskina, "Kelleran's family are here and are in great danger because of the Catlings who are trying to climb the trees to get at the family. They need your help in being rescued and brought to the safety of Sovorotskina."

"Thank you, Father. I will relay this message to the King and help with the rescue. Be safe, Father. I am worried about you and my fellow Sprites now that the Catlings can climb trees."

"Well, I wouldn't say they can climb but they could keep trying and eventually master it."

"All right. But be careful. Okay?"

"Yes, son. I never thought I would see the day that a son of mine would take care of me. Now, go quickly. The family is waiting."

Spindle flew back to the King's house and knocked on the door. King Gateskin was there waiting and opened it inviting Spindle in.

The Sprite explained what his father had said.

"Thank you, Spindle. Please convey my thanks to your father for keeping an eye out on the family until we can get there."

"Yes, I will, King Gateskin."

King Gateskin along with Spindle, Mitteran and several other guards went directly to the border of Skina Forest to rescue the family of Kelleran.

Mrs. Kelleran and her three children were perched up in a tree as the King and guards arrived. They could see in the distance the Catlings moving toward the tree.

King Gateskin whistled and got the attention of a wolf nearby and pointed to the Catlings who were gaining ground. The wolf called some of his fellow wolves together and they formed a barrier around the tree facing the Catlings enabling Spindle and the other guards to bring the family to safety.

One Catling, braver than the rest or maybe just inexperienced with wolves to know better, sprang forward and attacked the wolves. He was quickly bitten multiple times and left for dead as the wolves retreated safely into Sovorotskina with the guards and family.

The wolves turned to look behind them to ensure no Catlings were following and saw the Catlings attacking the injured one savagely.

King Gateskin heard the growling and made sure the family did not look back at the horror behind them as he closed the barrier with his powers.

CHAPTER TWENTY-NINE

Abason was waiting up in the tree as he observed the rescue. Spindle flew next to him and said, "King Gateskin requested I give you his gratitude for watching over Kelleran's family."

"It was my pleasure, Spindle. Please tell the King that. We are here to help one another."

"I will but please be careful, Father. The Catlings look eager to learn how to climb trees. They just might develop a taste for wooden creatures like us."

"No worries, son. I am still quicker than they are and I don't think they would enjoy the heartburn I would cause them if they tried to eat me."

Spindle chuckled at his father's words but still wore a concerned look on his face.

***

King Gateskin sent word to his wife, "The family of Kelleran are coming to our house."

Queen Solinara prepared a room for them in the extension and some food and drink to refresh them. Serena was there to welcome them too with her brother and sister.

Kelleran's wife, Francia, bowed down to King Gateskin and Queen Solinara in thanks.

"I don't know how to thank you both for saving us from those creatures and welcoming us into your home. I will do all I can to repay you for your kindness."

"No need, Francia. We are happy to welcome you and your children to our home for as long as you need us. We will find a home for you and your children soon. For now, please eat and then rest. You must have been through such a harrowing journey to get here."

"Yes, we were frightened all the way here. If it wasn't for the swift thinking and action of the Sprites, we would all be…" Francia couldn't go on. She looked over at her three children, two girls and a boy the ages of the King's own children, before breaking down.

The Queen hugged Francia and guided her over to the table for a hot cup of her special chamomile tea to calm her. The children were taken care of by Serena who gave them each a cup of her favorite hot chocolate and a sandwich with some of the cookies she had baked the other day with her mother.

Soon after the family was sent to the extension to beds that were made up and ready for them. The children were so exhausted they laid down and went right to sleep. The mother took a little longer as she watched over her children first then laid down and was soon asleep too.

***

"Thank goodness the Sprites watched over them, Gateskin. I can't imagine what would have happened otherwise," Solinara shivered.

"Yes, dear. I know. We owe a lot to the quick thinking and action of the clever Sprites. They are always coming to our rescue. I must get Spindle to convey my thanks once again right away."

Before Gateskin could go to the door and call Spindle, the Sprite was standing on his doorstep with a wide smile.

"Oh, Spindle. I was just going to call out to you. Please convey our sincere thanks to your father and fellow Sprites once again. I don't know what we would do without your help. You are quite a clever bunch, aren't you?" King Gateskin smiled as he shook Spindle's little hand.

Spindle's face blushed a greener shade and bowed to the King. "You are welcome, my King. I already gave my father your message."

He said, "'We are always here for you. It is our pleasure to assist you in any way we can.' Is there anything else I can help you with, my King?"

"I think you did enough for today, Spindle. Why don't you go home and rest? I will need you fresh for tomorrow for anything else that comes our way. Rest well, my little man."

"But don't you need me to watch over Serena some more?"

"No, she will be under my watch now."

Thank you, King Gateskin. Then, I will go home. It has been a long day. You sleep well too, Sire."

"I'm sure I will, Spindle. Thank you."

King Gateskin called Mitteran, his second guard in command, and the other guards who assisted him and Spindle on the rescue. He faced the men and said, "Thank you all for your assistance in safely getting Kelleran's family out of harm's way. They were grateful to all of you for your efforts. Now you must go home and rest. We don't know what tomorrow will bring. I only hope it will be better. Thank you again."

Mitteran bowed along with the other men and turned to go. But Mitteran let his men leave and walked back to the King.

"I want you to know, King Gateskin, I am here for you. If you need me to stay close to your home, I will do that tonight especially with the Catlings on the prowl. They may try to get through the border again."

"Thank you, Mitteran. I don't think that is necessary. The wolves are on the alert. I will have a conference with them through Serena to let them know what I want them to do. I appreciate your loyalty and help, Mitteran. I value you as much as Spindle to lead the men in the right direction at all times."

"My pleasure, King Gateskin. That is why I am here. You saved me and my family. This is the least I can do to keep you and your family safe too. You know I am always ready whenever you need me. Just send me a message and I will come. Good night, Sire!"

"Good night, Mitteran. Give my best to your wife and children. Sleep well."

Gateskin called his daughter into the dining room and told her to sit down at the table so they could discuss what he wanted her to tell Cantok.

"Yes, Father. Whatever you want I will tell him. He has been most helpful. Don't you think so?"

"I agree, Serena. Now this is what you should tell Cantok so he can relay the message to the other wolves."

Serena listened intently and nodded several times. "Okay, Father. I will tell Cantok to keep his young ones safely tucked in their shelters and to keep a watch for any sign of the Catlings again."

"I will go outside with you to meet with Cantok and then you must go to bed. I am sure you are tired from all the chores you had to do today."

Serena explained to the wolf what her father had said and he nodded and looked the King in the eyes and backed away to do his bidding.

"Cantok agreed with you about keeping his cubs safely tucked in the shelter. Catlings would love to gobble them up. He promised to watch over our borders behind the house and told the other wolves to do the same things around the village."

"Good, Serena. Thank you. Now off to bed with you."

"Oh, father, one more thing I forgot to mention to you. Did you know Arubane can also converse with the wolves?"

"Hmm, no, I did not know that. That's interesting to know. I guess with his abilities to change into animals, he must have a sixth sense about how to talk with them. That could be helpful to us in the future if you are not available to help."

"I am not going anywhere, Father. I will always be here."

"Oh, I know you will be here for a long time. But one day you will marry and maybe move away. I hope you don't but if you do, I will be prepared to use Arubane as my interpreter."

Serena turned in a huff, "Fine. If that is what you want to do."

"Serena, dear. Please don't walk away like that. I didn't mean to upset you. I shouldn't have said that. I'm sorry, honey. No one can converse with Cantok like you. After all, Cantok loves you, you know. I can see it in his eyes. They soften when he looks at you."

"He does? Well, I love Cantok too and his family," Serena sniffled and then smiled at her father. "Thank you, Father, for telling me that."

King Gateskin sighed and thought. *That was a close call. I nearly blew it with my daughter. I wasn't thinking too clearly. I guess I must be tired too. But I will have to speak with Arubane and his parents about this soon though.*

CHAPTER THIRTY

Simon and Catalina were in the back of their house doing pooper scooper duty once again.

Catalina exclaimed in surprise and delight, "Look, Simon! There's a little kitty in the bushes. How sweet he is!"

Simon reacted as quickly as he could by saying, "No, Catalina! Don't touch it! It's a baby Catling!"

By the time his words left his lips Catalina had the kitten in her arms and was cooing to it.

Sending his thoughts to his father's mind he alerted him about what was transpiring.

Gateskin came running as soon as he heard Simon's warning about the Catling kitten.

He came up behind Catalina and softly explained why she shouldn't be touching this little kitten. "Do you understand what I am trying to tell you, little one?"

"I don't see what's wrong, Father. It's not a dangerous one. It's only a baby."

"But, Catalina, babies grow up to be dangerous like their parents. Also, the mother is probably out looking for her baby now. You must put it back where you found it right away. Go into the house now, sweetheart, where it is safe. I will take care of this."

"But, Father! I want to keep it as a pet. It's so cute. It likes me too!" Catalina listened more closely to her father when she saw the stern look on his face and placed the kitten where she had found it.

Before Gateskin could say another thing to try to convince his youngest daughter of the dangers, a Catling appeared in the bush close to where the kitten was sitting. It sniffed the kitten and licked it all over to get the smell of the humans off of it. The mother Catling looked at Gateskin, Simon and Catalina and growled deep in her throat as she picked up her kitten and moved back into the woods.

"Simon, take Catalina back into the house immediately. I don't think the Catling is going to forget this. The mother will bring back more Catlings to punish us for touching her young."

King Gateskin sent word to Spindle and in turn Spindle alerted all the other guards to come quickly to the King's aid.

Queen Solinara came rushing out of the house after her children relayed what had happened in the yard with the Catling. She raised her hands over the borders surrounding their property and sent a powerful protective spell over the land as her husband was doing the same thing.

"Gateskin, thank God you were close by to keep Catalina from getting hurt. She is still so young and doesn't realize the dangers."

"I know, my dear, but I don't think the Catling will forget our daughter's scent. She will be back with reinforcements."

Gateskin looked deep into Skina Forest and beyond into the UT. He could see some scurrying of many animals as they gathered together. As he kept his focus there, Spindle flew into the King's vision. Shortly behind the Sprite marched many of his guards ready to protect and defend if needed.

Turning to his Head Guard and other men, King Gateskin praised them, "Thank you for your quick response. So far nothing is happening. But I can see them gathering in the UT. They will be back. That is why we must be vigilant. I have put a spell over the borders along with my Queen's help to protect the property deeper into the ground. That is how the kitten came through the border. It burrowed its way here. That is surely how the other Catling got through our defenses before."

"Yes, I agree," Spindle replied. "That is the only way they could have broken through. The spell does not go below the ground unless you put it there."

"Yes, Spindle. I wish I had thought of that sooner so this wouldn't have happened. My youngest daughter is now in danger because of my ineptitude."

"Oh no, King Gateskin. You are never careless with your spells. Who would have thought this could happen? I certainly didn't," Spindle bowed to Gateskin.

"Thank you, my good man. You are a wonderful support and good for my ego," King Gateskin smiled at Spindle's kind words of encouragement.

"Well, I hope I can always be that way for you, my King!"

"I must get Serena to speak with Cantok to prepare the wolves for the inevitable arrival of the Catlings."

Using mind messaging King Gateskin called out to Serena who was in the kitchen with her mother preparing lunch. She came out in a hurry, wide-eyed and alert to what had happened previously.

"Mother told me about the kitten Catalina had found. I will contact Cantok immediately, Father, as you requested."

"Thank you, Serena. We will need as many wolves as we can get to patrol the borders along with my guards. We have to keep a lookout in case they try to burrow their way in again."

"Of course, Father. Cantok will know what to do. I called out to him and he is on his way here with reinforcements. He told all the mates of his fellow wolves to keep their cubs safely away in their shelters until otherwise noted."

"Good idea, Serena. Thank you, sweetheart. Now go back into the house and watch over your sister and brother. I don't want them out here until I say the coast is clear. I expect some movement of the Catlings any time now."

"Yes, I will, Father."

Serena looked up at Spindle who was beaming at her from a tree near the border which he was guarding. She nodded back to him and threw him a kiss which almost knocked him off his feet when he tried to catch it in mid-air.

She giggled and turned toward the house but peeked over her shoulder one last time to wink at him.

Gateskin smiled at this exchange and shook his head. What was he to do with these two? They definitely liked one another but what would become of this mismatched couple? What could he do to make this match possible in the future? He would have to speak with Solinara.

She would certainly know what could be done.

That would be a discussion for much later. For now, he had more pressing concerns than a budding romance.

CHAPTER THIRTY-ONE

King Kaposkaran paced his Meeting Room waiting to hear something about the guards he had sent on a mission to bring back the Quintaroon. What was keeping them? How hard would it be to capture it and bring it back here? The food he had sent along to entice the creature was laced with enough sleeping potion to knock out a much larger animal. All the guards had to do once it was asleep was to tie its legs and arms to the wooden stake and carry it back. There were more than enough men to distribute the weight of it amongst them.

He couldn't stand the waiting so he called his chef to prepare his lunch and do it sooner rather than later. At least he could enjoy something to eat to take his mind off of the matter and maybe have a glass or two of his special wine.

***

In the UT the guards were unaware that the King was upset over the time they had been gone without any word back to him. They were more concerned about staying alive. They could feel that something was watching them as they crept along carrying the wooden stake, ropes and the food for the Quintaroon.

The Quintaroon had not detected the men yet for it was burrowing after the kittens who were escaping from its claws as it continued to dig for its supper. The Catlings were aware of it and pushed their kittens deeper into the burrows that went to the caves where they were all sheltered.

The guards stopped to take a rest and some sustenance to energize them since they had been walking all day. They lit some fires to keep any animals at bay as they settled down to eat their lunch. Some men laid down and fell asleep while others were too nervous to do so and kept watch. That was the only thing that may have saved them.

The Catlings came out of the woods growled and pounced on a couple of unsuspecting sleeping guards and dragged them away screaming.

The guards who were awake alerted the rest and they gathered around the fire with their spears ready for battle. A couple of Catlings were killed when they ventured too close to the guards and were stabbed and thrown into the fire. The smell of the meat cooking drove the rest of the Catlings back into the woods but attracted the Quintaroon who stopped digging in the burrows and followed the scent drifting up from the fire.

The Quintaroon stood in the woods bordering the guards and waited to see what they would do next. It watched the Catlings in the fire turning darker and scenting the air with an aroma which drove it mad with hunger. It moved closer to the fire and tried to pull one of the Catlings closer to itself with a stick so it could eat some of it.

The guards watched in horror as the Quintaroon was successful in getting one Catling with the stick by skewering it. It gripped the Catling in its claws and ate as much as it could in its massive jaws.

The men threw some of the tainted meat, they had brought with them, at the Quintaroon to entice it to eat a little. They observed the Quintaroon as it reached forward and grasped some of this meat and shoved it into its mouth.

Soon they could see the Quintaroon nodding its head and trying to shake off the feeling of sleepiness. They waited a little while longer to ensure it was asleep.

The men worked quickly to tie up the Quintaroon and made sure it was secure before lifting up the stake and walking forward as they balanced the weight amongst them.

They didn't waste any time and moved as fast as they could for fear of being followed by the Catlings. They were also not sure how long the Quintaroon would be asleep from the potion. It did not eat very much of it. Since it had swallowed nearly the whole Catling beforehand.

They passed through the UT bordering all the other villages until they came to the border of their own village of Parotovina. They stopped a few minutes to adjust the stake and ensured the ropes were still tight.

They moved forward and felt a resistance in the wooden stake as the Quintaroon awakened, startled by the fact that it was tied up.

One man was knocked off his feet as the Quintaroon whipped its head around at him, the creature's jaws just missing capturing the guard's head.

The other guards dropped the stake and ran when they saw the Quintaroon pull himself free of the ropes. They came into the village and yelled to the Gatekeeper, "Open the gates now! Quickly! The Quintaroon is right behind us!"

The sleepy-eyed Gatekeeper moved too slowly to open the gates for the guards who climbed up the high gate and jumped over.

The Quintaroon did not move when it reached the gate. He stood there looking at the village and remembered where he was. He turned and ran back to the UT.

When King Kaposkaran was alerted to this, he ran out of the castle and grabbed the first guard he would catch.

"Where are you going? Where is the Quintaroon?"

The guard mumbled and sputtered trying to explain what had happened, "So sorry, King Kaposkaran. The Quintaroon escaped and was running after us. We had to get away!"

"What is wrong with you? Can't you guards do anything right? Where is the Quintaroon now?"

The guard looked around and shrugged. "I don't know, King. He was just here behind us."

King Kaposkaran raced back to his castle and called more of his guards together. "Go find the Quintaroon! Don't come back without him. Do you hear me? Take some of the tainted meat and the stake and ropes with you. You had better be more successful than the others or you know what will happen to you."

The guards nodded anxiously and ran out of the castle, picked up the stake, ropes and meat that the other guards abandoned outside the gate. They held their spears in front of them as they moved stealthily through the border of the UT.

***

The Quintaroon returned to the UT and never looked back. He had remembered the messages he had received that the King was going to have him killed if he returned to the village. He would not let that happen no matter what. He was now free to do whatever he wanted with his life such as it was.

He could hear more messages coming into his brain now but from a different source. These were not threatening but held his interest. They were from the Wizards who created him. He remembered he had killed two of the Wizards but hadn't meant to do that. He hadn't known his own strength at the time.

He listened more intently as he got further into the UT. What did they want with him?

CHAPTER THIRTY-TWO

The four Wizards kept repeating their
mantra to the Quintaroon. "You must
come to the border of Sovorotskina right
away. There is something we must share
with you. We are your creators and do

not plan to harm you. Please heed our warning, do not return to Parotovina. King Kaposkaran only wants to harm you."

Marno sighed heavily after repeating the message to the Quintaroon several times. "I think we may have reached him. I felt a tremble in the connection. That means he is interested at least a little not to ignore us completely."

"That's good, isn't it, Marno?" Fortag queried with concern.

"Well, at least it opens up the channels for us to continue to converse, though one way only."

"What are we going to tell him if he comes this way?" Fortag asked.

Wassor added, "We could tell him that he is still partly human and that we can fix him."

"We can't promise to do that, Wassor!" Marno shook his head and gave his fellow wizard a stern expression.

"Why not," Wassor pressed on.

"For one thing, I don't think that is possible," Marno answered in exasperation.

"Wait a minute," Tornak interjected. "It might be!"

Marno looked at Tornak in surprise. "What do you mean? How is it possible? Do you know something that I don't, even though I am the Head Wizard? Have you forgotten that fact?"

Tornak ignored the bristling tone of Marno and continued to explain, "I think we can do something to help him get back to his own self."

"Please go on," Fortag and Wassor exclaimed in unison while Marno folded his arms across his chest and kept a stern expression on his face, not giving Tornak a second look.

"I have read of spells of old that can do this. It is somewhat dangerous but, what alternative do we have? The man, or should I say creature, is dangerous not only to others but also to itself."

"How is he dangerous to himself?" Wassor asked, in confusion.

"Well, he cannot think like a human and rushes into things. I don't think he knew what he was doing when he squeezed our fellow wizards to death. He was confused about what he was and how strong he had become."

"Ahh, I see," Fortag exclaimed in agreement. "I think you are right, Tornak. Yes, I think you are right!"

"What do you know, Tornak, that I don't know?" Marno inquired in frustration.

"Please, listen to me, Marno. I do not want to be disrespectful toward you, my friend. I respect you and your powers and only wish I was as powerful as you. But this I know from extensive reading in the old book of spells left to me by my father. There was a time when he had to use a spell on a goat who he had changed into a person. I know it is just the opposite but it may work on the Quintaroon."

"What happened to this animal, which was a goat, to make him want to change it into a human?" Marno asked, curiosity getting the better of him.

Tornak explained, "According to my father's notes, the animal was always rambunctious and getting into all kinds of trouble. He wanted to be able to fix its personality and the only way he could do that was to change it into a human and change it back into a goat."

"Ha ha," Marno laughed out loud at that. "A goat is known to have that type of personality anyway. How did he expect to fix something that was innate?"

Tornak smiled to see that Marno was in a better mood now. He continued to explain, "My father knew that of course but wanted to do something that would be unexpected. I guess he was essentially experimenting on the poor goat to see if it was possible."

The three wizards waited for Tornak to explain further.

He looked at the expressions of impatience on his fellow Wizards' faces and chortled, "Yes, I promise to explain. Sorry about that. Well, my father was a true pioneer and innovator, the first to do a lot of experiments others feared to perform. You could say he was a fearless and determined soul."

"Was he successful, Tornak?" Marno asked, clearly impatient to know the end result.

"Oh yes, he was! What he found out was quite interesting."

"Are you going to keep us in suspense forever?" Wassor asked, upset over being kept in the dark a moment longer.

"Yes, I am going to tell you. Just trying to build up the suspense a little more," Tornak snickered but then got serious when he saw the Wizards' exasperated faces.

CHAPTER THIRTY-THREE

While the guards watched the borders, Gateskin received an urgent message from the Wizards about a spell that could be used on the Quintaroon. He told them to come to his home to discuss it immediately.

The Wizards were at the King's door quicker than he was to answer the door in anticipation.

"Well, it seems we meet again. Maybe I should have you sleep in the extension instead of having to go back and forth between our houses?" King Gateskin joked to lighten the situation for himself and the Wizards who were definitely looking stressed but excited at the same time.

"Now, what was so urgent that could not wait a minute or two, my good men?"

"Sorry, your highness, for disturbing you. It looks like something important is going on here with all your guards around. Did we interrupt an important meeting or something else of urgency?" Marno expressed his dismay in case they angered the King.

"Well, we did have a scare a short time ago," Gateskin explained the situation about Catalina and the Catling kitten.

"Oh no, that is not a good thing to do. Is your daughter all right?"

"Oh, Catalina is a strong-willed little girl, not afraid of anything. She didn't realize the danger she was in and if she did, she would have persevered and not shown her fear."

"She is just like her father in that respect," Fortag bowed to King Gateskin as he said this.

"That's kind of you to say, Fortag. Turning to Marno he asked, "What was so urgent that you needed to see me right away?"

Marno cleared his throat and said, "Well, it has come to our attention, through our fellow Wizard Tornak, there is a spell that can be used on the Quintaroon."

King Gateskin's curiosity was piqued. "Well, explain this to me quickly. I must go check outside soon."

"Oh, sorry, King. I will let Tornak explain this spell and how we will perform it." Marno gave the floor to Tornak resignedly.

Tornak nodded to Marno and began to tell the story of the animal that was changed into a person.

"Do you think it will work on Quintaroon? He is much larger than a goat?" Gateskin chuckled at the thought but listened to Tornak explain.

"I know it is something we do not know yet until we try. This is the only thing we have at this point to do."

Marno stepped forward and added, "We sent a mantra that will keep repeating to the Quintaroon to stay away from Parotovina for fear of his life being taken by King Kaposkaran. We asked him to come to the border of Sovorotskina instead for a message. At the time we sent the message we were not sure what we were going to tell him. But now we do."

"Do you mean you will perform the spell on him without explaining what you are doing?" the King inquired.

"Yes, we plan to do just that. We have to do it quickly before he attacks us. We do not know if he will wait long enough to listen. His attention span as a creature is shorter than as a man," Marno explained.

"Yes, I believe you are correct, Marno. I have seen the Quintaroon in action and how quickly he can attack. It was not a pleasant sight or experience. Please be careful whatever you do. I do not want any one of you injured. You have become valuable citizens to this land."

The four Wizards bowed with respect to the King and their wrinkled faces blushed in surprise, as they swished their wide colorful cloaks around them. Their pointy and fringed hats wiggled in delight at the King's remark.

"Thank you, King Gateskin. We appreciate your kindness in welcoming us to this fine land. We are truly grateful to be here. We promise to be careful and do what is necessary to stop this creature from harming anyone else," Marno articulated his concern over the situation.

"It's not necessary to keep thanking me, Marno. What I need from you is all you can do to remedy what you were forced to do by creating this fearsome creature. I am sure you know what you must do. Continue to keep me abreast of what the outcome will be. In the meantime, I will be here watching our borders for the Catlings' return. I only hope the creatures do not intersect each other. I strongly suggest you steer the Quintaroon in another area outside of my home to perform your spell?"

"Yes, of course, your highness. We will do that right away," Marno bowed and left the King's home with his fellow Wizards in tow.

"Where should we tell the Quintaroon to meet us, Marno?" Wassor asked anxiously.

"Let's move away from here first and try to get a feel for where the creature is. Maybe we can sense his presence as we get closer to the UT border."

Fortag looked worriedly at Wassor and shook his head in alarm. "I don't know if we should get too close to the border. It may jump out and grab one or more of us like he did to Karno and Sufan."

Unbeknownst to the Wizards, the Quintaroon observed them through the trees on the border of the UT and Skina Forest. It listened to them as they discussed it. What were they planning to do, it wondered?

Wassor cried out before he could be stifled by his fellow Wizards when he spied the Quintaroon through the trees.

"What's wrong, Wassor?" Fortag asked as he held Wassor in a grip to hold him in place before he could run away.

"He, it…is here. It is watching us! We have to get away from here now!"

Marno instructed, "No, wait a minute, Wassor. Let Tornak do his spell. We need to stay together."

Wassor nodded but never took his eyes off of the creature as it met his gaze.

Tornak stepped closer to the border and raised his hands over the area where the Quintaroon was standing. Since the creature could not go any further due to the spell over the border Tornak felt safe enough for now. He worked quickly and waved at the other Wizards to add their parts to the spell.

Working together they completed the spell and waited for something to happen. The Quintaroon looked confused and then fell to the ground twitching and moaning.

"What happened to him, Tornak?" Fortag asked in confusion.

"Wait a minute. I think it is working. We will have to open up the border to get to him," Tornak stated in anticipation.

Marno announced, "I will send a message to Gateskin to open up this part of the border long enough for us to get to the Quintaroon. Once we pull him through, we can have the King close it again."

"Okay, but we must work fast. We don't want anything else to get in, along with him," Tornak stated urgently.

"Look at him. He has changed into a man! Oh, my goodness! If I didn't see it with my own eyes, I would never have believed this was possible!" Wassor exclaimed in shock.

Marno reached through the now opened portion of the border, and swiftly with the help of the other Wizards, pulled the Quintaroon, now a man, through to the safety of the border of Sovorotskina. He quickly sent a message to Gateskin to close the border.

"Wow, this is incredible, Tornak! You did it!" Fortag cried out in surprise.

"Yes, you did it!" Marno praised him too.

"Well, not just me. I needed all of your powers collectively to do this. I thank you too," Tornak stated with a smile. "But we are not out of danger yet. We must talk to Quintal and see if he remembers anything. We must make sure he understands he can be changed back."

"He can?" Wassor asked, bewildered.

"Yes, I can change him back. But I will not do that," Tornak explained. "It is not safe to assume he is still not a dangerous person because of his previous persona."

Quintal looked around in confusion. "Where am I? What happened to me?"

The Wizards were shocked to hear Quintal did not remember that he had been a Quintaroon.

Marno leaned in closer to Quintal and helped him up onto his feet. "You don't remember what happened, nothing at all?"

"No. Should I? The last thing I remember was I was going to be hung in the square for what I had stolen from the marketplace." He continued to look around him.

"Do you know where you are, Quintal?"

"No. Where am I? Is the King here? Will I be put to death?"

"You are in Sovorotskina now. You are safe from King Kaposkaran. But you must try to remember something. We need to pull out the hidden memories and take them away once and for all. They may be too frightening for you to endure."

"What are you talking about, Wizard?"

"You remember who we are?" Marno asked.

"Yes, I know who you are, all of you. Everyone knows who you are in Parotovina. You are the King's eyes, ears and powers."

"Yes, we once were. Now we are citizens of this land of Sovorotskina under the good King Gateskin, so will you be once we bring you to the King, Quintal," Marno explained.

"I will? How did I get here? Will King Kaposkaran come looking for me?" Quintal asked in fear.

"No, we are here to protect you and so is King Gateskin," Marno stated.

"But there are some concessions on your part that you must give back for your safety and exile here," Tornak added.

"What must I do, Wizard?"

Marno nodded to Tornak and let him continue to explain, "You must prove your allegiance to King Gateskin and promise to be a good citizen of this wonderful land. You cannot go back to your ways of theft and treachery."

Marno continued, "If you do not change your ways, Quintal, you will be deported back to King Kaposkaran and surely to your death sentence."

"Oh no, I cannot go back there. He is not a forgiving king. I have heard King Gateskin is such a king. Is that not so?"

"Well, he is known to be kind and benevolent but he is quick to anger if you do not change your evil ways. We have seen his anger firsthand and do not want to see it again," Wassor explained.

"Okay. When will I meet King Gateskin, Wizards?"

"Can you walk without assistance now, Quintal?"

Quintal looked at the Wizards in confusion. "Why shouldn't I be able to walk on my own? I am not helpless."

"No, you are not. Well, if you are ready to go meet your new king, then let's go," Marno ordered in a calm tone so as not to excite the man unnecessarily.

"Lead the way, Wizards!" Quintal walked along in a jaunty manner feeling like a free man, which he essentially was now.

CHAPTER THIRTY-FOUR

Gateskin kept his eyes and ears on the border behind his house. There had been no sign of the Catlings. He told his men, "You can go home now. I think the

Catlings will not be here until after dark. Get some rest and dinner and wait for word when to come back here.

Gateskin turned to go inside to see his family and explain what he planned to do about the Catlings. Just as he was relaying his plans to his wife and children, a knock was heard at his door.

He waved his family away and got up to answer the door. Before him stood the three Wizards and a man he did not know.

Marno explained to a surprised king who this man was, "This is Quintal, King Gateskin. He wanted to meet you."

"I see. Nice to meet you, Quintal," Gateskin extended his hand to the man who looked a little in awe at the King's size and aura. King Gateskin stood over six feet, four inches tall.

"I...I...am honored to meet you, King Gateskin. Thank you for welcoming me here. I am still confused about how I got here, but the Wizards' promise to take care of my memories."

"It is a pleasure to meet you. I'm sure the Wizards will take care of everything for you and help you get acclimated in your new home. I will have a cottage for you nearby to get settled. You will only be a short walk away from here. I will be keeping an eye on you to make sure you are okay." The King looked at Quintal with a steely-eyed stare to make sure he understood his connotation.

Quintal jumped back in alarm. "Oh, King Gateskin, I promise to be a good citizen and do whatever is expected of me to mend my ways."

"I certainly hope you will, Quintal, beginning right now."

Quintal was unaware of the King's message to Spindle to come quickly. Gateskin turned toward Solinara and whispered, "Make up a citizen award for Quintal."

Spindle quickly flew to the King's home and knocked on the door. He saluted King Gateskin as soon as he welcomed him in.

The Sprite flew up to the King's shoulder, much to Quintal's surprise, and smiled at the man. He waited for the King to tell him he was ready to present the Citizen Award to the man, which he now held in his hand from the Queen.

Looking at Quintal who had bowed his head and did not meet the King's fixed gaze, King Gateskin requested, "Quintal, look at me. Repeat after me, I, Quintal, profess to be an honorable citizen in my new home of Sovorotskina and do all I can to help my King and do whatever he requests me to do. If I do not do this as he requests, I will be remanded to my former home of Parotovina."

Quintal repeated this in a shaky and unsure voice but did manage to meet the eyes of the King in fear of being banished as he spoke.

"Now you are a citizen of Sovorotskina, Quintal."

Spindle handed over the award and whispered to King Gateskin. "Is there anything else you will need me to do, King?"

"No, Spindle. Go home until I call you back after dark."

"Yes, King Gateskin. I will await your word." Spindle looked around for any sign of Serena but she was not there.

Serena was watching from her doorway and sent a message to Spindle. "I see you and am sending you a kiss. Stay safe. See you later."

Spindle blushed and turned quickly toward the door so no one would notice his flushed face. But the King did hear his contented sigh and saw his eldest daughter looking sheepishly at him.

Gateskin smiled at her and turned toward Quintal and the Wizards to send them on their way.

"Escort Quintal to the new cottage down the path on the right that he had just conjured. Make sure he is settled before leaving him. Solinara has left him some food and made up the bed. If he needs anything, let me know."

"Yes, King Gateskin. We will be happy to do this," Marno responded.

The King whispered to Marno, "Do whatever is necessary to erase his memories safely. We do not want him to revert back to the creature in any way. I am depending upon you to make my land safe."

Marno bowed and nodded as he and his fellow Wizards escorted a still confused Quintal to his new cottage.

***

Marno shared his thoughts with the three Wizards about what they would do next to Quintal.

When they had settled Quintal in a chair at his dining table, they explained what they would be doing to him, "Now, Quintal. You must first of all relax so we can remove the memories that might not be good for you. This will not harm or hurt you in any way. But you must relax and fold your hands in front of you and place them on the table."

Quintal nodded and waited for whatever was to come. He watched the Wizards move around him and wave their hands back and forth. He was fascinated by these movements which put him into a trance-like state in order for them to remove the memories safely.

A pot appeared on the table in front of Quintal which he did not see because his eyes were now closed. Marno guided the first memory carefully out of Quintal's brain and placed it in the pot. Fortag, Wassor and Tornak followed with more white lightning-like coils that sprung up and out of the man's head and into the pot which was quickly filling. When there was no more room, the pot was magically lidded, locked and put away from sight. This pot would reside safely in Marno's cottage locked away on shelves for use later if needed.

The Wizards woke Quintal up and observed him for a few minutes before asking him a question.

"Do you know where you are, Quintal?"

Quintal looked around and smiled before answering, "Yes, I am in my new cottage and am a citizen of Sovorotskina."

"Ah, that you are, Quintal. Are you feeling all right?" Marno inquired.

"Yes, I feel the best I have ever felt, Wizard. What did you do to me?"

Marno smiled and said, "I am happy to hear that, Quintal. We only gave you a much-needed rest and now you can get settled in your new home. Food is in the cupboard for you and a bed is ready. If you need anything, we will leave a bell here for you to call us. Please only use it if absolutely necessary. We are going to our cottages where we will be having our dinners soon with our families and do not want to be disturbed. We will check back on you tomorrow. Sleep well, Quintal. Welcome to the Land of Light, new citizen!"

The Wizards left Quintal alone and excitedly whispered all the way to their homes about what they had just done, much to their surprise and delight. They only hoped the spell would hold and Quintal would be a changed man for the safety of Sovorotskina.

***

Quintal explored his cottage in wonder. He had never had his own place before. He had always lived off the streets and stole what he needed to survive. He remembered what King Gateskin had told him about being a good citizen and if he did not change his ways, he would be banished to Parotovina and surely to his death.

He smiled as he settled down to a tasty dinner provided by his new Queen and a warm and comfortable bed. What could be better than this, he thought?

He laid his head down on the pillow, closed his eyes and drifted off to sleep. He felt as if he were floating in the UT. In front of him was a creature he had never seen before with a massive jaw, huge teeth, sharp claws and multi-colored body with spikes. He screamed as it came closer to him. He sat up in bed in a cold sweat. *What's happening to me? What is this creature?*

CHAPTER THIRTY-FIVE

Hotenfaran and Procelina were awakened by a scream from their son, Arubane. They sat up and were going to see what was wrong when Arubane came into their room.

He appeared distressed and shivered as he got closer to his parents' bed. He sat down on the end and looked at them wide-eyed and shaken.

Procelina laid her hand on Arubane's arm and pulled him closer into a tight hug. "What's wrong, sweet boy?"

"I...I...had a dream about the animals in the UT. They are gathering to come here. I must stop them. They will be coming after the King and his family because of the kitten."

"Kitten? What kitten, Arubane?" Hotenfaran asked, clearly puzzled.

"Oh sorry, Father. I didn't realize you hadn't heard about that yet." Arubane explained about Catalina and the kitten.

"Oh dear!" Procelina exclaimed. "Please tell us about this dream. What did you see, sweetheart?"

"Oh, Mother! It was awful! It mustn't happen!"

Hotenfaran rubbed his son's back to calm him down and enquired, "Arubane, please try to tell us what you saw. I imagine it must have been frightful but you must get it out of your head so you can sleep again."

"I don't think I will be able to close my eyes until I see the King and explain what is going to happen to him. He has to be prepared."

"Okay, dear. We will contact the King and you will stay right here. Okay?"

Procelina closed her eyes and visualized the King and sent a message to him. He was surely sound asleep. She only hoped he would leave his mind open to receive her message of urgency.

Hotenfaran opened his mind too to receive the King's messages. They waited for several minutes then they both received a message from the King.

"What is wrong? I am awake. Sorry I didn't answer right away. I was checking outside for any activity from the Catlings. My men and the wolves have been on duty, taking shifts and rotating their sleep. It is all quiet here so far."

Hotenfaran and Procelina took turns explaining what Arubane had told them about wanting to share a dream he had.

Arubane picked up the message line from here and began to explain what he saw in his dream. "It was awful, King Gateskin. The Catlings were everywhere. They came over the border in packs and attacked the wolves and then went after you and your family. I tried to stop them by talking to them and convincing them to go back to the UT or they would be destroyed."

"I see, Arubane. It was just a bad dream. The Catlings will not be able to penetrate our defenses. If they do, we have the wolves who are bigger and stronger than the Catlings. The powers of the Wizards and my family combined will be too much for the cats to defend against."

"Okay. I guess you are right, King Gateskin. I'm sorry for disturbing you. But I can help by sending messages to the Catlings to confuse them. I can come to your house and stay there if you need me. Of course, if my parents will let me, that is." Arubane met his parents' eyes and pleaded.

"On one condition, Arubane. We have to come with you and stay there until all this is settled if the King and his family will have us."

King Gateskin chuckled, "Of course, you are family and always welcome. Come whenever you want and please come right in. I will leave the door unlocked for you. My family is still sleeping but I will be up and about when you get here. Oh, and thank you, Arubane, for your assistance."

King Gateskin looked out the window but it was still dark. He couldn't see anything unless he closed his eyes and concentrated and then opened them up and looked deeply into the UT. It appeared all quiet for now but he believed Arubane. He was foreseeing the future. A future that he would have to change quickly before it came to fruition. He sighed heavily and stepped outside to speak with Spindle and Mitteran about this portentous future.

Spindle listened and spoke first, "My King, this will not come to pass. We will not let it. I will double the guards and keep rotating them so they will be fresh and ready for anything."

"Yes, that is good, Spindle. But I think we will need more help. I will call the

Wizards to put a spell over all the weapons to ensure they can protect all my guards and prevent any injuries to them."

Mitteran stepped closer and whispered, "I think Arubane's dream is a warning for us to increase our patrol too, King. I trust Arubane who is so powerful that he can perform feats most of us couldn't even think to do."

"Yes, Mitteran. I agree. He is going to be a powerful wizard one day. We will need him on our side. He is coming here shortly with his parents. The three of them will be able to help keep us well covered with spells of protection. Keep your eyes, ears and other senses alert. Something is coming this way. I can feel it in my bones and my hair follicles are quivering in warning."

Within a short time Arubane came hopping along the pathway to the King's home and bowed when he stood in front of him.

"Welcome, my fine little man. It is good to see you again. My daughter Serena recently told me about your ability to speak to the animals. I am not surprised you can converse with Catlings. That is a good thing for us. We may need your help in contacting them to convince them to stay away for their own safety."

"Yes, I think that would be a good idea, King Gateskin. I can send a message to the leader of the Catlings and let him know it will be too dangerous for them to come here."

Hotenfaran and Procelina stood behind their son and beamed with pride at his intellect and powerful abilities. They were for once speechless.

"Good to see you both, Hotenfaran and Procelina. Why don't you all go in the house? I can hear Solinara up and about now and the children will be soon enough especially if they know that Arubane is here to visit for a while."

Hotenfaran shook Gateskin's hand and said, "I'm sorry if we disturbed you so early, but Arubane was clearly upset over the dream and would not go back to sleep until he could talk to you and warn you about the impending dangers."

"That's fine, Hotenfaran. Arubane is quite a remarkable young boy. I can't believe how much power he has in that little body. It will only grow stronger as he grows up. You must cultivate it and train him in every manner you can. He will become my most powerful wizard one day."

Procelina smiled as she listened to the exchange between her husband and his brother-in-law. She leaned in and added, "I agree, King Gateskin. Arubane may one day be the most powerful wizard of all time. We will do our best to train him to the utmost of our abilities. I know he will be beyond our powers soon, if not already."

Arubane went into the house to see Aunt Solinara and his cousins. He smiled to himself at the conversation he had heard. *Will I really be the most powerful wizard of all time? Wow! I can't wait!*

Procelina and Hotenfaran followed close behind their son and went to see Queen Solinara who was busy in the kitchen preparing breakfast for her family and guests. She had heard them talking and even though it was still not sunup, she knew she would be needed.

Serena and her brother and sister were up and about and greeted Arubane. He began to explain why they were visiting so early.

"Wow, did you see us get killed, Arubane?" Catalina asked.

"Catalina! Of course not!" Serena exclaimed in alarm.

"Oh no! I didn't see anyone harmed. I think this was just a warning to all before something like that could happen." Arubane looked at Serena and whispered, "Sorry!"

She nodded to him and gave her sister a silent warning not to ask such things.

Catalina bowed her head and sighed, "So sorry, Serena. I just had to know. But I know that we are too powerful even for the Catlings to try to harm."

Simon agreed with his little sister, "Yes, Catalina. We are too strong and powerful for cats to overpower. We are invincible!"

Catalina clapped her hands and high-fived her brother in agreement.

Solinara called out to the children to help set the table and stated firmly, "Stop the nonsense about anyone getting hurt. It will not happen."

"Yes, mother. We will set the table," Serena pulled her siblings along to help.

Arubane grabbed some dishes and began placing them around the table quicker than Catalina could.

She gave Arubane a silly face and stuck out her tongue at him and said, "Show off!"

Arubane giggled and let Catalina finish setting the table as he went out to the kitchen to see what else he could do to help.

He stopped at the door of the kitchen when he heard his mother telling Solinara about the warning he had in the dream. Procelina's voice shook with worry and tears formed in her eyes.

He pushed open the door and announced, "I am here to help. What can

I do? The others are setting the table. Can I help cook?"

Procelina blotted the unspent tears that threatened to fall with the edge of her apron and turned toward Arubane. "Don't tell me you know how to cook too, my son?"

"Well, maybe a little. I can cook eggs, hard boiled. I used to do that with the chickens' eggs when I lived in the barn in Parotovina. I would steal, oops, I mean borrow some eggs and put them in a pot and hold it over a fire I made in the woods to cook. They always tasted so good, especially since I had only been eating grass and yucky stuff."

Solinara and Procelina giggled at Arubane's escapades.

Queen Solinara said, "You were quite a talented little boy from the very beginning."

Arubane smiled and responded, "I always tried, Aunt Solinara. I would have starved if I hadn't figured something out." He laughed as he looked at the stove and stirred something in a pan for his aunt.

"Thank you, Arubane. You are such a big help."

"Yes, he certainly is, Solinara," Procelina hugged her son from behind feeling so much love for him that her tears returned, misting her eyes.

Arubane stopped stirring and turned away from the stove as he went into a trance. "It's coming!"

"What? What is coming, my son?" Procelina asked in alarm.

CHAPTER THIRTY-SIX

King Gateskin and Hotenfaran discussed, outside away from the women and children, what Arubane said about being able to converse with the Catlings.

The sun was rising, bringing a brightness to the world around them. All appeared to be safe with no dangerous creatures in sight, just the wolves who were poking around and searching for a Rabbinel to eat for breakfast. The two men watched the wolves as they scurried around to get a scent of the little creatures.

King Gateskin continued, "I recently learned about your son's abilities to converse with animals, like I told you, but I never got to discuss this further. I think it would be a good thing to let him converse with them at a safe distance. I will be right next to him. Is that satisfactory to you and Procelina? I will never let any harm come to him," the King promised.

"I know my wife will not be happy about this. She is extremely anxious as it is that he dreamed this could happen. I will have to convince her it is the thing that has to be done to protect all of us. I only hope Arubane can convince the Catlings we do not want to harm them or their kittens in any way."

"After you speak with Procelina, we will discuss this more. For now, let's have breakfast. We need to be ready for whatever comes our way. Besides, I can smell something cooking that is making my stomach growl."

Hotenfaran laughed and agreed, "I'm with you, Gateskin. I'm starved!"

As they entered the house Arubane was standing at the doorway to the kitchen in a trance-like state. Everyone was looking at him and not moving.

Hotenfaran rushed to his side and took his hands, directing him to a chair before asking, "What do you see, my son?"

Arubane mumbled at first, then looked at his father in surprise. "What, Father? What do you mean?"

Confusion was evident in Hotenfaran's expression as he looked over at his wife who was also perplexed.

Procelina stepped closer to Arubane and asked in a soft voice, "You said, 'it's coming.'"

The young boy shook his head and concentrated, scrunching up his face as he tried to extract his memories of a short time ago. "I know I saw something but...it now escapes me. I'm sorry. I know it will come back to me but..."

"That's all right, Arubane. Just relax. If it is important, it will come back to you, I'm sure," Procelina said as she gave her son a hug to reassure him all was well.

She exchanged concerned glances over her son's head with Hotenfaran and shrugged. They shared a few words through their minds.

"I don't know what that was about, dear," Hotenfaran said.

"Well, I'm sure he will remember shortly. It definitely was something that shook him because he went into a trance-like state for several minutes before he came out of it when you spoke to him."

'Don't worry yourself, Procelina. He will remember soon. Because whatever it was, he saw something dangerous. It could be here soon. At least he gave us a warning to be on the lookout."

"Yes, dear. I agree. Let's eat something first and then we must explore further what is coming."

Hotenfaran looked around at the others who were waiting for him to explain what he and his wife were discussing.

"No worries, everyone. We will soon know what is ahead. Let's eat while we can and then see what we can find. I'm sure Arubane will know something soon and share with us."

Looking at his son, he directed his inquiry, "Won't you, Arubane."

The boy had his mouth full but just nodded in agreement causing everyone to chuckle and lose their anxiety to an extent.

It wasn't long before they had all finished breakfast when they heard a noise outside.

King Gateskin was the first to rise and look out the window. He didn't see anything but sent word to his men outside to keep a lookout a little longer and go in shifts again so they could all have breakfast at one time or another.

Spindle responded, "Yes, King Gateskin. I am sending some of the men home to rest and eat and others are taking their place. All has been quiet all night and now at sunrise. The only animals stirring are the wolves. They are quite busy searching for something to eat – probably the Rabbinels. Oops, I think they caught one – I heard squealing."

"Good man, Spindle. I know you will keep me abreast about what is happening out there. But I must share that Arubane has spotted something coming this way. It could be dangerous so keep a close eye and ear out for it."

"Yes, of course, my King! I will do that."

CHAPTER THIRTY-SEVEN

Arubane finished his breakfast and went to the window to look out. He squinted his eyes and turned to his parents. "I think it is here now. But it is not the Catlings. It is the Quintaroon."

King Gateskin, hearing this, swiftly opened the door and raced out to Quintal, the new citizen's cottage, without a word to anyone else.

They all watched him as he ran up the path to Quintal's house. He didn't even knock as he got there and threw open the door. Quintal was sitting at the table in a trance similar to Arubane's.

He poked Quintal in the back and waited for him to wake up.

"What is it, King Gateskin? You startled me!"

"Did you have a dream now?"

"Um...no not now but earlier when I was sleeping. I was just thinking about it now. I don't understand what it means though."

King Gateskin asked, in a stern voice, trying to control his anger, "What did you dream about, Quintal?"

Quintal met the King's eyes and stuttered, "I...I...don't know what I saw. It was a strange creature with massive jaws, sharp teeth and claws and multi-colored with spikes all over its body. It was really frightening. I woke up with a shock. It was coming after me."

"How do you feel now?" King Gateskin inquired as he watched Quintal's expressions.

"I...I...am still shaking from it. Does that mean this creature is coming after me?"

King Gateskin mulled this over before answering, "No, I don't think it can come after you unless you let it out."

"What? What do you mean, let it out?"

"I think it is time to explain something to you, Quintal," King Gateskin began to tell him of what he was and had done before his transformation by the Wizards.

"Oh no! I couldn't have done all that! I was a monster? I don't understand? How?"

"Well, maybe I should have the Wizards explain in more detail. I think they were fearful of telling you this in case you changed back into it. Evidently, they did not get all the memories out of your brain."

"Oh, is that what they were doing to me when they cast a spell over me when I first came here?"

"Yes, that is correct. If you need more explanation and details, I can ask the Wizards to come here."

"Yes, maybe that would be a good idea. Then they can work to get more of those horrible memories out of my brain. I don't think I could take another night like last night. I was so frightened. I can't imagine how I could be that creature. I know I wasn't a good person but I don't want to become like it again. Please help me, King Gateskin!"

The King sent word to his Wizards to come to Quintal's cottage immediately. Before he closed off his mind to them, they were at the door.

Gateskin opened it and explained to them in their minds, avoiding shaking Quintal up more.

"I had to explain to Quintal about what he was before you changed him back. He has a lot of questions for you. He is experiencing flashbacks of the creature coming after him. It is trying to come out again. I think it would be a good idea to extract more of these memories to ensure they are all gone for good. Arubane has seen this too. He warned us about the Quintaroon coming back. Work quickly, Wizards, and make this right." Gateskin turned and left the cottage to go back to his own home. He knew he would have to explain his sudden departure to his wife and extended family.

The Wizards bowed to the King, nodded and went to work on Quintal once again. He was sitting at the table with his hands folded and ready to begin.

They explained to Quintal about how they had to change him into the creature. He nodded and said, "Please hurry. I fear it is trying hard to come back. I don't want it to destroy anyone else."

The Wizards pulled another pot out of thin air and extracted more memories from Quintal's brain and placed them securely inside the pot and locked it down for good and sent it to the shelves in Marno's house. This time they were sure they got every one of the memories from the Quintaroon.

Wizard Marno asked Quintal, "How do you feel now? Is there any sign of the Quintaroon?"

Quintal looked puzzled as he tried to recall anything about the creature. He shook his head, "I think he is gone. But I will know more when I sleep tonight especially if it comes back to me."

"If that happens, ring the bell we gave you that only we will hear and we will come immediately. It is of the utmost importance we get it all out of you, once and for all," Marno explained.

"Yes, I agree, good Wizards. By the way, I forgive you for creating the monster in me because I understand that you were under duress. I also have to thank you at the same time for saving me from a death sentence."

Tornak nodded and smiled, "Yes, I guess we did save your life. We are truly sorry for what we had to do to you but we had no choice."

Wassor added, "Yes, we had no choice. If we hadn't used you to create the creature, we would not have been able to do anything about it. It would still be roaming the UT and killing whatever was in its path."

"Well, I guess it was a good thing then, Wizards. I thank you. Now if only it will stay away. What if King Kaposkaran brings it back?"

"No, he cannot do that now. We have extracted all the memories. If he does try to summon you, do not listen to him. Ignore all messages and report them to us right away. We will take care of them and stop them from reoccurring."

"Ahh, thank you, my friends. I consider you to be my friends now that all has been explained and forgiven."

"Yes, we are now friends, Quintal. Please alert us to any problems at all. We are as close as the bell is," Fortag added.

"We must be on our way. We have more to do to assist the King if any other creatures come this way. Rest well today and tonight, Quintal."

"I'm sure I will or at least I hope I will be able to sleep."

The Wizards waved their hands over Quintal to relieve some of his anxiety before leaving. They looked back at him and noticed he was looking much better now. He had a peaceful expression on his face and was calm.

CHAPTER THIRTY-EIGHT

King Gateskin arrived back at his house where his wife and extended family were still sitting at the dining room table sipping chicory coffee. They looked up at him expectantly.

Queen Solinara spoke first and asked, "Is everything okay, my dear?"

"Oh, yes. All is back to normal, whatever normal is. The Wizards have it in hand and are taking care of Quintal's errant memories that somehow escaped them before. He should be fine now. Evidently, he was having dreams and visions of the Quintaroon going after him. It was truly frightening to him. He had never seen this creature since he was inside it. In fact, he never knew he was a creature or at least he says he doesn't remember it."

"That's good to hear," Solinara sighed in relief.

"Yes, I guess we don't have to worry about the Quintaroon anymore," Hotenfaran expressed in relief.

"Thank goodness," Procelina stated as she looked at her husband and smiled.

"I don't see the Quintaroon anymore, Father and Mother. It must be gone for good," Arubane announced as he came into the room from where he had been playing with the other children.

"Yes, my son. He is gone for good. You need not worry about it anymore." Procelina patted her son on the head as he came closer to her.

Arubane laid his head on his mother's shoulder and sighed heavily, clearly relieved of not having to see this creature in his head ever again.

King Gateskin addressed Arubane, "I appreciate, dear boy, you keeping us up to date on whatever creatures are coming our way."

Arubane nodded and smiled, "I am happy to be of service to you, King Gateskin."

His words made everyone laugh for such a young boy to be so intelligent and powerful.

Serena came looking for Arubane. "Where did you go, Arubane? We were waiting for you to finish the game. I am winning and I don't want to start all over again. I may not be so lucky with the next game."

"Okay, Serena. I am coming! Women, what are you going to do with them?" Arubane shrugged his shoulders and smiled.

More laughter was heard as he left the room by all the adults who just shook their heads in amazement at what came out of this little boy's mouth.

King Gateskin stated in a snicker, "He is one special little boy, Hotenfaran and Procelina. You have quite an amazing little son. I know he will become quite powerful as he grows into adulthood. I plan to keep him busy helping me around here. He is a mastermind at seeing things and talking to the animals."

Hotenfaran and Procelina beamed with pride at the King's words. "Thank you, King Gateskin, for your kindness toward our son. We are constantly amazed at him too. Every day there is something else he can do. He will be much more powerful than all of us put together. That is a frightening concept."

"Yes, it can be but also a marvelous one to think over. He will surely take over for the other Wizards one day helping my children when they rule this kingdom. He will be their Head Wizard."

Procelina's eyes opened wider in disbelief. "Do you really think so, King Gateskin, Arubane will be that powerful?"

"Yes, I do. Of course, he is still a little boy and has a lot to learn from the both of you. Maybe you should think of having him coached and taught some spells by the Wizards too."

Arubane's parents exchanged wary glances before answering, "We don't think it is necessary to teach him any more spells at the moment. He has been teaching himself some from the Book of Spells. He said he and Serena have been working together on some spells."

"Really? How interesting. Serena never mentioned that to us," Solinara said in surprise as she looked at her husband for any sign that he knew about this.

"No, Solinara, I did not know about this," Gateskin responded in her head.

"Okay. I'm happy to hear that you were not keeping this from me. We may have to speak with our daughter to ensure that she is not teaching him anything that could get him into trouble with his parents."

"Yes, I agree, dear. I will speak to her soon. Now let us get back to more important things. I need to check up on my guards to see if anything has been spotted outside."

Solinara nodded at her husband and refilled the guests' coffee cups to keep them busy as she snuck off to speak with Serena before her husband did.

***

Solinara watched from the doorway of the playroom as the children played a game with whoops and hollers as they won or lost. Serena looked up at her mother when she sensed her presence.

"Hi, Mother. Do you need me?"

"No sweetheart, just checking up to see if you are having fun."

"We are! I just won another game against Arubane, Simon and Catalina. Well, Catalina doesn't count because she is still learning the game."

Upon hearing her name and what her sister said Catalina responded, "I do know how to play this game. I play all the time with my friends." She sulked as she turned away from Serena.

"Now don't let me interrupt you. We can talk later, Serena. I believe you, Catalina. I know how smart you are," Solinara smiled at her youngest daughter. She moved closer and kissed Catalina on the cheek before leaving the room.

Catalina looked at her sister and stuck out her tongue, "See, Mother believes me! So there!"

"Okay, I believe you too. Now let's play one more of this game and then onto another one. Remember, using magic to win is not allowed."

Arubane sat up straighter and said, "All right. I'm ready. I will beat you all this time!"

"Ha-ha. I don't think so," Serena egged him on.

Simon stayed quiet, not sure if he would win this time either. He sighed and finally said, "Okay I'm ready too."

Catalina just smiled broadly and nodded feeling sure she would win this game even if she didn't win that much.

***

King Gateskin was outside looking deep inside the borders of his kingdom and into the UT for any sign of trouble. He had been surprised the Catlings had not attacked all night.

He turned to speak to Spindle, "What do you think is the reason the Catlings have not attacked us yet?"

Spindle took a deep breath and expelled it before answering, "I think they may have something else in mind. I will check with my father to see if he knows anything. He can contact the Sprites in the UT and see if they have seen what the cats are up to."

"Good idea, Spindle. Maybe something has stopped them from coming."

CHAPTER THIRTY-NINE

King Gateskin continued to think over what had happened to prevent the Catlings from attacking. It didn't make sense after he had seen how the mother

Catling had cleaned her baby and stared back at him with a fierce expression. She was clearly looking for revenge. That was the main reason he had to keep his youngest daughter inside for as long as necessary. So far, she hadn't complained about not being outside to play with the wolf cubs.

He cleared his head and listened to some new messages from the Healers, rulers of the Land of Merona in the central part of the Noella Province. He hadn't spoken with them since the attacks from the Parotovinans. He wondered what they wanted or needed from him.

He listened more intently and their message became clearer. "King Gateskin, we have some visitors here that would like to come see you immediately. Are you available for a conference? They are citizens of Parotovina and have escaped the wrath of King Kaposkaran. They need your help."

"Yes, of course. Send them along and alert King Cavelan of Votovia they may try to cross his borders."

"Yes, of course. I have already done that in case you did accept these visitors."

"I see. You are ahead of me, Healers. If I can be of any assistance to you, please let me know. I am here and my door is always open to you. Take care."

"Thank you, good King Gateskin. We will keep in touch. Things have been quiet here but I know what you have been dealing with in the UT. We can't hear the creatures like you can but we sense they are there. Stay safe."

"Yes, we are doing all we can to do just that, Healers."

The messages ended as King Gateskin proceeded to the borders of his land and that of Merona. He brought along Mitteran and some other guards with him since Spindle had not gotten back from seeing his father.

Things were abnormally quiet as they got closer to Merona's borders. King Gateskin looked deeper into the Merona Forest and spotted several visitors coming his way.

He opened the border and waited for them to step forward.

There were two women, two men and a few young children in tow. They all bowed low to King Gateskin and stood up when he asked, "Please rise and introduce yourselves. Welcome to Sovorotskina."

The couple holding hands looked up with hesitancy but answered, "We are Henno and Jenara, husband and wife. We are citizens of Parotovina. We have heard you are a benevolent king who has taken in many of our fellow Parotovinans. We seek exile here too."

King Gateskin nodded at them and turned his attention to the others who appeared to be a family of five. "Who are you? What can I do for you?"

The father, Danko, stepped closer to the King and bowed in respect. "I am King Kaposkaran's guard of Parotovina and this is my family. We are seeking exile also, King Gateskin. It is a sincere pleasure to finally meet you. I have heard so much about you from King Kaposkaran most of which was not good because of his jealousy of you and your powers. I know none of what he said is true though."

"I see. Nice to meet you all. What are your names?"

Danko's wife answered timidly, still bowing her head, "I am Garita, Danko's wife and these are our three children." She turned to them and tapped each one of their children on the head to respond to the King.

The oldest one said, "I am Harmony, eight years old." She bowed and stepped back for her siblings to come forward and answer.

The second oldest said, "I am Celdrick, six years old."

The youngest one looked up with tears in her eyes and shook her head.

"What is wrong, little one?" King Gateskin asked in a soft voice.

"I am afraid of you. Are you evil like the other king?"

"Oh no, I am kind and not like him at all. Please do not be afraid of me. Now tell me your name. If you do not want to say it out loud you can whisper into my ear.

He leaned forward for her to do that and heard, "I am Aneka. I am four years old – almost four and a half."

"Hmm. I see. It is important to get that half in there. It certainly makes you a bigger little girl," King Gateskin chuckled, clearly smitten with the adorable child.

Addressing the whole group, the King said, "You are welcome to the Village of Sovorotskina and will be guests of my family and me. Please follow my guards. We have much to discuss. I am sure there is a story behind your request for exile. I look forward to hearing all about it."

The group followed closely behind the King and his guards and heavily sighed, feeling somewhat better being in the Land of Sovorotskina with this kind king.

The children chattered away as they passed by all the cottages and citizens working in their gardens. They gasped in surprise when they saw their first wolf. It was walking along the border of Skina Forest and stopped to look up at them.

Aneka pointed and shouted to her family, "Look at that animal. What is it, Mommy?"

Her mother looked in alarm at the large wolf and exclaimed, "Oh dear, it's a wolf, an extremely large one at that." She poked her husband and he turned to look.

King Gateskin heard their chatter and explained, "No need to worry about the wolves. They are our friends and live here with us. They have promised to protect us and our borders from any dangers."

"Oh, but what do they eat?" Celdrick asked with curiosity.

"They have plenty of food to eat that we have prepared for them. I'm sure you would enjoy hearing about that more from my children. They will be happy to introduce you to the wolves and their cubs."

"Cubs? They have little ones?" Garita asked in surprise.

"Oh, yes. They have many cubs. My children have grown quite fond of them in the short time they have been on our land. But like their parents, they are growing larger by the day."

Aneka's eyes grew wider as she exclaimed, "Can I meet them, King?"

"Of course. I will have my oldest daughter, Serena, introduce you all to Cantok and his family."

"Will they want to eat us?" Harmony asked in a shaky voice.

"No, not at all. They only eat what we have provided for them. Come into our home. We are here. I will explain all this to you. There is no need for you to worry about them. In fact, you will find them quite friendly." King Gateskin smiled to ease their nerves.

Serena, Simon and Catalina were at the door waiting, after their father sent word, they had more guests to welcome.

Serena smiled at them and opened the door wider for them to come in. "Welcome to our home. It is so nice to meet you all. I am Serena, oldest daughter of King Gateskin. This is my brother, Simon, and my sister, Catalina."

Everyone entered and were met by Queen Solinara who had set the table with all kinds of food and drink. She waved the way forward for them to sit down and enjoy it all.

"Welcome. I am Queen Solinara. Please refresh yourselves."

Danko and Garita guided their children along with Henno and Jenara to the table where they suddenly realized how hungry they all were.

The children were seated at a smaller table with Serena and her siblings who chatted like they were old friends.

Questions were flying back and forth between them as Serena explained about the wolves. "They have been here for a short time but have kept us safe from the Catlings. I will introduce you to the Cantok, the head of the wolves and his cubs. They are so cute. You will love them even if they are already growing larger and are no longer easy to pick up. They are much too heavy," Serena sighed.

"Catlings? What are they?" Celdrick asked, with curiosity.

Simon explained, "Well, they are like large cats who keep growing due to the food they are eating that makes them stronger and bigger. This food was supposed to be for another creature."

"Will they eat us?" Aneka asked as her voice shook.

"Umm…well, they could but the wolves won't allow that to happen. They are here to protect us. You do not need to worry about the Catlings."

Harmony patted her sister on the head and reassured her, "Don't worry, Aneka. The wolves will protect you and all of us. Serena just told you that."

"I know but the wolves don't know us yet. They may think that we are enemies because we do not belong here."

Simon couldn't help himself when he said, "Yes, that is true. That is why we must introduce you to Cantok right after you finish eating. Once he meets you and realizes you are friends, then he will protect you like he does the rest of the citizens of our land."

Serena gave her brother a fierce look of warning and whispered, "Simon, that is not nice to say. You will frighten our guests."

"Sorry, Serena. I didn't mean to scare anyone." He nodded at the guests and shrugged his shoulders as he left the room to go outside to see the wolves.

The children followed him and waited to be introduced. When they got closer to the wolves, they gasped in surprise to see just how large the animals were and how fierce they appeared.

Cantok listened to Serena explain who these new people were and introduced each one to him. He bowed and nodded his head at each one.

"Are you talking to him, Serena?" Celdrick asked in wonderment.

"Yes, I know how to converse with him. No one else does, except one other, that is."

"Can I learn to speak with him too," Celdrick asked.

"No, I don't think I can teach you how to do that. It is one of my powers and not something that is shared."

"Oh, okay." Celdrick frowned and slumped his shoulders.

The cubs stepped forward and sniffed the guests as Serena introduced them.

Aneka stooped down next to the smallest wolf and put her hand out so it could sniff her. She giggled when it tickled her palm with its tongue and whiskers.

Danko and Garita watched their children in awe as they interacted with the fierce creatures, showing no fear at all.

"How did you train these creatures to be your protectors, King Gateskin?" Danko inquired.

The King explained all about the wolves and how they came to live there in peace and provide protection for him and his village.

"That is amazing, King Gateskin! I would never have believed it if I hadn't seen it with my own eyes and heard about it through your words."

Garita continued to watch her children with some uneasiness she couldn't quite shake. She turned toward her husband to question him, "Do you think it is wise for our children to play with these creatures, Danko? It makes me nervous to see how they interact without any fear."

"No, I do not think it is a problem for us to worry about, my dear. Look how kind and gentle these huge creatures are toward our children. I am not worried and neither should you be, Garita. Relax and enjoy our new home and be thankful King Gateskin has welcomed us here."

"Yes, I'm sorry, Danko. I can't help being a mother who worries about everything.

I can see how sweet and gentle these wolves are with our children. You are right, dear. I guess I will be able to relax a little."

Danko patted his wife's hand as she slipped it into his own and leaned her head on his shoulder. He heard a heavy sigh leave her lips and smiled. He looked around for King Gateskin to ask him about when they could officially become new citizens of this fine land but he was nowhere in sight.

CHAPTER FORTY

King Gateskin watched from his kitchen window how the wolves interacted with the new visitors. He had a lot to ask these visitors about why they had come to Sovorotskina. Were they spies of King

Kaposkaran or just others who were escaping his evil kingdom?"

Danko looked up and spotted the King in the window watching the wolves. He waved at the King to get his attention and was requested to come back inside.

"I was just going to look for you, King Gateskin. I have much to ask you and also to share about my family and myself. You are probably wondering why we are here."

"Well, that was one thing I was going to ask you, Danko. Why are you here?"

The Parotovinan guard cleared his throat and began to explain about how he met Henno and Jenara.

"I see. So, you are saying that they convinced you to escape with them to Sovorotskina to get away from King Kaposkaran?"

"Yes, King. We had no choice. Once we made the decision we could not go back. I took my family with me immediately and here we are."

"What are Henno and Jenaro to you and your family, Danko?"

"We are not related but have the same feeling about King Kaposkaran. We fear him and do not want to live under his reign another minute. We all heard about you from other travelers who passed through. They said you were kind and generous and always welcomed others into your kingdom."

"What about Henno and Jenara? What is their story?"

"Oh, I think that should come from them, King Gateskin. It is not for me to say," Danko looked away as he said this in the direction of the couple.

Danko waved at the couple to come inside. He excused himself and left the

King with the couple who looked confused and a little frightened being summoned like that.

"What...what can we do for you, King Gateskin?" Henno asked anxiously as he met the King's eyes.

"There is nothing to worry about, Henno. I would like to talk to you and Jenara for a few minutes to learn more about you. I need to know what your story is and why you came to be in my land of Sovorotskina."

"Yes, of course, King Gateskin. We apologize for not explaining sooner. It was all this about the wolves that made us forget the purpose of our visit here."

King Gateskin waited for Henno to collect his thoughts before he continued.

"I...I mean we have been wanting to leave Parotovina for a long time, King Gateskin. We didn't see any way to do it until we met Danko. But before that we

408

were forced to meet with King Kaposkaran."

Jenara nodded to her husband and picked up the explanation, "Yes, we met with the King once he discovered our powers. He forced us to summon the Quintaroon since he had been unable to do that himself without any of his Wizards."

"I see," the King smiled. "I understand now."

Jenara smiled back at him and continued, "Yes, we did what the King wanted but added our own mantra telling the creature not to return home since he would be put to death by the King."

"Oh, that was clever, indeed," Gateskin chittered.

"Yes," Henno added. "We thought that would work to keep it at bay until we could escape. We didn't want to run into it and be forced to stay to help the King control it."

"Smart thinking, Henno." King Gateskin stated.

"Well, we did manage to escape and here we are now. We convinced Danko to come with us when he showed some sympathy toward our predicament."

"Yes, he did tell me that."

"Now, good King! What can we do? Will you let us take asylum here or do we have to return to Parotovina or another village for safe keeping?" Henno bowed his head as his shoulders shook.

King Gateskin placed his hands on Henno's broad shoulders and Danko pulled his head up to meet the King's eyes. "You need not worry about that, Henno and Jenara. You are welcome to stay here for as long as you want. If you plan to make this your permanent home, then you can become citizens of

Sovorotskina as many others have done before you."

Jenara's eyes opened wide and tears brimmed in her eyes as she nodded briskly to her husband, "Yes, please, King Gateskin. We would be happy to make our home here. Wouldn't we, Henno?"

"Yes, dear. I think that would be a good thing to do, most certainly," he chuckled as his wife hugged him tightly in gratitude.

"Well, it is all settled then. I will have you recite the pledge and you will become new citizens of Sovorotskina. But first we should check with Danko and his family to see if they agree to do the same."

"Oh, I doubt if you will have any resistance there, King Gateskin." Henno smiled and headed out to see Danko's response when the King asked him.

***

A short time later Spindle came back to speak to the King about what his father had told him about the Catlings in the UT.

He promised to help with presenting the awards to the new citizens first before he went into depth about his report.

Once the new citizens were fully installed and grateful, he and Spindle sat down in the King's private meeting room at the back of his house, opposite the kitchen and dining rooms, to discuss serious matters about the UT. Gateskin knew Solinara would keep the new citizens busy with refreshments and a place to rest away from him and Spindle so they could conduct their business in private. He did not want to worry the new citizens about any dangers that could soon come to pass their way.

Spindle looked at the King and queried, "Do you think these citizens should have waited longer before becoming citizens of this great land, King Gateskin? I am so sorry for my brashness in asking this."

Gateskin smiled and nodded. "You may be right, Spindle. But this was my way of keeping them in line. They may be more careful how they act now that they are official citizens of Sovorotskina. I can keep the threat of sending them back to their former home in the back of their minds."

"Hmm, I see, King. That could work. Forgive me for my boldness. I do not want to insult you in any way, King Gateskin."

"No, you did not insult me, Spindle. I was thinking along those lines too. But this will work, I'm sure."

CHAPTER FORTY-ONE

Back in Parotovina King Kaposkaran paced in his meeting room so many times that he had worn a path there. He called his guards, who were outside the castle, to come in immediately.

"Come in, you imbeciles! What are you standing there for? Didn't you hear me? I need you now!"

The two guards stumbled over one another to get into the King's Meeting Room.

"So sorry, King Kaposkaran. We didn't hear you right away," one guard apologized but shook in fright as he stood there.

The second guard explained, "We were coming, King, but we got tripped up by some things going on outside the castle."

"What? What is going on outside the castle?"

The second guard shrugged his shoulders and said, "There were guards entering the gate in a hurry. They ran helter-skelter as if something was chasing them."

"What are you talking about, you fool?"

"I didn't see what was chasing them because I came in as soon as you called. I didn't get to see what it was, King Kaposkaran."

The King pushed aside the two inept guards and headed back to the castle door to peek out. What he saw was chaos. There were guards running every which way and behind them were large cats that growled showing their teeth and trying to snap at the men's behinds as they ran.

The King rang a gong at his door that sounded throughout the kingdom and finally got the attention of his men who looked up but did not stop running around in circles to avoid the creatures.

"What is going on here?" the King yelled.

One guard ran up the walkway to the castle but kept his eye on the creatures that were running around. He pulled out his sword and stood in front of the King to protect them both in case one cat came their way.

As they guard looked away, trying to explain to the King what happened, a cat came up and grabbed his leg and pulled him off into the woods.

The man could be heard screaming in terror as the cat dragged him all the way out into the UT. No one dared to go after him. The man could be heard for miles away still screaming. The citizens looked on in horror trying to keep out the terror from their families as they went home and closed their doors and ears to it all.

Some of the guards turned their swords toward the cats once they had cornered a couple and killed them. They planned to roast the cats in the square to see if they were good to eat. If not, these creatures would be burned until incinerated.

King Kaposkaran called all his guards to order and requested they destroy the cats and gather in his Meeting Room right away.

There wasn't much that could shake the King but this had affected him in a way he never expected. He shook off the feeling of being dragged like his guard through the UT and eaten alive. He didn't want to think about it.

These creatures had to be destroyed at all costs or they would come back again.

The King looked around his massive Meeting Room with its multi-chaired table at all the serious faces of his guards. They had been shaken by this recent horrific event also.

He raised his hands and told his men, "We cannot let these creatures come back. Once they have tasted our bodies they will be back for more. You will guard our gates around the clock. Take turns if you must. But you will not sleep and leave us unprotected. Do you hear me?"

All the guards grunted their assent and nodded solemnly.

"All right, men. You are dismissed. I want some of you posted around the gate. The rest of you go home and get some rest and begin taking turns to keep our land protected." He looked around at the men and waited to see if they would try to ask a question. He dared them to do that.

The men watched the King's face and knew they would all be on a death watch from now on to keep the village safe from these horrific creatures.

One guard whispered as they left the castle, "We are in dire trouble. These cats have overcome our borders and will return. How are we going to keep them back and for how long can we do that?"

"I don't know, my friend. I just don't know. The man who was taken was my cousin. How do I explain to his wife and family about how he met his death?"

"It is too horrible to even think about," the first guard replied as he visibly shivered. "I'm sorry for your loss and his family's too."

They exchanged worried looks as they tried to think about what they would have to do to survive in the days ahead.

CHAPTER FORTY-TWO

"Are you sure about this, Spindle?"

The Sprite sighed heavily as he nodded. "Yes, I couldn't believe it either, my King."

"Your father said the Sprites in the UT outside the Village of Parotovina saw this horror?"

"Yes, unfortunately, they did. They were quite shaken up about it all and felt helpless for the first time in a long time. They could do nothing to help the poor man who was dragged away. Other guards were attacked but escaped with many grievous wounds."

"It sounds like the Catlings are on a rampage to go after everyone. But something must have happened to bring this on. We know what my daughter did – handle one of their young kits. But what did the guards do in Parotovina?"

"I think the Catlings were provoked, King Gateskin. By the sounds of it, they were definitely incited to violence."

"How did that come about, Spindle?"

Spindle collected his thoughts and shook off the shiver of terror that held him as he recalled his father's words, "The Catlings were attacked by the guards who were in the UT. They were hunting once again for the Quintaroon which is no longer there. We know that, but they don't. When a kitten came too close to the fire, one of the guards speared it and threw it into the fire for food. The guard was not aware at this time that the mother Catling was close by keeping a watch over her kitten. When the mother Catling heard the shrieking of her kitten when it went into the fire, she attacked the man who had caused the kitten's death and tore him to pieces. The man didn't even know what had hit him. But the other guards watched in horror as it all played out. They raced away back to their village as fast as they could. Of course, the Catling alerted the other Catlings and they many came to her rescue to get their revenge."

King Gateskin shivered in disbelief as he replayed the horrifying scene over in his head.

"Now I understand why they did not return here. What we did was not an egregious act like the ones the Parotovinan guards had committed. I feel sorry for them but they should not have done that. But just the same, no one should have to be killed in this horrendous way. Please do not share this with anyone, especially my family. I do not want them to have nightmares about such horror."

"Yes, of course, King. I don't like to think about it. I had a difficult time learning about this from my father and then having to share it with you was even more awful. I am still shaking from it all. I can't get it out of my head."

"Yes, I agree, Spindle. I think I may have nightmares about this for a long time. Let's not talk about it anymore, little man. It is over now. Let's worry about other things. We can only hope the Catlings will finally stop their dreadful killings and find something else to keep them occupied."

"I hope so too, King Gateskin. But what if they come back here after their killing spree in Parotovina?"

"We will have to deal with them the best way we can - with magic, Spindle. Plenty of magic will be their undoing."

"Yes, if anyone can do magic, it is you, King Gateskin and your powerful family. Or course the Wizards will probably help too."

"I agree, we will need the assistance of the Wizards to keep the magic strong and powerful for a long time. I don't think the Catlings are going to forget the taste of human blood. They just might discover that they like it."

"Yikes, I don't want to think about that, my King. Thank goodness, I don't carry that blood inside me. Catlings would never like the taste of Sprites. We are too tough and hard to swallow."

"Well, that is good to know, Spindle. I don't think you will ever have to worry about anything wanting to taste your tough skin," King Gateskin smirked as he shook his head at Spindle's humor in these trying times.

Spindle suddenly looked confused and directed his next question to the King, "What about Parotovina? Who is going to keep them safe, King Gateskin?"

"I don't know, Spindle. I would think King Kaposkaran will be doing what he can to protect his kingdom in every way. He must first begin protecting his borders against the Catlings. They are getting in and will do so again."

"Should we do something to help them, King?"

"I don't know yet. It is up to the King to request assistance. I cannot go over his borders without his permission. Besides, the Catlings are there right now and will most assuredly return to seek more vengeance upon the guards for what they did."

"I guess so, but I feel badly for them, just the same. I know how they have treated us in the past but not all the guards are evil like their king."

"Yes, I agree with that, Spindle. We have seen this first hand with Mitteran, and now with Danko. They are good men just trying to keep themselves and their families safe and alive in a terrible situation. I will pray they are safe and that the Catlings will grow tired of more vengeful acts toward them."

"I will keep asking my father for updates of any more activity going on there. Okay, King Gateskin?"

"Yes, most definitely. That would be a good idea, Spindle. I need to be kept abreast of any new developments that may take place in the UT involving Parotovina."

***

Solinara was waiting for her husband to surface from his meeting with his Head Guard. They had been in the back room for a long time. She didn't want to disturb them or listen in. She knew her husband would share what was discussed soon enough. At least she only hoped he would share it.

As the two surfaced from their meeting, Solinara observed their pale faces and rounded shoulders as if in defeat. She wondered, what happened to them? Was it too horrible to even consider hearing? Her curiosity would not abate until she had heard every word no matter how terrible that could be.

Later that evening when the children were in bed, Gateskin discussed what had happened in the UT to the guards. His wife listened in shock, visibly shaken to her core, after the tale was finished.

Gateskin hugged his wife and held onto her for a long, long time until he could feel her body stop quivering in shock.

Gateskin continued to hold his wife as they lay down to sleep. They only hoped that they would be able to sleep through the night.

He whispered, "I'm so sorry to share this with you, my love. It was too frightening to think about but I know you would not stop asking me about what was bothering me. Now you know. Let us forget it. Okay?"

"Yes," Solinara shivered and sighed as she hugged her husband for warmth that she could not feel since she had heard this.

"Our children must never know about this."

"Yes, I said as much to Spindle. I requested he keep all this to himself and not share it with anyone, Solinara. I do not want our children to have nightmares about it. I can't sleep right now for fear of seeing it all play out in a dream."

"I know what you mean, Gateskin. I fear that happening to me too. But if I can just hold on tightly to you until I fall asleep, I will not be afraid of anything coming after me if I am in your arms, dear."

"Okay, snuggle up and hold on tight. I promise not to let go of you all night. We are safe together against any nightmares, my love. Sleep well."

Gateskin kissed his wife softly on her lips and tightened his grip on her so she would feel safe. He still felt her shivering, even though it was not cold in the room. He feared for her health and was sorry he had shared this horrific scene with her.

He would have to talk to her in the morning and see how she was feeling. He prayed she would forget some of it soon enough before it could all make her sick.

Gateskin lay there holding onto his wife as her shivers began to dissipate and she fell into a deep sleep. He only wished he could sleep too.

CHAPTER FORTY-THREE

Gateskin rose earlier than usual and was relieved that his wife was still asleep. Her face was serene in sleep. He only hoped her rest had not been disturbed by the events they had discussed the night before.

He went out to see the wolves who were prowling for their breakfast. Cantok looked up at him when he came closer to try to speak with him through his mind.

They stared at one another for several minutes but nothing seemed to pass through their minds and back again. Gateskin shrugged his shoulders and leaned over to pat Cantok's head. He noticed Cantok was growing even larger than before. It must be all the meat that was filled with nutritious ingredients that increased their strength and size exponentially, he thought. He would have to ask Solinara about this possibility.

King Gateskin turned back to his home and entered the kitchen where his wife was now up and preparing breakfast for their family and guests who were still sleeping.

"How are you doing, this morning, my love," Gateskin inquired.

"I'm fine. I did finally get to sleep and don't remember anything after that. No, umm, you know."

"Yes, I do, dear." He leaned in to give his wife a kiss and hug in relief.

"How did you sleep, Gateskin?"

"All right, I guess. I don't remember falling asleep, but I guess I must have." He shrugged his shoulders and smiled as he began to set the table to keep his hands and mind busy.

Solinara frowned in concern as she watched her husband setting the table in an odd manner. She would have to fix it afterwards. She went back to her work and tried not to worry too much about him at the moment because the children were up and about now and so were their guests.

Henno and Jenara came out to help in the kitchen when they smelled the delightful aromas that had woken them up.

Behind them came Danko, Garita and their three children who were exclaiming, "We are starving, Momma!"

"Yes, I bet you are!" she retorted back. "Go wash up and get into your clothes and then you can sit down to eat."

They all nodded and ran off to do just that as they nearly knocked Serena aside to get to the sink and tub Serena had filled with freshwater for washing for their guests. Serena had just pulled out enough water to bring to her mother for her to wash the vegetables.

"Someone is in a hurry this morning, Mother."

"What, dear?" Solinara turned to hear her daughter's voice.

Serena looked at her mother's face and noticed it was a little paler than usual. "Are you okay, Mother? You look a little pale this morning. Can I get you something?"

"Oh no, sweetheart. I'm just fine. I guess I need a little fresh air to brighten up my cheeks. I have been busy lately inside with all the guests we have been having."

"I guess you are right. But I'm here to help you in any way, Mother, and so are Simon and Catalina. We can take some of the load off your shoulders so you won't be looking so peaked."

"Yes, dear. Of course."

Serena was puzzled over her mother's response. Something was up. She could feel it. Her mother was keeping something from her. Her next step was to go see her father. He may confess what it is.

"Good morning, Father. What are you doing here? This is our job. Why don't you go get a cup of coffee while we finish setting the table?"

Serena looked down at the mismatched mess of table setting her father had created. What is going on here? He never sets the table, and certainly if he did, he wouldn't do it like this in such a scattered way.

Simon and Catalina came alongside their sister and looked down at the mess on the table. "What happened here?" Simon asked.

"My question exactly," Serena stated in confusion.

"What's wrong?" Catalina quizzed as she looked at the table.

"It's a mess. Who did this?" Simon inquired.

"I think Father was trying to do it but didn't succeed. He must have a lot on his mind. When he is thinking about something that has upset him, he does have a tendency to mess up ordinary things like this."

"I see what you mean," Simon responded and chuckled.

Solinara walked into the room and noticed her children in deep discussion about the table setting. She stepped closer and said, "Can you please fix this up before our guests come to sit down. It does look quite a mess."

"We are fixing it, Mother. I don't know what happened for Father to do this. He never sets the table. I think he knows how to do it but he always says it is our job to do," Serena announced.

"Yes, it is your job. We are almost ready with the food. So, make sure it is all done right. Okay, Serena?" Solinara announced.

"Yes, mother. We will!" She saluted her mother and turned to see her father watching her with a faraway look in his eyes.

"Are you okay, Father?" Serena asked.

"Ok, sure. I'm fine, sweetie. Nice job on the table, by the way."

"Thanks." Serena watched her father sit down at his end of the table where a cup had been placed by their mother. He sipped it slowly but was not quite awake or maybe deep in thought, she guessed.

She just may look into his thoughts to see what was going on. She was getting worried about both her parents because of their strange behavior this morning. What happened last night? They were fine when she last saw them.

Spindle flew by the window and knocked to get Serena's attention. She looked up in delight and waved. "Hi, Spindle. Do you want to come in for breakfast?"

"I don't mind if I do." He appeared beside her in a blink of an eye and blew her a kiss.

She blew one back to him right in front of her father who did not appear to notice. That was even stranger, she thought. He would surely have said something about that display.

Serena watched Spindle as he sat down on a chair just for him with a plate his size in front of him. She always had that ready for him in case he appeared.

She whispered in Spindle's ear, "Do you know what is going on here today?"

"What? What is going on here? I don't know anything." Spindle jumped back in alarm.

"Spindle, spill it! You know something. Don't you?" Serena gave Spindle her scariest stare.

"No, no I don't know anything at all. I better eat up and go on duty. The King will have my head if I take too long to get out on the border."

Before Serena could ask Spindle another thing he had disappeared and so had his chair and plate which were put back where they were supposed to be.

Serena sighed and helped her mother place the food around the table as their guests sat down to enjoy it all. She wasn't sure she would until she could figure out what was going on around here.

***

After eating everyone thanked the King and Queen for their hospitality. They promised to work hard farming the land and tending to the animals on the King's land in return.

CHAPTER FORTY-FOUR

Gateskin knew he needed to converse with Cantok but how could he do that without sharing what he saw with his daughter? He needed her help to do this. He thought this over before calling her for assistance. Instead, he contacted Hotenfaran and Procelina to see what they could do to protect their son but at the same time allow him to converse with Cantok for the King instead of Serena.

Hotenfaran and Procelina met in the barn with Gateskin to hide from his children who were still in the house helping their mother clean up. He knew they would be in the barn soon enough to do their chores so he had to hurry and explain what he needed to do using the Wizard and Fairy's son, Arubane.

Gateskin tried to leave out most of what had transpired between the Catlings and the guards but he still told them he needed to warn the wolves about a possible attack soon from the Catlings. The Wizard and Fairy agreed to let their son send messages directly from the King's brain into Cantok's brain without reading them. They did not want their young son to be frightened either by these horrific messages.

Hotenfaran could feel the King's angst about this subject but did not pursue it any further. He felt the horror from what little was shared with him and his wife. He could only imagine how horrendous it must have been for King Gateskin to learn all about it in minute detail. He shivered and looked at his wife.

"Is everything okay, Hotenfaran?" Procelina asked as she watched her husband's face pale.

"Yes, dear. Everything will be all right. I assure you. Arubane will not know anything that is passing between the King and Cantok. Gateskin promised me this is the only way he could do this. He knew his daughter would not cooperate in this manner and insist on receiving all the messages herself. It would be too horrible for her to take."

"Oh dear. I will keep my magic all around Arubane's head to keep the messages from seeping in. If we work together, we can be successful at doing this, Hotenfaran. We must protect our son at all costs."

Hotenfaran nodded and pulled his magic closer to his wife's as they concentrated on sending messages from King Gateskin's brain through Arubane and then into Cantok's head.

Arubane was outside the barn waiting for his parents to tell him when they would need him. He had no idea what was happening inside his head. They put a magic spell all around the words that flowed back and forth. He did not know it was all happening as he supposedly waited to be called to assist the King in some way.

They worked quickly between themselves and the King and were soon pleased with the results. Cantok had responded in kind and said he would do all he could to protect everyone and find out anything he could about the warring Catlings.

Arubane called out to his parents, "Do you need me now?"

King Gateskin called out to Arubane, "I don't think we will need you after all, Arubane. I appreciate you coming by with your parents. Would you like to spend some time with my children? They would love to see you again. They are in the house if you would like to go find them."

"Okay, thank you, King Gateskin," Arubane replied and ran off to find Serena and her siblings.

Hotenfaran sighed in relief. "Thank goodness Arubane had no idea what was going on between you and Cantok. It did work well but I am still a little anxious about doing it again. Arubane is so clever he may figure something isn't right here. We ask him to help and then tell him that we don't need his help. Don't you think he would wonder about this if we do it too many times?"

Procelina agreed, "Yes, most definitely, dear. I don't think we can do it again. At least we can't for a long time, that is."

"I don't plan on doing it ever again. It was only this time. If my daughter got wind of this, there were be no end to the complaining I would hear."

"Ha-ha!" Hotenfaran couldn't stop laughing over this. He slapped the King good heartedly on the back. "Are you really fearful of your oldest daughter, King Gateskin?"

"Well, maybe just a little. She is head-strong like her mother and opinionated. She and I have locked horns before, especially about this very subject. She does not want to even hear about Arubane taking over her job of conversing with the animals."

"Oh, oh! That is not good. What if she gets wind of this, Gateskin?" Procelina asked, frowning.

"We won't think about that now. It is over. I only hope I don't have to converse with Cantok about some other horrendous acts by these Catlings."

"Yes, I agree, Gateskin. Let's not think about such things for now. By the way, what did Cantok say he would do about the Catlings?"

"He plans to keep a watchful eye out and spread word to his fellow wolves about the attacks. He assures me no Catlings will get through our borders unless through him and the other wolves."

***

Arubane found the children in their large playroom. Serena was watching over her little sister to ensure she did not go outside to play with the cubs or get too close to the borders because of the

Catlings. Serena's father had instructed her to keep an eye on Catalina since she had picked up the kitten.

"How come you are not outside on this perfect day, Serena?" Arubane asked.

"Well, my father said I cannot let Catalina out until he gives me the all clear."

"What's that about – all clear from what?" Arubane pushed for more information.

"Oh, didn't you hear about the Catlings? Catalina picked one up and played with it. The mother Catling didn't like that. Father said we could be attacked because of that."

"Oh yes! That is terrible, Serena! I will keep a watch over Catalina too along with you."

"Thank you, Arubane. You are too kind, but you don't need to do that. You are welcome to stay in and play cards or other games with us until it is safe."

"Maybe that is why King Gateskin asked for my help even though he said he didn't need it after all."

"What? Help? With what?" Serena asked, puzzled at this.

"Oh, I don't know. I waited outside the barn for a long time but they never asked me to go in. They were doing something in there."

"Who was doing something in the barn?" Simon asked.

"Oh, my parents and the King were involved in something but didn't need my help, I guess."

"Do you know what they were doing, Arubane?" Serena asked, inquisitively.

"Not really. Let's play some cards. Do you want me to deal?" Arubane reached for the cards and began the game while

Serena sat there stupefied that her father had just tricked Arubane into doing something he had no idea he had done. Now, what did he do? Serena was determined to find out just that.

CHAPTER FORTY-FIVE

King Gateskin contacted the Wizards to keep them on alert also since the attacks. They came swiftly to his door and knocked loudly making everyone jump at the sound.

The King opened the door and welcomed them in but not before saying, "Were you trying to frighten my guests with your boisterous knocking?"

The Wizards shook their heads and bowed saying, "Sorry, King Gateskin. We didn't realize how strong our knuckles were collectively when we knocked."

"Next time I will knock alone," Marno exclaimed as he gave his fellow Wizards a stern reprimand in his expression.

The three other Wizards visibly shrank back giving their Head Wizard front place control. They would wait for Marno to call them forward.

"I would appreciate that, Wizards. Next time do it more quietly especially when we have visitors," King Gateskin said in a calmer voice.

"Of course, my King!" Marno bowed and waited to hear why he had summoned them.

"Now, the reason I called you here was of utmost importance. We need to speak in private away from everyone. Put us in a bubble spell to keep our thoughts inside for only us to hear and continue to my Meeting Room."

Marno spread his hands over himself, King Gateskin and his fellow Wizards who he beckoned to move closer forward to be included in the bubble as they entered the King's Meeting Room.

Solinara moved their guests and children away from the bubble and into the extension. She gave them places where they could get settled with their own beds, lockers and hooks to store their belongings. She knew her husband had much to discuss with the Wizards and did not want to frighten the guests and their children to hear anything or somehow discern what was being discussed.

***

The Wizards were horrified by the vicious attacks after King Gateskin's description of the events. They felt badly for the guards who were mostly good men imprisoned by an evil king.

"What can we do to help you, King Gateskin?" Marno asked first.

"I need to know that our borders cannot be breached. Evidently the Catlings crossed over all the borders of Parotovina without any resistance."

"Yes, it appears that way. I don't know what spells were spread across the borders. We did not put any back then because there were no dangers we knew of, to keep out," Marno explained.

"Do you mean you never strengthened your borders ever?" King Gateskin questioned in surprise.

"Yes, we never had any enemies that tried to enter our borders. It was always the Parotovinans who were the enemies of everyone else. That has now changed with the Catlings. King Kaposkaran will have to do something to put a spell over the borders to keep them out," Marno stated.

"We did put a spell over some of the borders at the back of the village where our citizens might escape. But this was mainly to keep them from leaving," Tornak interjected.

"Oh, that is right, Tornak. We did do this one time but then didn't bother after a while," Wassor added.

"What about the area around the castle? We also put a spell all around that too, to protect the King and his family from an attack from within," Fortag announced.

"Yes. I remember we did that too. But King Kaposkaran never asked for our spells to be reinforced on a regular basis. He believed they were strong enough as they were, I guess," Marno stressed.

"Well, were they still strong enough later on or did they wax and wane in strength?" King Gateskin enquired.

Marno paused to think that over. "Well, I guess by the looks of the attacks our spells were most likely gone completely."

"I see," King Gateskin said as he sighed. "It is too sad to see how King Kaposkaran treats his kingdom so callously. He has lost many men this way."

"That is why we are here instead of there now, King Gateskin. We never felt safe there no matter how strong our powers,"

Marno expressed this with a deep sigh of relief.

"I am happy to have you here too, Wizards. Your lives will never be in jeopardy if I can help it."

The Wizards bowed and said in unison, "Thank you, good King Gateskin. We are happy to be here with you."

"Now get some spells together and send them out in all directions of the village borders to keep the Catlings away. Can you create something that will repel them such as a noxious smell only cats can detect?"

"Well, that is something to consider, King. We will get to work on some right away," Marno stated as he stood at attention.

"That is perfect, Marno. Get to it right away. I don't think the Catlings will be taking a break. I expect them to come this way again especially if the Parotovinan borders may be closed to them now."

"Yes, I agree," Marno nodded to the King.

"Well, off you go, Wizards. I appreciate your efforts and coming so quickly when I need you. You have a lot to do."

The Wizards bowed and let themselves out of the King's home.

CHAPTER FORTY-SIX

Back at the village of Parotovina, King Kaposkaran was on a rampage. He had his men running all over the village to make sure there were no more Catlings hiding out in the barns. They had found one there eating a few sheep. The guards had trapped it, put it into a metal cage and dragged it over to the dungeon. The King was looking for some powerful citizens to help him keep the creature contained until he could do something with it.

The citizens of Parotovina lived in fear and would not admit to having powers of any kind. They knew what would happen to them if they did share this information with the King or his men. They had seen how the young couple, Henno and Jenara, had been pulled into the King's castle and never heard from again.

The Catling growled at the men who were in the dungeon guarding it. It tried to reach through the bars and grab one of the guards but the man jumped away in time.

"What are we doing here? This thing wants to eat us and will not rest until he does. How are we going to keep it contained?" one guard asked in a shaky voice.

"I don't know. All I know is if we don't stay here to guard it all night until the King relieves us with other guards, we will be dead from his hands and not the creatures. If we stay far enough away from it, we should be okay," the second guard stated just as anxiously.

The Catling prowled the large room he was in. It had metal bars on all sides that were too strong for it to break. It kept trying to gnaw the bars with its sharp teeth but the metal didn't seem to be affected. He kept his golden eyes on the two guards who were sitting a distance away and not within reach. He was getting hungry and didn't see any way to reach them to feed. If he didn't get something to eat soon, he would try digging out of this room. The floor was partly dirt and felt soft to his claws as he tested it. He listened for any sounds from the forest around the area but could not detect any of his fellow Catlings nearby.

The guards were struggling to stay awake now. They kept looking over their shoulders at the creature. It hadn't moved since the last time they had looked. It appeared to be sleeping, as tired as they felt.

One guard whispered to the other guard, "Do you think it's sleeping?"

"Maybe. That is what I want to do right now but I don't dare."

"Why don't you dare? I will keep watch so you can catch a nap. Then when you wake up, I will catch a few too. No one will have to know. Okay?"

"Sounds good to me." The guard fell asleep quickly while the other one struggled to stay awake. It wasn't long before both were sound asleep while the Catling was wide awake and watching the two men sleep.

The Catling began digging in earnest until he had a good-sized hole. He sniffed around to see if he could find a way out if he kept digging in the same place.

Morning dawned and the two guards stretched and yawned as they looked at each other and shrugged their shoulders.

"Hey you never woke up to relieve me."

"I know, but you got to sleep anyway."

"Yeah, I guess I did. I feel a lot better now. How about you?"

The second guard didn't answer. He was looking into the dungeon room where there was a huge mound of dirt and no sign of the Catling in sight.

"Oh no! We are in trouble! Where did it go?"

"I don't have a clue. We had better find out soon before the King takes our heads!"

The men went into the room and looked down into the hole. It was too dark to see very far into it. They grabbed a lantern and lit it, pushing it into the hole so they could see where the hole went.

"I can't see the end of it. It's pretty deep and appears to keep going underground. We can't go in there. We will never get out," one guard announced in fear.

"I agree. We will have to tell the King. It's not our fault it could dig like that. How were we to stop it?"

"Right. We couldn't have stopped it even if we were awake."

The Catling was long gone back to his burrow gathering with his fellow Catlings for another attack, this time through the hole the male Catling had dug that eventually connected it to their main burrow. It had taken him all night digging.

The guards reported to the castle to explain what had happened to the Catling in the dungeon. The King's voice could be heard all over the kingdom as he yelled at the incompetent guards.

King Kaposkaran ordered the two guards strung up in the square for all to see.

The guards struggled to free themselves from their fellow guards who dragged them to the square to be hung. They begged and cajoled the guards and explained they would do anything to be free, even offering all the riches they had.

The four guards, who were instructed to hang the two guards who were derelict of their duties, talked it over. They didn't see how they could not do what needed to be done. If they did not hang their fellow guards, they would be next.

The two convicted guards tried to delay their deaths by saying, "Don't you want to see the hole the Catling dug first?" They were hoping to find a way to escape their fate.

The four guards nodded, curiously. "Okay, let's go see it."

When they arrived at the hole in the dungeon room, they lit the lantern and looked into the hole. What they saw was not expected. Two golden eyes were glowing back at them.

CHAPTER FORTY-SEVEN

Marno stood up from the table where he had been working with his fellow Wizards when he received the urgent summons. It was not from his new king but from his former one.

Fortag, Wassor and Tornak received a similar message shortly thereafter. They looked at each other in alarm.

Marno was the first to voice his concern. "What is going on? King Kaposkaran is out of his mind! He requests our presence immediately! He said if we do not come, Parotovina will no longer exist."

"What is he talking about?" Wassor asked in confusion.

"It doesn't make sense to me either. I don't believe him for one minute," Tornak expressed his concern and reluctance to listen to the messages that kept coming into their heads.

"We know he is only doing this to get us there. Once he does, we are lost forever. He may even put us in the dungeon after he gets all he can out of us," Fortag said in disgust.

Marno was only partially listening to the Wizards' complaints because there were different messages coming into his brain now that alarmed him even further.

"What? What is it, Marno? Did you get another message that was different from ours?"

"Yes," Marno said and stopped to listen again.

Fortag poked the other Wizards as they all observed the color change in Marno's face at the latest message he received. The other Wizards were no longer receiving the messages now, for some reason.

"Why aren't we getting the same messages as he is?" Wassor quired.

"I don't know. Wait. Let's ask Marno. His coloring is returning somewhat to his face," Wassor stated, with concern.

"Can you speak now, Marno?" Tornak asked as he waited for Marno to look him in the eye in acknowledgement.

Marno sighed heavily, and sat down to collect his thoughts before answering, "Yes, I can speak but you won't believe what I just heard."

The three Wizards waited on pins and needles to hear what the Head Wizard had to say.

Before they could realize what was happening, Marno waved his hands over himself and the other Wizards. They suddenly disappeared from Marno's home and appeared in front of the King's house.

The Head Wizard knocked on the King's door as calmly as he could and waited.

***

Back in Parotovina it was utter chaos. The six guards who were looking down the hole never stood a chance. They were decimated by all the Catlings who poured out of the hole.

The citizens locked themselves away from the creatures who now freely roamed their village. They dared not go outside, in fear of their lives.

Even the castle was locked up tight and all the guards were inside along with the King and his family.

The only creatures that were stirring were the animals in the barns who continued to squeal and scream in fear as they were cornered by the Catlings and eventually feasted upon.

King Kaposkaran paced his meeting room wearing a deeper hole in the carpet. He did not know what to do. He needed help but there was nowhere to turn. He was alone. For once he was alone with his guards who were useless. He had to think fast. There had to be someone who could and would help in this dire time of need. But who? He had made so many enemies over the years. There was no one left who would do anything for him.

He suddenly thought, what about the Quintaroon? He would help his king. After all, *I am his father, well sort of.* He chuckled to himself to steady his nerves. *Yes, the Quintaroon will come if I command and tell it about what is happening here.*

CHAPTER FORTY-EIGHT

King Gateskin looked down on the Wizards who were much smaller than he, and were looking quite glum. He never noticed how small they really were until now. They had always flown up to meet his eye when they came to his door. Something was definitely wrong. He welcomed them in with a wave but they floated in without a nod to him and sat down at his table. The Wizards' colorful hats vibrated according to the tension they were feeling and the tassels at the tips of the hats shivered and swayed back and forth as if they had their own emotions.

Marno spoke up at first in a whisper as if he was afraid someone else would hear him. "We have something to tell you, King."

The other Wizards gathered close to him for support and shivered as they looked up at King Gateskin with frightened eyes.

The King led them into his private Meeting Room at the back of his house and covered them over with a Soundproof Spell to keep what he knew was not going to be something he would share with his family by the looks of their pale and terrified faces. There wasn't much that would cause expressions like that on such powerful people.

"Please go on, Marno. What is bothering you so much?"

"Oh, some terrible things have come to pass. Believe me, King. We are not responsible for such heinous things. We would never wish all this upon King Kaposkaran and the citizens of the Village of Parotovina. It is too horrible to even think about."

"Will you be kind enough to explain what you mean, Head Wizard? You are confusing me."

"I'm sorry, good King Gateskin. I should begin at the beginning. Well, we were sitting down together working out some spells to use around our borders to ensure our safety from the creatures in the UT. We had almost completed them when I began to receive urgent messages from King Kaposkaran. He was shrieking about something in the village that was happening. It was almost impossible at first to make out what he was trying to say with all the noise he captured along with his message. He sent all of it to me."

Tornak, Wassor and Fortag added almost in tandem, "He sent some of that to us at first but then stopped."

"I see. What were the messages and sound effects? Please explain," King Gateskin tried to keep the urgency out of his voice but was getting impatient to hear what this was all about. It still did not make sense.

"I apologize, King. It was so difficult to listen to. The screams and horror that were taking place there. It sounded like many people were being killed in some horrible way."

"What? Who was killing them and why? Are the Catlings back?" Gateskin asked in urgency.

"King Kaposkaran explained his kingdom was being overrun with cat-like creatures. Yes, most likely the Catlings were back."

"Why didn't he protect his borders from them?"

"He mentioned in his messages that his borders were protected by spells he put there with the help of us in the past which he thinks are still effective. But the Catlings did not come that way. They came from underground."

"What? Where?" Gateskin gasped in shock.

Marno took a deep breath and continued, "One Catling was put into the dungeon and left there guarded by two men. The men evidently fell asleep leaving the Catling alone to his own devices. He began to dig and burrow so deep under the dungeon that he opened up a tunnel to go to his main burrow where all the other Catlings were living. He opened up…"

"Yes. I see. I got the picture. He opened up a connection that could not be broken. Now they will forever be able to come and go as they please unless something is done to stop them."

Marno exchanged air as he said, "Yes!"

King Gateskin announced, "We must help them!"

"But, King, we can't go there. How will we help them?"

"I will contact all the other rulers in the villages and we will have a meeting to decide how to do this. We will need the help of all of you, Wizards, from every land to put your heads together and come up with a way to stop the Catlings in their tracks. If we do not stop the

Catlings, these cats will take over all of our villages."

"Of course, we will help you in any way we can, King Gateskin. Tell us what you want us to do."

***

Quintal shook his head to clear it. What was that? He kept hearing noises, unpleasant ones at that.

He looked around his cottage and then outside the windows. There was nothing out there that could have caused such a racket.

He closed his eyes and listened closely. It was coming from inside his head. He heard his name or at least the creature's name, Quintaroon. Who was calling it?

He gasped as he heard many screams of agony and closed his hands over his ears to shut out the horror of the sounds. He couldn't take it anymore and raced out of his cottage to see King Gateskin. He would know what to do to stop these sounds from coming to him.

He stumbled all the way to the King's house and fell up the stairs as he knocked loudly on the door.

When the door opened, he passed out at the feet of the King.

King Gateskin bent down and picked Quintal up as if he was light as a feather. He brought him inside and laid him down on the wide padded bench. He brought a cup of water to Quintal's lips but he wouldn't drink.

The Wizards gathered around the man. The King waved some Pepper Salts under Quintal's nose and abruptly he sat up looking startled.

He looked around him and said, "I don't know what happened. One minute I was outside your door and the next I am here."

"Why are you here, Quintal?" King Gateskin asked.

Quintal shook his head and listened. The noises were fainter now but still there in the distance. He explained, "I was sitting quietly at home minding my own business, not doing anything wrong and suddenly my head was filled with all kinds of noises, terrible noises of people screaming and crying. Oh, it was awful! Then I heard King Kaposkaran calling me."

"What did he say to you, Quintal?"

"He was calling me Quintaroon and requesting me to return. I am no longer Quintaroon. Even if I was, I would never go back there. I was told by many messages in the past that King

Kaposkaran wanted to kill me if I did go back."

The Wizards exchanged wary glances at this comment.

Quintal looked over at the Wizards and said, "Did you send those messages to me when I was a Quintaroon about my death being imminent?"

"Well, maybe once. But that is all. We are not responsible for any other messages. We have been here for a while now and have not sent you any," Marno insisted. "I am surprised that you still remember the message, Quintal," Marno stated.

Quintal glanced at Marno but ignored his remark. "I don't understand what these new messages are about. Do you?" Quintal looked at the King and then the Wizards in confusion.

"No, we did not recently send those to you. We have been receiving them too," Marno explained.

"But what are they? What is happening over there?" Quintal asked in alarm.

King Gateskin took over explaining, "We think that Parotovina has been overrun by Catlings. The village is in danger and needs help. That is why King Kaposkaran is reaching out to you and the Wizards for help."

"Oh. But I cannot be of any assistance to him. I am no longer a creature of strength and power. I am only a man." Quintal bowed his head.

"Yes, you are. There is nothing you can do, Quintal. You should not worry yourself over this. I will take care of it along with the Wizards. You can go home now."

"No, I can't. The messages are still there and won't stop. Please help me rid my brain of them as you did before," Quintal begged.

The Wizards nodded and stepped forward close to Quintal and waved their hands over his head.

Quintal closed his eyes and waited for the noises to disappear. Once they were gone, he sighed and cried in relief.

Marno patted Quintal on the shoulder and said, "You are going to be all right now. Go home and rest. Forget about this. Please do not share any of these messages with anyone."

"Of course. I only want to forget them. Thank you for helping me once again. If I can be of service to you, please let me know." Quintal got up from the bench, bowed to the King and shook the Wizards' hands in thanks and left. He shivered from the after effects of the messages as he walked home.

CHAPTER FORTY-NINE

King Gateskin created a Channel Spell to open a connection to all the other villages except Parotovina. He kept that window closed. Once he had all the rulers of the villages virtually in his Meeting Room, he called the meeting to order.

He explained what had happened in the Village of Parotovina and the dangers they faced from the roaming Catlings.

"We need to help Parotovina. I know all of you have had unfavorable treatment by King Kaposkaran and his guards, so have I. But we cannot let these people suffer like this. We have to do something."

"Will we have to use dark magic to take out these creatures, King Gateskin?" King Cavelan asked.

"Never! We have to try something else. Please let's use first names only here. We are all rulers and don't need to use the pomp and circumstance in these serious times."

"I agree, Gateskin," Cavelan said.

Noderan of the Village of Amora asked, "Do you have something in mind, Gateskin?"

"Well, I think I can come up with a few spells with the help of all of you and my Wizards. Please let me introduce you to the former Parotovinan Wizards."

Gateskin spread his hands across the table and pointed out the four Wizards to the rulers. They all nodded and waited for more information about what they would be doing.

"These Wizards are powerful and can create spells to capture these creatures. Can you not, Marno?"

"Well, yes. I think we can, King, I mean Gateskin. We need to try out some of these spells and see how they work on one of the wolves as a subject. Would that be all right, K…Gateskin?"

"Yes. That would be a good idea. But be careful not to harm the wolf. They are friendly but won't be if we do anything to change how we treat them."

"Of course, good K…Gateskin."

The Healers of Merona asked a question, "How do you plan to do that, Wizards?"

"Well, we have many spells and tricks up our long sleeves to try out that could work. But we will need your help – all of you."

"Of course. We, Healers, know a few tricks of our own that may help you."

"I am sure you do. You are known for your powers of healing all over the lands. We welcome your assistance in any way," Marno bowed his head at them in respect.

Zuri, ruler of Merlina, listened and then added, "May I be of assistance to you, Wizards?"

"Of course, you may, K…Zuri."

"I had a problem with some critters that kept getting inside my castle. They were a lot smaller than these huge cats but I did use a potion to scare them away. It was quite noxious though and it took a long time for the annoying smell to leave my quarters," Zuri explained.

"Oh, I see," Marno said and added, "but it would be nice to check that out. If you would be kind enough to share the potion, we can work on it and change it so it would disappear quicker."

"Yes, that would be perfect. I would like to keep some just in case I may need it again one day. Let me know when you can do this." Zuri whisked the potion through the window Gateskin opened for the Wizards to catch.

Cavelan added, "I will have my Wizards confer with yours, Gateskin. Together they will be stronger. The rest of you, Kings, can do the same."

"Yes, I agree, Cavelan. We need the Wizards from all the lands to keep in touch and share their powers to get this done. My Head Wizard, Marno, will be in charge of coordinating the spells."

Marno nodded and said, "Yes, King Gateskin. I will take care of that. We will get to work right away. I will have my fellow Wizards spread the collective magic over the borders first to test our spells. We don't want the Catlings to sneak up on us too."

"Yes, most definitely do that right away," Gateskin exclaimed, relieved things would be safe sooner rather than later for his village.

Turning toward the ruler of Merlina Marno said without hesitation, "Thank you, King Zuri, for the potion. We will work on that right away. "I'm sorry I cannot call you by your first names. Please forgive me. I will use King when addressing each of you. Okay?"

Gateskin nodded and smiled, "That is perfectly all right, Wizards. Please continue to explain what else you have in mind for spells."

***

In Parotovina the screams of the animals had abated since they were all dead now. The Catlings had feasted on them and left the carcasses scattered all over the village. King Kaposkaran looked out of his third story window and gagged at the sight of his village and all the carnage that was there. He had to do something.

He tried once again to reach the Wizards and Quintaroon to no avail. It was as if the windows were blocked off from him. He couldn't wait any longer. He had to come up with a spell to chase the cats away. There must be one in his book of spells that would work.

493

If he could not find a spell, he would be forced to turn to King Gateskin and his powers to save them. This, he didn't want to do unless there was no other way. He was King Gateskin's enemy and not someone he wanted to depend on. He knew Gateskin would not want to help because of what he had done to him in the past. It was all unforgivable but he did not feel sorry for any of it. That was a fact. He knew he was evil and could not help it. These Catlings could be the end of him and his land.

All he needed to do was find a way out of this chaos himself so he did not depend upon anyone for his welfare and that of his village.

He would find a way no matter what. After all, he was King of Parotovina and no one was going to take that away from him – not even these creatures!

CHAPTER FIFTY

Henno and Jenara, Danko and his family were settled in King Gateskin's home in the extension that was continuing to be a good thing to have since unexpected visitors kept coming to Sovorotskina.

They watched as King Gateskin from outside his Meeting room as he scurried back and forth gesturing with his hands to the Wizards. The visitors could not see the virtual conference and all the other rulers who attended since they were not included in the spell.

Henno whispered to Jenara and Danko, "What do you think is going on in the King's Meeting Room? There appears to be something important to make King Gateskin so upset."

"Yes, I think so too, Henno. The King keeps looking outside the window for something. There is definitely something serious going on."

"Maybe we should ask him what we can do to help," Jenara suggested.

"Well, are you prepared to break the spell that he has purposefully put in place to keep us out?" Danko asked as he raised his brows in enquiry.

"No, but we may be able to do something to assist him in some way, however small," Jenara asked, somewhat hesitantly.

"No, I think we should wait it out and see. King Gateskin will come to us," Henno stated assuredly.

They all agreed to wait a little longer before doing anything to interfere with the meeting of the Wizards and the King.

The meeting ended soon afterward and King Gateskin closed off the Channel Spell. He could feel his guests' eyes on his back before he turned around to face them.

"I did not forget you. I had an important meeting to attend that couldn't wait. I think it is time for you to have a place of your own. I will have my men begin construction immediately on two cottages for you and your families."

"Thank you, King Gateskin, but may I ask you a question?" Henno met the King's eyes as he prepared to ask, "This is your home and we are your guests but I must ask if we can be of service to you for your kindness to us?"

"I don't think so, Henno. But maybe I should share this with you since you were once citizens of Parotovina."

Henno, Jenara, Danko and his wife, Garita waited with confused expressions for the King's explanation.

"I don't want to frighten you but Parotovina is under attack by the Catlings."

"What? Catlings? What are they?" Henno asked in alarm.

"Catlings? Are they from the UT?" Danko enquired.

"Yes, they are the very same creatures," the King explained further, leaving out the gross details somewhat. He told them enough to cause them to gasp in disbelief.

"Oh, my goodness! What can we do to help them?" Danko asked hurriedly, shocked over the needless death of some of his friends.

"I'm afraid that there isn't anything you can do at this time. I am working along with my Wizards and the other Rulers of the neighboring villages to come up with some spells that would help to keep the Catlings from continuing to burrow into Parotovina."

"Does King Kaposkaran know you are trying to help him?"

"No, not yet. I plan to contact him soon and explain what we want to do."

"Do you think he will accept your assistance, King Gateskin?" Danko asked.

"Well, we hope so. As one of his guards, how do you think he will react to our interference?"

"I don't think he will like it at all, King. In fact, I think he will refuse your help and insist on doing it all by himself. It would be a blight on his self-respect to accept your help."

"Yes, I agree. I think he will refuse our help at first until he can't do anything else to stop them. Then he will be forced to accept what we can do."

Henno looked puzzled. "Do you think you can stop these Catlings, King Gateskin?"

"Yes, I think we can. We have very powerful Wizards from Parotovina who are now citizens of Sovorotskina. They believe it can be done with the help of the powers of all of us Rulers. Collectively we are stronger than apart. We will do this," King Gateskin stated emphatically but turned quickly away before a tick could be seen over his right eye.

Danko said, "Well, if you need us in any way, King Gateskin, we are here for you. We have to repay you in some way for your kindness in letting us stay here in exile. I know we will never go back to Parotovina."

"Yes, we will never go back either, King Gateskin. Can we stay here if you find us worthy now that we are citizens?" Henno asked with concern.

"I think you are on your way to being worthy," King Gateskin answered and nodded to all. We will give you much to do to prove yourself after this business is taken care of."

Jenara sighed in relief and said, "Thank you so much, King Gateskin. I don't know how we will ever be able to show my appreciation for this chance to live in freedom without fear. We have waited so long for this to come to pass."

Henno nodded in agreement and bowed to the King in thanks.

Jenara whispered to Henno, "Should we share my power to fly with the King?"

"Yes, I think it is time to do that," Henno said.

"King, we need to share something with you. As we told you before we helped King Kaposkaran with messages to Quintaroon. What we didn't share was one other power that could be helpful to you."

"Yes? What would that be?" Gateskin queried.

Henno stated, "I can disappear and appear again in different places and blend in with my surroundings which I think I mentioned previously."

Jenara stepped forward and said, "I didn't mention, however, I can fly besides sending messages as I did for the evil King."

"Hmm, I see. These powers could be helpful to my village. I will keep this in mind. Now don't worry about anything but getting settled here in your new home."

"We are grateful to you, King Gateskin," Henno and Jenara said in unison.

Danko and Garita hugged and smiled as they also responded, "Thank you so much, King. We are truly indebted to you."

"You are all welcome to make your homes here. Now let me instruct my men to quickly construct your cottages so you can get settled. With a little bit of magic thrown in for good measure, they will be completed before the day is done."

Jenara jumped up and down like a kid when she heard this and pulled her husband in for a tight celebratory hug.

"Can we watch them being built, King Gateskin?" Jenara asked with enthusiasm.

"Of course, just walk down the path until you come to some building going on as we speak. You can watch safely from the roadway."

"Oh, thank you!" Turning to her husband she pulled him along saying, "Come on, Henno. Let's go see our new home being built!"

Henno smiled and shrugged his shoulders as Jenara tugged him by the arm until he caught up with her.

Danko and Garita followed close behind but not before calling their children to come with them. Their children had been busy with Serena and her siblings in the children's rooms.

Spindle was in charge of the men who were building the cottages. He watched the parade of people coming down the road to stand in front of the construction site.

He flew over to greet them and explain, "I am Spindle and in charge of the construction of your new homes. Please stay clear until I say it is safe for you to go near the cottages."

The group nodded in excitement as the cottages went up quickly with so many men working on them. Soon the buildings were closed in and work was being done inside each one.

The children were so excited to see the construction and kept jumping up and down. Their parents had to keep them back or they would have run right into the houses.

Spindle explained, "We call these cottages but they really are houses. We make them larger for a family of five like you are. The other one will be smaller but can be enlarged if and when more family members are added."

Henno and Jenara nodded with broad smiles. "That is a good thing. We may be adding three or more to our family eventually."

Jenara looked at her husband and said, "Really? Three or more?"

"Well, we can do two if that is enough, dear," Henno stated as he blushed in embarrassment.

Jenara smiled and nodded, "Sounds good to me, Henno."

Spindle hurried back to the construction to move it along.

Henno sighed in relief and listened as the construction sounds suddenly ended. He poked his wife and walked closer.

Several minutes later Spindle flew back to the party and announced, "Your homes are ready for you. You are free to go inside. We have placed furniture in there and some supplies. If you need anything else, please let me know. All you have to do is call out my name and I will hear you and respond."

"Thank you, Spindle!" The two families yelled out in delight as they ran over to see their homes.

The Sprite laughed over their exuberance as he dismissed his men and left the site to report to the King about a job well done.

Spindle looked back at the new cottages and smiled. The Village of Sovorotskina was certainly growing exponentially, he thought.

CHAPTER FIFTY-ONE

Gateskin was conferring with his Wizards about the spells they had wanted to try on the wolves. He was a little anxious about how the wolves would react to being guinea pigs. He called his daughter to help explain to Cantok what they needed to do.

Serena listened to her father's explanation and relayed this message to Cantok.

"It's all set, Father. Cantok is accepting of this. He wants the Wizards to do the experiment on him and him alone. He does not want to harm anyone else in case something goes wrong."

"Okay, tell him not to worry. It will all go well."

King Gateskin looked at his Wizards and sent his message to their minds. "Make sure you do not make a mistake and injure Cantok."

Marno responded in kind, "Yes, King Gateskin. We assure you there will be no mistakes made. We know how important Cantok is to you and your family. We will be careful."

Instructing his fellow Wizards, Marno stepped together with them and they all raised their hands over Cantok's head as he looked up at them in hesitancy.

Serena kept sending the same thoughts to him, "You are going to be all right, Cantok. Please don't worry. We just need to find out if this spell will work to keep the Catlings at bay if they try to dig inside our borders. All you have to do is begin digging and don't stop until the Wizards say so."

Cantok nodded and began digging in earnest so fast that his paws were a blur.

Serena watched in awe as the hole Cantok was digging grew wider and deeper. Soon they could not see Cantok because he was inside the hole.

The Wizards clapped their hands and announced to Cantok, "Stop."

Serena sent this message to the wolf and he stopped digging but did not appear yet.

The Wizards asked Serena to tell Cantok what to do next, "tell him to try and come out of the hole."

Cantok still did not appear as Serena conversed with him, "Come out of the hole, Cantok."

He could not move. He was stuck inside the hole and told Serena, "I cannot move out of the hole. The spell must be working. I am stuck and cannot move an inch."

Serena told the Wizards and her father what Cantok had said. There were celebrations and clapping from all when they heard this.

"It worked, King Gateskin!" Marno announced in jubilation. "It worked!"

"Yes, it appears to have worked, indeed, Wizards! Good work!" Gateskin announced happily as he clasped the hands of his Wizards in thanks.

Serena moved closer to the hole and looked down. She help a lantern over the hole into the darkness and saw Cantok's eyes glowing back at her.

"We must let Cantok out of the hole, Father!" Serena announced in alarm. "He looks frightened."

The Wizards quickly responded and waved their hands over the hole and the wolf suddenly appeared next to the hole.

Cantok bowed his head and expressed his relief and gratitude to the Wizards through Serena, "Thank you, I am all right. It did work!"

Serena patted Cantok on his enormous head and smiled. She said, "He is thankful and happy to be able to move again. He's also surprised at the outcome. It worked on his digging!"

"Hurray!" the Wizards jumped so high in exuberance that they flew up and around the hole Cantok had dug. They waved their hands over the hole and it quickly filled up and smoothed out.

"Wizards, you did good work in taking care of the hole. I was wondering about that. I didn't want to leave a hole in the middle of the yard for someone to fall into."

Hands were high fived and slapped as the Wizards continued to celebrate their success.

"It looks like we are ready to try it out on the Catlings, King Gateskin," Marno announced in glee.

"Yes, I think it may be ready. But first we must lay the spell all around the borders on top of the spells we already put there. I don't want to take a chance that a little kitten will get through and cause more trouble than we need right now."

"I agree, King. We will begin right away. Will you contact the other Kings about this good news?"

"Yes, I plan to do that now. Excuse me while I set up another conference. You can continue covering the borders with this new spell in the meantime."

The Wizards bowed in compliance and continued on their way to secure Sovorotskina's borders with the Halt Spell conferring with the Wizards of the other lands to do the same.

***

Serena spoke to the wolf about what had transpired. "Are you all right now, Cantok?"

"Yes, it was not a problem. I could feel the power of the Wizards stopping me from moving. It was a strange feeling. I have never felt anything like that before. They are quite formidable for little critters."

"Oh, you are too funny, Cantok. You call them critters. That is so funny. I guess to you they are little critters. Just like you are a large critter to them."

"Yes, I am getting bigger all the time," Cantok's voice was edged with concern.

"What is wrong, Cantok? Don't you want to be bigger?"

"No, I think if I get too big, I may change somehow. I do not want to be a danger to any of you. Can you stop us from getting any larger?"

"Okay, don't worry about it. I will ask my mother right away to do something to stop your growth at a certain point. Okay?"

"Yes, thank you, my friend. I fear I am changing inside along with my body. My mind is not as clear when I speak with you as it once was. That is not a good thing. I want to be able to converse with you. If I couldn't, I would be terribly sad."

"Oh, I would be devastated if that happened too, Cantok. You are one of my best animal friends. In fact, the very best animal friend and only one I can converse with so far. I do talk to Milly the cow and our chickens but they have never answer me back."

Serena frowned when she saw Cantok's face change to confusion. He no longer looked happy. She rushed to see her mother to fix this problem before she lost complete control of the connection with the wolf.

CHAPTER FIFTY-TWO

Gateskin was deep into a conference with the other rulers as he explained what had transpired with the Halt Spell over the wolf to prevent him from digging. He looked up when he saw his daughter's face as she came into the house. She skirted around her father and went in search of her mother.

Serena sent a message to her father's mind as she passed by him, "Don't worry about me, Father. I am all right. I need to see Mother about a problem with the wolves."

Gateskin nodded to her as he went back to his meeting. The rulers had much to ask about the spell. He tried to keep his mind on them but his daughter's sad face kept surfacing in his head. *I wonder what is so wrong all of a sudden?*

"Gateskin, are you still with us?" King Cavelan asked concerned with Gateskin's distracted manner all of a sudden. "Is everything all right?"

"Oh, it's just my eldest daughter. She appears to be distressed about something. I must find out what it is. Do you have any other questions about this spell? If you do, I will summon my Wizards to answer them."

"That would be a good idea," King Zuri said. "I am not sure how this will work long distance."

"Yes, I agree," King Noderan added.

The Wizards appeared, when summoned, in front of the virtual conference window to answer any questions as Gateskin made a quick escape.

Gateskin went in search of his wife and daughter to find out what was going on. He didn't like the feeling he kept getting about Serena's anxiousness that was seeping into his own head now.

He saw them in the kitchen washing vegetables as they talked softly. They looked up when they felt his presence and welcomed him forward into their conversation.

"Please come in, dear. I think this is something you must listen to. It is quite serious."

Gateskin looked at his daughter as she met his eyes. Her eyes were brimming with unspent tears as she hugged him.

"Father, I am so worried about Cantok. He doesn't sound like himself. He is changing. But I don't like what he is changing into. He warned me about it. We have to do something or we will be in danger of him and the other wolves. He told me so."

"What? What do you mean, Serena?" Gateskin hugged her back then released her so he could hear her explanation.

Serena explained, "He thinks it's the food source that was created for him. It has something in it that is changing him. It's making his mind foggy making it difficult for him to converse with me as before. He is concerned he may harm us if we don't do something right away."

Gateskin exchanged wary glances with his wife as she explained, "Yes, I think I know what is doing that. I will call Hotenfaran right away. We will work on it and change it immediately. We can add something else to counteract the problem."

"Thank you, Mother. Can I help you and Uncle Hotenfaran? I want to be a part of fixing Cantok. He is my friend."

Solinara nodded and said, "Okay, sweetie. Come with me. We will fix your friend and all the other wolves. They will not be a danger to anyone."

"Well, we still have to make them hate the Catlings and the Parotovinans. Right?"

"Ha-ha! Yes. Okay I will make sure they still keep us safe from the Catlings and the Parotovinans."

Gateskin sighed in relief. He knew Solinara and Hotenfaran would take care of this while he returned to his conference.

***

A short time later Solinara, Hotenfaran and Serena completed the change in the content of the meat and added another dash of some fig root and chick seed to fix the problem. They went out to try it on Cantok who was laying down next to his shelter and looking confused.

Serena moved slowly toward Cantok but stopped when he looked up at her and growled.

"Wait, Serena. Don't go any further. Let me toss some of the meat near him and see what he does."

Hotenfaran took a large chunk of meat out of the bag and handed it to Solinara. They watched the wolf gulp it down and then sit up as if he was now awake from a long sleep. He shook his head back and forth and nodded to Serena.

"I am sorry, my friend. I didn't mean to growl at you. I am feeling a lot better now, and my mind is clearer. Thank your mother and uncle for me. I will make sure all the wolves eat this new meat right away. What about the Rabbinels? Are they tainted too like the meat was?"

Solinara looked at her daughter and asked, "What did Cantok say to you, honey? Is he okay?"

"Yes, he wanted me to know he was sorry for growling at me. He said he feels much better and his mind is clearer too. He wants to know if the Rabbinels are tainted like the meat was?"

"No, I think it is just the meat we created. I will make sure though by testing a Rabbinel just in case."

"That would be a good idea, Mother. Thank you for healing Cantok."

"Of course, honey. Now please ask Cantok to capture a Rabbinel and bring it to me alive. I will put it in a cage and test it in our shed with your uncle's help."

Hotenfaran had a cage ready out of thin air and waited for Cantok to bring one out of the forest. Cantok raced in and out with a large Rabbinel in his mouth. It was struggling to escape but he held it firmly in his large jaws without harming it. He placed it inside the open cage and backed away.

"Thank you, Cantok. You are such a good fellow and a real gentle soul. I never worried about you harming my daughter for one minute. I appreciate how hard you fought against the fact you could have but didn't hurt her. I made a special treat just for you in gratitude. Please let me know if you like it."

Solinara reached inside the bag and pulled out a stick which was a bright blue. She held it in front of Cantok and waited for him to take it.

"What is that, Mother?" Serena asked, in awe.

"I call it a Tooth Stick. It is coated with a substance that cleans teeth and freshens breath much like our wooden teeth cleaner. It can be used again and again and it rebuilds itself. It will also strengthen their teeth as they gnaw on it. I will make plenty of them for all the wolves if Cantok likes it."

Serena explained this to Cantok and watched the wolf take it in his mouth, give it a lick and then a chew. He smiled as only he could smile. A deep contented sigh was heard from deep inside him.

"Wow! He loves it, Mother!" Serena exclaimed.

"Ask him about it, Serena. I know he does look happy but I want to know how it tastes," Solinara requested.

Serena asked Cantok and he quickly answered, "It is quite tasty, Serena. I like it. I know the other wolves will like it too. It makes my mouth tingle in a pleasant way too. My throat was sore but now it's not. It helps my stomach feel better too. I had what you call an upset stomach but now it's gone. Do I chew on this every day after each meal?"

Serena asked her mother the question and she answered, "Yes, if he doesn't feel well that is what he must do. It will not harm him to chew on it as many times as he needs to feel better."

Cantok listened to Serena's response and happily nodded as he continued to chew on his now favorite gnawing toy.

Serena laughed as she watched Cantok play with the stick, toss it up and catch it in his mouth and chew on it again and again. The cubs, who were growing much larger now and were getting close to their father's size, tried to grab it out of his mouth.

Solinara and Hotenfaran came back out of the shed with a bag full of these sticks and passed some out to the cubs and Cantok's mate. The wolves settled down to have a good chew.

Hotenfaran picked up the bag and flew over to each wolf shelter and passed out the new meat along with the rest of the sticks much to the delight of all the wolves. Serena went alongside him with his help flying to explain to the wolves what the meat and sticks would do for them.

Serena smiled in relief when she heard several exclamations of satisfaction from the wolves for both the new meat and the Tooth Stick.

As they left the wolves, they looked back to see several of the wolves happily chewing on their new chew toys.

CHAPTER FIFTY-THREE

King Kaposkaran continued to work some spells with his wife's help. She was a much more powerful wizard than he was. He never wanted to admit that to her though. In fact, she would be a more formidable ruler if he died first. He knew she would be fiercer than he could ever be. This thought frightened him.

Queen Beregina worked her magic using dark magic whenever she could. She knew her husband was not capable of doing that. She knew he would be afraid to use it.

A black cloud appeared over the Village of Parotovina as she worked her spells to stop the Catlings. The cloud descended onto the land and covered it with a moss-like texture. The Catlings sniffed this moss and tasted it. Once they did, they fell asleep.

King Kaposkaran looked outside his castle windows and noticed all the Catlings were asleep all over the village. He called his men to order, "Listen up, men! Your job is to rid this village of Catlings. Drag the bodies back into the UT as quickly as you can."

He looked toward his wife as she continued to work her spell. The moss grew thicker, covering almost the whole village now. The men struggled to move the animals' bodies as the moss built up.

"You must stop creating this substance, my dear," King Kaposkaran announced in a soft voice, fearful of angering his powerful wife.

"I will stop when the Catlings are dead," she announced without looking at him.

"But they are asleep. Now is the time for us to move them. Let my men do their job, dear. You must desist."

King Kaposkaran watched in horror as his men fell asleep now too. They were all over the village sleeping next to the Catlings as soon as they touched the cats' bodies.

He began to beg his wife, "Please, Beregina. Please stop. I need the men to do my bidding. If I don't have them, I do not have anyone to help me."

"Yes, so I see. You are quite helpless without them. All right. I will wake the men up so they can move the bodies. But I need to keep working a spell to reach the other Catlings underground who may try to burrow their way here."

"Okay, I see, my Queen. I understand. As long as I have my men to complete their work in ridding our village of these creatures. We must get them out of here before they wake up. How long will they be asleep, dear?"

"They will stay asleep as long as I continue to work this spell. If I stop, they will wake up. Tell your men to hurry and do their jobs," she announced as more of a command than a request.

As soon as the Queen awakened the men, King commanded them to do this quickly or they would be killed if the

Catlings woke up. Hearing this, the men raced around as quickly as they could, working in teams of four men dragging each cat out through the gate into the UT. There were so many Catlings all over the village. It took hours to move the creatures as the Queen continued to work her spell to keep them asleep.

King Kaposkaran watched from his windows in the castle as the cats began to dwindle now in number. The men were exhausted but were not able to stop for fear of being attacked if the Catlings woke up.

The King was fearful that this was not the end of the creatures. He did not trust his Queen to handle this situation completely. She was losing control using Dark Magic like this. He did not like it.

He went into his private room and tried to summon some help. The only one who he could trust was Quintaroon. He would ask Quintaroon to get King

Gateskin to speak with him about this problem. He did not want to do this but there was no other way. He feared his land was going to be destroyed by his wife's hand.

He wasn't sure if Quintaroon could do this. After all, he could not speak. He only hoped he could reach the human side of the creature to make him see how important it was for him to do this.

He prayed King Gateskin would not kill Quintaroon before the creature could get his message across to the King.

If this didn't work, he was going to try to reach Botular again. He never heard back from him about what he had been doing with his request to spy on King Gateskin for him.

Something strange was going on with his messages. Maybe the Wizards who escaped from Parotovina are responsible for the messages getting lost. He had to figure out why he could not reach anyone.

He went out of the castle to see how his guards were doing, clearing out the Catlings. They were exhausted he could see but he wouldn't let them stop until his village was clean once again.

He came back inside to his wife's private room where she was still performing dark magic to keep the Catlings under a spell. She looked tired. He touched her shoulder and she jumped in alarm.

"What do you want, Kaposkaran? Don't you see I am busy? I have to keep this up until all the Catlings are gone from our village."

"I know, my dear. But I can see you are tired and cannot keep this up much longer. The magic is taking over your body. Your aura is getting blacker than ever. I feel I will lose you completely if you don't stop."

"Ha-ha! Your aura, my dear, is blacker than mine. No need to worry. Are you afraid I will become stronger than you and take over the kingdom?"

King Kaposkaran's eyes widened in alarm. He shook his head and left his wife's room to enter his own private area with the statues of the gods of Darkness and Evil, Goddess Quilarena and God Quilottan. They would be the only way to stop his wife from becoming too strong.

CHAPTER FIFTY-FOUR

Quintal finished his dinner and laid down to sleep. He was feeling strange. He couldn't figure out what was happening to him. His head felt heavy while his body felt as if it was floating up from his bed. How could that be, he thought. Maybe I'm dreaming. He looked around him but didn't feel as if he were sleeping. In fact, when he looked down at his bed it was a couple of feet below him. He *was* floating.

What is happening to me? He tried to move himself back to his bed but found he was stuck in the air and could only go up. He was now nearly at the ceiling. When he floated up to the rafters, he grabbed onto one and tried to rappel himself back to his bed.

He tried to remember if he had been able to fly when he was a Quintaroon. He closed his eyes and tried to bring back some of those memories. As he thought this over, he found himself slowly floating back down to his bed.

Quintal had to ask the Wizards about this. But at the same time, he was thrilled with the idea he had a power no one else had or at least not the normal people of the village. He could not tell anyone about this. It would be helpful if he needed to get away quickly from someone or something.

He could not sleep with this new ability flooding his brain with exciting possibilities. He found that if he thought about it more, really concentrating on flying, he could do it. After some concentration and practice he was flying all around his cottage ceiling. He quickly came back down when he heard someone coming.

Quintal looked out his window at the path that led to the village and to the Wizards' cottages and then to King Gateskin's larger one. He saw a wolf pacing back and forth along the border of Skina Forest. He wondered what the wolf was looking for. It appeared to be agitated about something.

He stepped outside his door, looked around and listened closely. He found that his senses were keener all of a sudden too. Something was happening to him. Was he becoming a creature again?

There was a message coming into his head now. He could tell it was King Kaposkaran. He sounded frantic to reach him.

"Quintaroon, you need to go to King Gateskin. I need his help immediately. We are being attacked by Catlings. They have overrun my village. My Queen has put them to sleep with a spell but I don't know how long they will stay that way. My guards are moving the Catlings into the UT. They will come back. Please go to King Gateskin and tell him this. I need his help."

Quintal sent a message and said, "I am not a Quintaroon anymore, King Kaposkaran. But I will go see King Gateskin for you. I don't know if he will help you though."

"What happened to you? Who changed you back into a man?"

"It is a long story, King." Quintal did not want to share anything with King Kaposkaran for fear it would be used against him.

"I see," the King said, not in a happy way.

Kaposkaran continued, "I know King Gateskin does not like me. I have not been kind to him or his family. But please tell him I will do all I can to change my ways."

Quintal raced over to the King's house and knocked on his door and waited.

King Gateskin looked out at Quintal who stood on his doorstep. He looked into his mind and saw many jumbled-up thoughts.

He opened the door and said, "Quintal, this is a surprise to see you so late. What is wrong? I can see you are quite upset about something."

Quintal followed the King in and sat at his table and waited for Gateskin to sit next to him before beginning his explanation.

After several minutes of listening to Quintal's explanation about King Kaposkaran's situation King Gateskin sighed, "I see. That is why we haven't seen the Catlings for a while. They have been busy in the Village of Parotovina. I am sorry to hear King Kaposkaran lost a guard that way. What does he expect me to do?" The King did not share he knew of the attacks through his Wizards already and had been working on a plan.

"I don't know, King Gateskin. I guess he wants you to use your magic to make them disappear."

"Well, it is not as easy as that. They have found a way to get into our villages by burrowing. It appears that is how they arrived in Parotovina too."

"Well, I did tell the King you might not want to help him because of the way he has treated you and your family."

"Yes, he has behaved badly toward us. But that is not the reason I hesitate to help. I don't know if what we have developed would help him. So far, the Catlings have not been back here but I suspect they will be soon."

"Do you mean they will come here too?" Quintal asked with a frightened look on his face.

"Yes, I believe they will be back. We are developing something that could work however. But it needs to be tried out on these creatures. It worked on the wolves."

"Wolves? What did you do to the wolves?"

"We did not do anything to the wolves. We just tried out a spell on one of them when he tried to dig."

"Oh, I see. Did it stop him from digging?"

"Yes, it did. I will contact King Kaposkaran. Why don't you go back home and sleep? You do look tired."

Quintal nodded and turned to leave. He looked back at King Gateskin and said, "I had a... No, never mind."

"What?" King Gateskin met Quintal's eyes and noticed something strange. The look he saw there was similar to the look Quintal had in his eyes when he was a... The King shook his head to rid it of these thoughts. It couldn't be.

"Go home, Quintal. We will talk more tomorrow. Let me know if anything else comes to you from King Kaposkaran or if something else is bothering you."

"Um. Yes, King Gateskin. I am a little tired. You will take care of these messages now?"

"Yes, I will contact him and tell him that he should send messages to me and not to you from now on."

"Thank you, King Gateskin. I appreciate that. Good night."

"Good night, Quintal."

King Gateskin sat for several minutes to digest what Quintal had told him about the messages. He knew Quintal was holding something back. He had seen something in his eyes he did not like. It could be a portent of what was coming.

CHAPTER FIFTY-FIVE

King Gateskin contacted the rulers of the other villages. He would include King Kaposkaran after they completed their discussion about the Catlings' attack on Parotovina.

King Cavelan announced his concern, "Do you think it is a wise idea to help King Kaposkaran?"

"Well, I understand why you say this, Cavelan. I thought of that too but I cannot refuse someone's help if they and their villagers are in danger."

"Yes, of course. I understand. You are right, Gateskin. Sorry," Cavelan apologized.

King Noderan said, "Yes, I think Gateskin is correct. We need to help Kaposkaran. But there has to be concessions on his part."

The Healers of Merona agreed, "Yes, concessions are needed. We can come up with some if we put our heads together. These concessions are to include all of us."

King Zuri said, "Of course, we will need more than concessions with Kaposkaran. He is not an easy man to trust. He could turn his back on us in a moment's notice once we help him."

"Yes, I thought of that too, my friends. I will open up the Channel Spell now to include King Kaposkaran. Are we ready to speak with him about concessions or do you need more time to consider them?"

All the rulers nodded and agreed. "Yes, please give us a few more minutes to put them together before we open it to him."

Gateskin said, "Let's make our list now and then we can read it to him and have him sign it in agreement."

Gateskin added, "Okay, each one of you can give me a concession and I will record it. When we have all of them, I will open the Channel Spell to King Kaposkaran. Let's begin."

***

While the rulers were working on their concessions, Botular was also receiving messages from King Kaposkaran.

Botular was restless in bed and tossed and turned when the messages began. He sat up abruptly and shook his head to clear it.

"No, it cannot be! What do you want, King Kaposkaran? I cannot help you."

"Yes, you can, Botular, and you will!"

The King explained what he needed Botular to do. "I want you to spy on King Gateskin. I want to know what he is doing at all times to help me. I sent word to Quintaroon, or I should say Quintal, now that he is changed back, to give King Gateskin a message about the Catlings' attack on my village. I want to know what King Gateskin is doing to help me. Is he going to trick me? I need to know. Do you understand, Botular?"

"Yes, umm, yes, I understand, King Kaposkaran. I will do what I can. But please do not send me any more messages. I cannot take them. They hurt my head and I fear that someone will know what I am going to do. I need to clear them out. Please help me. I do not want to be killed."

"Who is going to kill you?" King Kaposkaran asked in confusion. "I am the only one who wants you dead, you imbecile. For now, I need you to do my bidding. If you don't, well, you know what will happen to you."

Botular shook all over with fear as he nodded even though King Kaposkaran couldn't see him. He answered in a quivering voice when the King repeated his question, "Yes, King. I understand."

***

The Channel Spell was opened to King Kaposkaran now that the rulers had six concessions to present to the King.

Kaposkaran blinked in alarm when he saw the channel open and all the faces of the other rulers looking back at him. "What is this?"

King Gateskin began by explaining, "We received your message from Quintal. My Sprite Guard also told me of something that was happening in the UT. We are here to try and help you with this unfortunate situation."

"I see. But something more is happening now. My wife is performing dark magic which has put all the Catlings to sleep. While the Catlings are sleeping, my guards have been moving them back into the UT. I fear that these cats will return once they wake up. I don't want this dark magic to take over my kingdom. I am the ruler, not the Dark King, Dargonet."

The rulers all held their collective breaths at the mention of Dargonet. They knew how formidable he could be once he took over. They may never gain control of any of their villages if he is allowed to come forth. He was much more dangerous than King Kaposkaran could ever be.

"That must not happen, Kaposkaran!" Gateskin announced with fervor.

"I know, but my wife Beregina cannot stop or will not stop the spell. I fear Dargonet is taking over her spirit as we speak. I must stop her before she is lost forever."

"Yes, I agree. What do you want us to do? We cannot use Dark Magic to counteract her spell."

"No, I don't think that would be a good idea. It would only give him more strength if we do."

The rulers put their heads together and whispered as they discussed what their next step would be.

"Can you help me?" Kaposkaran asked in a soft voice filled with worry.

"We will have to work together to stop her from continuing the spell. Take us into this room where she is. I will open this spell there once you arrive. Say the word NOW when you arrive there."

"Yes, I will. Thank you, Gateskin." King Kaposkaran rushed into the room and stopped short of his wife who was turning darker. He yelled out, "NOW!"

The Channel Spell opened into the large room allowing the rulers to see the darkness that was all-around Queen Beregina. The Kings of the other lands raised their hands up toward Queen Beregina and recited a Disconnectus Spell to interfere with the spell the Queen was performing.

Working together, the Dark Magic was lessening now and the aura around Beregina was brightening.

What the Kings didn't notice right away was a black wisp of smoke, escaping from her hands and moving towards them.

CHAPTER FIFTY-SIX

Botular was moving toward King Gateskin's house now per the request of King Kaposkaran. He needed to find out what King Gateskin was doing to help the Village of Parotovina. If he did not do his part for King Kaposkaran, he knew he was doomed.

While he was stealthily moving along behind the King's house, he did not notice someone watching him.

Quintal was doing much the same thing at the request of King Kaposkaran. Only he was not as avid in fulfilling this need. He knew King Kaposkaran had no control over him now that he was a man once again.

Quintal had woken up with a thirst he could not squelch. He drank from the well on the King's property until he was bursting. He looked down at the ground beneath his feet but did not see his feet. They were gone. What happened?

He raised his hands in front of his face but they were no longer there either. In fact, his whole body was gone. He could still feel it but couldn't see it. What was going on?

How could this have happened? He looked around and went to find the Wizards. They would know what to do.

He ran over to the cottage of Head Wizard Marno and knocked on his door. Marno looked out but could not see anyone. He concentrated and then could see a shadow of a man. It was Quintal.

He quickly opened the door and welcomed him in. "What happened to you, Quintal? Where are you?"

"How do you know it is me, Wizard Marno, if you cannot see me?"

"I have powers to do that, Quintal. Is that why you are here to get me to help you?"

"Yes. Of course! I need your help. I don't know what happened to me. One minute I was drinking from King Gateskin's well and the next I had disappeared. Can you help me?"

The Wizard guffawed then responded, "Yes, I know what has happened to you, Quintal."

"Are you going to explain that to me?"

"Well, I guess I should explain a little about when we created you."

Quintal tapped his feet, impatient to hear what the Wizard had to say.

"I am getting there, Quintal. Be patient. There were some things we had to do in order to control you and keep you out of the King's control. The only way we could do that was to give you strengths and weaknesses.

We gave you these powers:

1. Ability to fly
2. Formidable size and strength
3. Dangerous claws and jaws
4. Ability to become invisible if you drank water

Your weaknesses are:

1. Afraid of the dark
2. Blinded by bright light
3. Fear of rodents like squirrels, mice, rats
4. Allergies to nuts

"Ah, now I understand. I drank a lot of water. But I drank water before and nothing happened to me. But I guess I was in bed and didn't notice I had disappeared because it was dark in my room."

"This is quite strange that it's happening now that we changed you back into a human again. I don't understand why. I must confer with the other Wizards. Let me call them here now."

Before Marno could blink, the other Wizards were standing in front of him quite confused.

"What do you want, Marno? I was just about to have breakfast with my family," Fortag announced, quite upset.

"Yes, so was I," Wassor exclaimed.

"Me too," Tornak stated grumpily.

"Sorry, my fellows, but there is a problem we must solve right now. Do you not see we have a guest in front of us?"

The Wizards looked around in confusion. They blinked and squinted and shook their heads.

"Don't you see him?" Marno asked. "Look more closely and concentrate."

Tornak jumped back in alarm when he spotted a shadow close to him. "Yes, I see him! It's Quintal!"

"What? Is that Quintal?" Wassor asked in confusion.

"What happened to him? Why is he a ghost?" Fortag queried.

"Ahh, now that you see him, let's put our heads together to find out why he is invisible."

Quintal spoke up startling them all, "I think it is your fault I am a ghost. You did this to me. Now you have to fix me."

Marno explained, "Don't you remember the powers we gave him? If he drinks water, he can become invisible.

"I remember now," Fortag exclaimed in relief.

"How do we fix him?" Tornak asked.

"That is what we must work out together. We have to reverse the spell we put on him even though he is no longer a Quintaroon."

"But if we do that, will he turn back into the Quintaroon?" Wassor asked, confused.

"I am not sure about that. We will find out soon enough, won't we?" Marno answered, anxiously.

"Shouldn't we tell the King right away?" Fortag asked.

"Yes, I suppose we should. But first let's see what we can come up with so we can present our findings to the King."

"Good idea, Marno. That way we will be ahead of the situation. Because most likely King Gateskin will ask us to fix it anyway," Wassor agreed.

"Yes, I believe he will, my fellow Wizards," Marno said with a smile. "Now let's get to work."

With their heads together the Wizards discussed their options.

"What do you want me to do, Wizards?" Quintal asked.

"Sit still and do not talk. We are working to help you and do not need your interruptions," Marno stated in a firm voice.

"Oh, sorry, Wizard Marno. I will sit here quietly. But I do have some questions for you."

"Quiet!" the four Wizards yelled in unison to Quintal.

CHAPTER FIFTY-SEVEN

Spindle flew over to the King's house to report what his father had told him about the Catlings in the UT. Abason had told him that the Sprites had seen about a hundred Catlings all sleeping in the UT in piles. They looked like someone had put them there like that.

The Head Guard knocked on the King's door and waited to be received. He looked around and spotted Botular trying to hide in the back of the house. He flew up and over the roof to find out what Botular was doing here.

"What are you doing, Botular?" Spindle inquired.

"Oh my. I didn't see you there, Spindle. So sorry, I was just looking around. I thought I saw a Catling roaming around in the back. I was just going to report that to King Gateskin."

"Oh, were you?" Spindle asked with a furrowed brow.

"I guess maybe I was wrong. I don't see it now," Botular said as he backed away from the Sprite.

"Where are you going, Botular? I think you should come with me."

"Umm, no I think I will go home now. I was mistaken," Botular said in a shaky tone.

Spindle gripped Botular and pulled him along as he flew back to the front door where King Gateskin was waiting.

"Where did you go, Spindle? I heard you out here a minute ago and then you were gone," King Gateskin asked.

"Oh, sorry, King. I was talking to Botular who was skulking around in your backyard."

"What do you have to say for yourself, Botular?"

"I...um...I don't know. I should go home now."

"Go home now. I will be by there shortly. Don't you go anywhere until we have had a chat," King Gateskin announced with a scowl. "Spindle will be by to watch over you for me until I can get there."

Spindle nodded in agreement to the King.

Botular raced home with his head down and didn't look back.

"Spindle, I can see this wasn't the reason you came to see me. Something has happened, hasn't it?"

"Yes, King. I received an urgent message from my father about the Catlings. He said that the Sprites noticed a hundred or more Catlings piled up in the UT. Someone was leaving them there all night long. They said they think it might be the Parotovinan Guards who were doing this, but weren't sure. It was quite bewildering."

"I am in a conference with King Kaposkaran right now and the other rulers. Let me tell them this. Please come in. If they have any other questions, you may be able to answer them or at least ask your father to answer them."

Spindle watched in awe as the rulers grasped the wisp of black smoke that came in front of them. They twisted it into a knot, put it into a pot they had conjured up, and placed it on the large table in front of them. They put a cover on the pot and locked it down. The pot shook and rattled; the dark magic trying to escape.

King Kaposkaran watched his wife as her aura returned to normal and she fell to the floor in exhaustion. He pulled her into his arms and held her close.

"Are you all right, dear?"

Beregina looked up at him and said, "What happened? Why am I on the floor. I was working on a spell and then I don't remember anything else."

"That's okay, dear. You are fine now. The other rulers helped bring you back. The Dark King, Dargonet, had a grip on you. He is gone now."

"Oh, that is why I felt a heavy weight on my shoulders. It was as if someone or something was pushing me down."

"It's gone now, Beregina. You must rest. You did a good deed and helped rid the village of the Catlings, but the Dark King took over and tried to capture your soul."

The Rulers listened to Kaposkaran as his Queen came around. They waited until he turned to them before saying anything.

"Thank you, all, for what you did to save my wife. I am grateful. But we are still enemies. I will not bother you until there is a need to protect my land from you."

"You are welcome, Kaposkaran. But we will keep a close watch over you. We will be ready to protect our own too," Gateskin announced.

"I see you are not using titles when you speak to me," Kaposkaran stated.

"Yes, during these conferences we are not using them. It is very informal and less tedious to keep saying king this or king that. Don't you agree?"

"Well, I suppose. But I expect to be addressed as King Kaposkaran outside these conferences."

"Of course," Gateskin sighed in exasperation as he raised his eyebrows at the other rulers.

Heavy sighs could be heard all around then a few giggles to relieve the tension.

Gateskin cleared his throat and announced, "The meeting is now ended but there is something else to add." King Gateskin turned to Spindle, "Please explain what you told me before."

Spindle stepped forward and flew up to meet everyone's eyes as he retold his tale, "My father shared something that the Sprites in the UT saw. There were a hundred or more Catlings piled up all over the UT fast asleep or maybe they were dead. It was hard to say. The Sprites thought the Catlings were being brought there by the Parotovinan Guards."

King Kaposkaran hemmed and hawed and finally responded, "Yes, they did that by my orders. I told you all about the Catlings coming into my village and my wife putting them to sleep. Well, that is when I had my guards move them back to where they came from before they woke up."

"When will they wake up?" Gateskin asked.

"I don't know. I don't think Beregina will be able to tell me either. She was under the control of Dargonet. She doesn't remember anything."

"All you can do is make sure your borders are covered by a strong spell. We cannot share ours with you but I'm sure you have someone who can do that."

"Unfortunately," King Kaposkaran sighed, "I do not have any Wizards or people with powers. They have all left Parotovina to come to you or the other villages. You probably already know that."

"Sorry to hear that, Kaposkaran," Gateskin responded softly.

"I am relying on my own powers and that of my Queen for now. I will keep my options open to other means."

"I'm sure you will," Gateskin said in a whisper.

"What?" Kaposkaran asked.

"Oh nothing. I think it is time for us to part, King Kaposkaran. The meeting is over. Best of luck to you and your guards keeping the Catlings in the UT."

"Thank you, King Gateskin, and you other rulers. I appreciate your kindness. But don't think I will change my ways because of this."

Before anything else could be said, King Kaposkaran disappeared from the Channel Spell leaving everyone else speechless.

"Well, I guess we are all safe for now. Let's keep the concessions aside until we need them in the future. I'm sure there will be another time when they will come in handy.

I want you to know Queen Solinara and her brother Wizard Hotenfaran are working on a spell to keep the Catlings away. They developed a spell to stop them from burrowing their way into our village. I will have her share this with you all to keep your villages safe also.

Once she has it completed, I will open up this Channel Spell again and share it."

Many thanks were heard as the rulers said their goodbyes. It was once again quiet in the King's house. He and Spindle sat down to discuss the business of Botular before he went over to speak with him.

"What do you think Botular was doing in my backyard, Spindle?"

"I just happened to see him lurking around close to the house. I think he was trying to peek inside to see what you were doing. He was close to the window and was probably trying to listen in."

"Hmm. I see. Well, I think it's time to find out what he has to say for himself." King Gateskin left his house and walked along as Spindle flew next to him to Botular's cottage.

CHAPTER FIFTY-EIGHT

Botular was rocking nervously back and forth in his rocking chair trying to think of what he would tell King Gateskin when he came to visit. He had to come up with something. He just couldn't tell him about King Kaposkaran's request to spy on him.

A knock was heard at his door as he jumped up from his chair and went to answer it.

"Hello, King Gateskin and Head Guard Spindle. Please come in." Can I get you some coffee or tea?"

"No, not for me. What about you Spindle?"

"No. I am fine. Thank you, Botular."

"Well, why don't we sit down and discuss what you were doing in my backyard, Botular."

"Umm. Well…I…thought…I…"

"Yes. What did you think, Botular?" King Gateskin asked as he watched the man's face for any signs he was lying.

"I don't know, King Gateskin. I'm sorry that I was on your property. I apologize. Will you forgive me?"

"Let me think about this. There always seems to be something you are doing. But you never have an explanation for what you are doing."

"Yes, I guess I am confused, that is all, King. I can't explain my behavior. Sorry about that."

"I think there is something you want to tell me, Botular. Isn't there?" King Gateskin met Botular's eyes with a steely gaze.

"I don't think so. I...I..." Botular stuttered and looked away from the King's eyes.

King Gateskin concentrated and looked into Botular's confused mind and saw something there that he was not happy about, and sighed. "I think I know what is bothering you, Botular."

"What? How can you know?" Botular looked frightened and covered his face in his hands as he trembled in fear.

"No need to be frightened, Botular. I think I know what is on your mind. It is something that is out of your control. I understand. I can help you get rid of it."

"Can you?" Botular asked, in relief, but still wary what the King was about to say.

"Has King Kaposkaran been sending you messages again?"

"Yes...yes...he has. But I don't want to listen. I don't want to do anything for him. I am afraid he will come and get me and I will be put to death. He told me if I didn't do what he requested, I would die."

"What does he want you to do, Botular?" King Gateskin waited for a reply even though he saw what the message said already.

"I can't do it. He wants me to spy on you. He wants to know what you are doing at all times. If I don't tell him…I will be put to death, I'm sure."

"I see. But why were you at my house then if you do not want to do what he requests?"

"I don't know. I'm sorry. I won't do that again. I promise."

"Hmm. It appears I have heard that from you in the past. You always promise not to do something you shouldn't but then here you are doing something you shouldn't again. What am I going to do with you, Botular?"

Botular shrugged his shoulders and sighed. "I don't know, King Gateskin. I have no idea."

"Well, it looks like I need to give you a job to keep you busy and out of trouble. Why don't I have you become one of my guards? You will be under the control of Spindle here. He will tell you what to do. You will obey him. If you do not…well, we will discuss that further. Do you understand, Botular?"

"Yes…umm…yes, I do, King. I will do as Spindle asks."

"Good, now take him away and keep him busy, Spindle, if you will."

"Yes, my King." Spindle bowed and pointed the way out to Botular as he flew next to him with his hand on the man's shoulder for guidance.

Botular walked with his head down and shoulders slumped like the weight of the world was sitting there.

King Gateskin followed them out of Botular's cottage and closed the door. He stood on the pathway but kept his eyes on Botular as the man walked along resignedly with Spindle flying by his shoulder.

Gateskin shook his head and turned toward home. One more problem put to rest for now, he thought.

CHAPTER FIFTY-NINE

Back in Parotovina King Kaposkaran was keeping a close watch over his wife Queen Beregina. He told her to rest so she could get her strength back after her ordeal with the Dark King, Dargonet.

She was reluctant at first but finally succumbed to sleep after a little help from a sleeping elixir that King Kaposkaran had left over from his Wizards' potions.

He went back to his meeting room and called his guards to discuss the Catlings. The village was now clean of all the bodies. He only hoped it would stay that way.

The guards slumped against each other, too exhausted to hold themselves up alone. They had worked all day and night moving the bodies of the Catlings back to the UT.

The oldest guard stepped forward when asked by the King, "Report what you have done to keep the Catlings at bay."

"We have locked the gate and put the Gatekeeper on alert in case any of the creatures came back. We also filled the hole the Catlings dug in the dungeon and replaced the soil with rocks and spikes in case they tried once again to burrow their way back. On the top layer we spread poisoned meat that if eaten would kill anything that ingests it. We also buried all the carcasses of the sheep and other animals eaten by the Catlings."

"Good. Now you will take turns guarding the dungeon in case they do somehow manage to come back."

The Head Guard sighed heavily and said, "Yes, King Kaposkaran."

"You are dismissed," King Kaposkaran announced with a wave of his hand.

The guards stumbled out and headed home to rest all except a couple who were chosen by the Head Guard to stay on alert at the dungeon.

These guards grumbled and moved begrudgingly toward their post. They mumbled their words of woe back and forth to keep awake.

"I can't believe we were chosen to do the first post. I can barely stand up at this time. How about you?" the first guard complained.

"You're not the only one who is tired! For goodness' sake, stop whining, man. Let's try to stay awake. We only have to stay here for four hours, then our relief will be here, the second guard stated.

"Yeah, but it will feel more like ten," the grumbly guard said, as he yawned and stretched his arms over his head. "What is that smell?"

"It's probably the feces of the cats who came through here. They ate all the small animals around and then left their deposits," the second guard replied.

"No, I think it is something new. It's getting stronger," the first guard stated.

"Let me go look in the dungeon. Maybe some other animals are in there," the second guard announced.

"Okay, I'll stay here," the disgruntled guard said nervously.

The second guard looked inside the dungeon but couldn't see anything. He grabbed a lantern on the wall and lit it. He raised it up over the hole. What he saw was beyond belief. He called out to the other guard to come quickly.

***

In Sovorotskina the Wizards had finally come up with a way to help Quintal without changing him back into the Quintaroon.

They brought Quintal to King Gateskin to explain what they were going to do about his recent episode of invisibility.

King Gateskin welcomed them all into his house and listened to what they had to say. He was shocked by this new situation.

"What? Quintal is having some issues that involved when he was the Quintaroon? How can that be? I thought you changed him back to a human."

"Yes, King. We did. But it appears some of his powers may have latched on to him."

"Are there any other powers we have to deal with from now on?"

"I'm not sure, King," Marno said as he exchanged puzzled looks with his fellow Wizards.

"Well, don't you think we need to find out if there are any others still there?"

Quintal was still in shadow and listening intently to the conversation. He cleared his throat and announced, "Yes, there is another one. I can fly, well a little bit off my bed at night. I woke up one night recently and found myself floating up from my bed at least several feet. In fact, I reached the ceiling and grabbed onto the rafters and pushed myself back down."

"What?" Marno asked in alarm.

"Are you sure you weren't dreaming, Quintal?" Fortag queried.

"No, I was awake. I pinched myself to make sure," Quintal answered.

"You must have been dreaming, Quintal. That is not possible," Wassor exclaimed.

"Well, it could be possible," Fortag stated as the others gave him a look of disbelief.

"No, I don't think that is possible," Tornak said.

"Stop arguing. Anything is possible. Let's think this over," Marno reprimanded as he raised his hands over his fellow Wizards to calm them down.

King Gateskin told everyone, "Wizards, please sit down. You too, Quintal. I want to keep you close by until we get this settled."

Quintal's shadow moved toward the side chair next to King Gateskin and sat down. He announced, "I am sitting next to you, King Gateskin. I will tap my fingers to let you know I am still here from time to time."

"No need to do that, Quintal. We will have you fixed up in no time. Be patient. We have a spell that should work on erasing both of your powers and still keep you human," Marno explained.

Quintal nodded, then retorted, "Will you get rid of all my fears too, Wizard Marno?"

"No. Your fears are part of your human form and not attached to your creature form. But they will still be there to be felt."

"Yes, I am still afraid of the dark, don't like bright lights, fearful of rodents and have allergies to nuts."

"Some of these things you will just have to get used to. You have had them all these years now."

"Yes, I know. But it would be nice to not be afraid of these things."

The Wizards dismissed this statement from Quintal as inconsequential.

"Let's begin, Wizards!" Four pairs of hands were raised over Quintal's shadowy form and sent a steady stream of light toward his head.

Quintal's head swayed back and forth as if being pulled this way and that. He mumbled unintelligibly as he shook all over.

Several minutes passed as they waited for Quintal's body to calm down and appear in front of them.

King Gateskin watched in amazement as Quintal was suddenly standing there with a smile on his face.

"How do you feel, Quintal?" King Gateskin asked.

"I am feeling better. It's as if a weight was lifted off of me. My head is clearer too."

"That's good to know," Marno said in relief.

"It looks like your spell was successful, Wizards," King Gateskin announced with delight.

"Yes, I think we got it right this time. But we still need to keep watch over him at night and during the day to see if anything happens again," Marno stated with some concern.

"You need to take turns to do this, Wizards," King Gateskin directed his words toward them.

"Yes, King. I will take care of that. We will take turns in his house at night while he sleeps. Other times we will watch him as he walks around to make sure he doesn't disappear again," Marno stated.

"I will walk Quintal home and stay with him tonight. Tomorrow someone else can take over," Tornak stated.

"Okay, I will take the second day and night," Wassor replied.

"Well, I guess I will do the next," Fortag stated resignedly.

"Yes, that will do. I will do the fourth day and night. I think that should do it. If nothing shows up after four nights, we have been successful," Marno expressed his opinion.

"That is perfect, Wizards. It looks like you have this situation in hand. Check in with me in four days to let me know how everything is," King Gateskin instructed.

Turning to Quintal, Marno said, "Let's leave King Gateskin to his business. I am sure he has much more to do. Tornak will take you home and stay with you."

Quintal nodded and followed Tornak out the door with the rest of the Wizards right behind. Marno bowed to King Gateskin before leaving.

King Gateskin went to look for his wife who was in the kitchen preparing his dinner. She had been listening to the Wizards as they performed their spell.

"Sorry, dear, but I did overhear what was happening in the dining room. Is everything back to normal?"

"Well, I guess so. At least for now. We will definitely know in four days' time, so Marno announced."

"That is too bad for Quintal. He must be so confused or at least he was," Queen Solinara said with concern.

"Yes, I guess he was a little muddled about it. I'm sure it will all work out."

"What is bothering you, dear? Is there something else that is nagging you?" Queen Solinara asked.

"Well, Botular is another problem I am dealing with now."

"Botular? What did he do now, dear?"

"What didn't he do? It is always the same thing with him. He is a spy and will always be a spy. I have put Spindle on watch to stay with him and keep him busy."

"Poor Spindle. He is such a nice young man and never refuses whatever you give him to do. But this is a little too much, don't you think, Gateskin?"

"No, I don't think anything is too much for Spindle. He is an amazing little man."

"Yes, he is."

Listening in behind the kitchen door was Serena. "What did Spindle do that makes him so amazing, Father?"

"Oh, Serena. What are you doing there, eavesdropping?"

"Well, I didn't mean to, Father. I was following the scent of what Mother is preparing. It smells wonderful, Mother."

"Why don't you set the table for us, Serena," Solinara announced to change the subject.

"Okay, Mother. But I still want to know about Spindle." She gave her father a smile with an arched brow and winked at him.

"She is something else, too, isn't she, Solinara?" Gateskin chuckled.

"Yes, she is a special young woman. She is growing up too fast, dear." Solinara agreed, sharing a laugh too.

Gateskin's chuckle disappeared as he thought over everything that had transpired recently with King Kaposkaran, the Catlings, Botular and now Quintal. Would there be more problems coming?

He would have to contact Procelina and Hotenfaran about helping keep eyes and ears on Botular and Quintal in case they act up again. He would need all the help he can get.

CHAPTER SIXTY

"What is that?" the disgruntled guard asked as he looked closely at the dungeon floor.

"It looks like small Catlings. They are dead," the second guard said.

"How did that happen?" the first guard asked in a shaky voice.

"I don't know. But at least they are not alive. They must have burrowed through and eaten all the poisoned meat."

The first guard asked warily as he looked around, "Does that mean the large ones are coming back?"

"I don't know. But it looks strange that the young ones would come up like this and ..."

The second guard didn't finish what he was saying when a large head was seen burrowing through the soil and pushing aside the small dead Catlings.

"Oh no! What's happening here?" The first guard turned and ran in the opposite direction as the second guard disappeared as he was grabbed by the Catling and pulled downward.

By the time the relief guards arrived there was no sign of the original guards at the dungeon. They looked around and went into the dungeon where the lantern was sitting on the ground next to the multiple bodies of small Catlings.

Once the two guards relayed what they saw, King Kaposkaran called all his guards to order once again and queried them about the missing guards. "Did you see the guards who were on their post in the dungeon? If anyone sees them, report them to me. I will not stand for insubordination."

The Head Guard stepped forward to explain, "I think something has happened to them, King Kaposkaran. There were dead bodies of small Catlings all over the ground where we had put the poison. Evidently, they managed to get through, ate the poisoned meat and died. There is no evidence of any large Catlings coming through though."

"Well, that is good but we must fortify our borders again. I need some wizards. Are there any villagers that have exhibited powers of any kind? If you know of anyone, you must bring them here now." King Kaposkaran looked around at his men who hung their heads and didn't meet his eyes.

One guard stepped forward to reply, "Yes, King Kaposkaran. I know of one such person who can help you."

"Well, speak up, man. Who is this person?" King raised his voice as he stared at the guard.

"He is an old villager. I will get him right away." The guard raced away from the castle, before the King could ask him anything else, to find the man who could help.

The guard knew the man in question would refuse to help. But if he didn't come back with him, the King would have him killed for not following orders. Also, the Village of Parotovina would be in danger of being destroyed by the return of the Catlings.

He would have to convince the man that he had to do this deed just once to save them all.

***

King Gateskin sat sipping his chicory coffee after a robust meal of beef stew. His wife had outdone herself once again. He sighed contentedly but that didn't last too long for he felt a deep disturbance in the air.

He opened a Channel Spell to the other villages. He couldn't believe what he saw.

THE ADVENTURES CONTINUE...

Watch for Books 3-6 in the coming years with more adventures.

ABOUT THE AUTHOR

Janice Spina is a retired administrative secretary from a public school system in Massachusetts. She has always loved writing poetry, novels and children's stories. She published her first book in 2013 and hasn't stopped since.

This is the 39th book Janice has published. She also has two mystery series of six books each, one for boys and the other for girls even though they both are enjoyed by either sex. She has published 19 children's stories for young children. She also writes under J.E. Spina and has published five novels and a short story collection for 18+.

She can be reached at these links.

Website: http://Jemsbooks.com
Twitter:
http://twitter.com/janice_spina

FB Main Page:
http://facebook.com/janice.spina.9
FB Author Page:
http://facebook.com/janicespina7
FB Novelist Page:
http://facebook.com/jespina7
Blog: http://Jemsbooks.wordpress.com

Janice lives in New Hampshire with her husband, John, and two tanks of fish. John is the illustrator of her children's books and designer of all her book covers.

If you enjoyed this book, please leave a review where you purchased it and spread the word to your family and friends. Janice loves to hear from readers and welcomes reviews from wherever her books are purchased. She says, 'It's like Christmas each time I receive a review!'

If you would like to be on Janice Spina's email list to receive updates, newsletters, and special deals on books, please follow her blog at link above.

Watch for more books coming from Jemsbooks.

A NOTE FROM THE AUTHOR

Book 1 of this series was written over ten years ago. At that time, I wasn't ready to publish it. There were too many other books I wanted to publish first. I've always enjoyed reading fantasy and wanted to create my own fantasy series for young adults. This is Book 2 with the continuing saga of Gateskin Chronicles.

This series is written for young adults – Ages 13-17, but can be enjoyed by adults too. I consider this series to be PG-13 and up. It is up to parents to use their discretion about whether your children read this series. Some things may not be suitable for young children. There is never any vulgar language in any of my books but there are some situations that may be too violent for young readers.

I hope you enjoyed this work of fiction. Watch for more books in this series coming over the next few years.

Thank you for purchasing one of Jemsbooks. I appreciate your kind support of me and my books. If you like this book, a review would be greatly appreciated wherever you purchased it. Reviews and word of mouth are the best way to spread your thoughts about books. Please share your review with friends and family. I would love to hear from you. You can reach me at jjspina(at)comcast(dot)net.

All my books are available on Amazon and Barnes & Noble. Watch for more books coming for all ages.

With Blessings & Love,

Janice Spina

YA BOOKS BY JANICE SPINA - PG 13+

*The Legend of the Taken Ones
(Gateskin Chronicles Book 1)*

OTHER MG/PT/YA BOOKS BY JANICE SPINA

Davey & Derek Junior Detectives Book 1:

The Case of the Missing Cell Phone

(Pinnacle Book Achievement Award,

Honorable Mention- Readers' Favorite Book Award)

Davey & Derek Junior Detectives Book 2:

The Case of the Mysterious Black Cat

(Pinnacle Book Achievement Award)

Davey & Derek Junior Detectives Book 3: The Case of the Magical Ivory Elephant
(Pinnacle Book Achievement Award & Reader's
Favorite Book Awards – Silver Medal)

Davey & Derek Junior Detectives Book 4: The Case of the Brown Scraggly Dog
(Finalist in Red City Review Awards & 5-Star Book Review –
Readers' Favorite Book Awards)

Davey & Derek Junior Detectives Book 5:
The Case of the Sad Mischievous Ghost

Pinnacle Book Achievement
Award & Authorsdb
Cover Contest – Silver Medal)

***Davey & Derek Junior Detectives
Book 6: The Case of the Mystery
of the Bells***
(Pinnacle Book Achievement
Award, Finalist – Readers'
Favorite Book Awards, Finalist –
Book Excellence Awards)

Abby & Holly School Dance
(Pinnacle Book Achievement
Award & Bronze Medal from
Readers' Favorite Book Awards)

***Abby & Holly Series Book 2:
Unfortunate Events***

Pinnacle Book Achievement
Award, Readers' Favorite Book
Awards – Honorable Mention)

*Abby & Holly Series, Book 3,
Secrets of the Trunk*

(Pinnacle Book Achievement
Award)

*Abby & Holly Series, Book 4, The
Hidden Stairway*

(Pinnacle Book Achievement
Award)

*Abby & Holly Series, Book 5, The
Copper Key*

(Pinnacle Book Achievement
Award)

Abby & Holly Series, Book 6, Faulty Timeline

(Pinnacle Book Achievement Award)

BOOKS BY J.E. SPINA FOR 18+

Hunting Mariah (Finalist in Authorsdb First Lines Contest)

Mariah's Revenge (Finalist in Authorsdb First Lines Contest)

How Far is Heaven

An Angel Among Us: A Short Story Collection

In A Second

Lubelia Alycea: One Hundred Years

More books coming in 2024 and beyond